ALL'S FAIRE IN LOVE

Copyright ©2025 Line By Lion Publications
www.pixelandpen.studio
ISBN   979-8-9988123-5-4

Edited by Susan Travis
Cover Design by Adam Prack

For more information, email www.linebylionpublications.com

LINE BY LION
PUBLICATIONS

This book is dedicated to everyone who has wanted ren faire to last a little bit longer or wished that the magic of it all could be real!

Author's Note

Our beloved MMC Donnchadh's name is pronounced Dun-A-Kah.

And our dear FMC Mairead is pronounced Ma-raid.

Prologue

"Lairds and Ladies! Welcome to our celebration! His Royal Highness King James IV has deigned to grace our humble little hamlet, with his exalted presence during his coronation tour! We have prepared a grand market with wares from across the land, a feast that is indeed fit for our king, and a tournament amongst the strongest knights in the realm!" Walter, the town crier, announced with a contagious exuberance. The man had an uncanny amount of charisma, and it spread through the gathered crowd like wildfire.

Meanwhile, toward the back of the gathered crowd where they would not be heard by the crier and higher-ranking officials, two women watched the proceedings. "Do ye think he might have some handsome kilted noble Scots in his retinue that are lookin fer ladies tae run their keeps?!" Rose, a petite blonde woman in a tan bodice and blue skirt who served at the Inn waiting tables, whispered rather loudly.

Mairead, another inn wench, stared wide eyed at her disruptive friend. Several people turned to look at them, some with amusement and others with annoyance at the interruption.

"Haud yer Weesht!" Mairead hissed. "Ye are like tae get us a day in the stocks if ye continue tae make a scene!"

"Och, but would it no' be worth it if the lad were fine?!" Rose winked. A woman nearby gawked at them, unsure of what to make of Rose and Mairead.

Mairead laughed and tossed her long brown curls over her shoulder, "guess it would depend on the lad in question."

"To that end," intoned the crier, "We hope that His Majesty will enjoy our offerings! Throw wide the gates!" The cannon roared and belched an impressive cloud of smoke. The crowd began to dissipate, moving through the market. Mairead shifted her basket of cheese and fruits as she made her way to the Inn. The Inn cook had promised to make a grand feast at dusk, and each of the workers were contributing something to the meal. She wound her way through booths that had been set up along either side of the road. She smiled as music filled the air. Pipes and drums could be heard across the market, and she knew that her friends would be amassing an audience. Heaven knew she had sat and watched them; even danced along as they played in shaded areas in the market plenty of times. She adored them and their music.

The early morning stroll through the market was one of her favorite parts of the day. The little village was just waking up and she would stop to chat with the shop owners or wave in greeting to passersby. Today was a grand day, and she was in a fine mood. She had just purchased a new skirt and bodice, and was eager to see what her friends at the inn thought of them. They were a bit nicer than her old ones. The skirt was of a heavy burgundy fabric, and the bodice was of a lighter brocade with a square neckline that had been all the rage at Queen

Elizabeth's court. She wore them over her white chemise, and utilitarian black boots.

Winding her way through the crowded market she happened upon part of the King's entourage that had been slowed by the crush of people. She caught the eye of a particularly handsome guardsman and winked, blowing him a kiss as she passed. He checked to see if his captain was looking, and then dramatically acted as if he had been struck through the heart; smiling and clasping his chest as he stumbled. Hearing the commotion of people laughing, the captain turned to look. The guard quickly snapped back to attention in an attempt to hide his tomfoolery. His Captain eyed him and then glared at Mairead. Once he turned around again, the guard winked at her and then resumed his stony composure. She laughed as she continued on her way.

The Inn was a two-story half-timber building with a dusty inn yard; a smaller structure next to it contained an oven and served as a kitchen. Trees on one side surrounded the Inn, and across the yard was a small lake. Mairead stopped to take it all in as she often did on beautiful clear mornings when the sky was almost a sapphire blue. She loved the beauty of the village she called home. "Och Lass get yer head out of the clouds!" Angus, the Inn's cook, yelled as he leaned out to the kitchen door upon seeing her loitering in the yard. He was a barrel-chested man, with a baldhead and wiry brown beard that was steadily becoming greyer with each season. He wore a sleeveless tunic that may have been white at one time and brown breeches with a heavy leather apron. "What have ye brought me this morn?"

"I canna say as I am sorry Angus! Tis simply tae bonnie a day tae no enjoy it!" She grinned at him and gave him her basket. "Goat cheese with herbs and some melons. You like melons aye?!"

He threw his head back and roared with laughter as she withdrew the melons from her basket and held them in front of her at chest level. "Aye lass tha I do! And ye have some fine melons indeed!" She promptly dissolved into giggles at his response. Some of the patrons of the Inn that were sitting on benches in the yard turned and looked scandalized by the exchange; which made them laugh even more. Angus was still chuckling, as he took the basket back to a bench in the kitchen.

Mairead ducked inside the Inn, and it took her eyes a moment to adjust. It was still early in the day, so there was not much of a crowd; only two patrons sat conversing. She went to the back of the Inn, through a door to a small storage area, and grabbed some containers. Rose was wiping down tables, and Sybil, the innkeeper's wife, was opening windows and making sure that they had enough light and airflow. Mairead set about laying out various cheeses, hard breads, and dried fruit on platters on a table along the right wall. The three had been working together long enough that they each knew their part, and for the most part they functioned like a well-oiled machine. On occasion, it degenerated to chaos, but that was to be expected. Once she had set out the spread, she put away the containers with leftover food. Rose bounded over asking her about her schedule for the day. It was a Sunday, so the morning would be a bit slow. "I plan tae visit with the pipers a bit this morn' or check in on a friend of mine that is hawking for a leather vendor. Or perhaps any number of things, until I am due here tae relieve ye just before nooning".

A short while later, Mairead was making her way down one of the sun-dappled lanes lined by booths. Before she could get close to the leather booth, her friend Ian came bounding out dressed in his hunter regalia. His clothing was shades of muted green and brown, and they fit well on his lean frame. He wore a light brown tunic with a deep green capelet over his shoulders, and dark brown pants. His long straight brown hair hung down to the middle of his back, and he wore a pointed green bycocket much on his head, much like Robin Hood or even Peter Pan wore. As soon as he got close, he scooped her up in a hug, spinning her around. "It is good to see you!" His smile was sweet and genuine; warming Mairead's heart as his eyes shone in the sun.

"I missed ye as well Ian!" she smiled. Once he put her down, she leaned over to kiss him on the cheek. But at the last moment, he turned his head so that she kissed him on the lips. "Och ye're incorrigible!" she teased, shaking her head and pushing him away.

"You can't blame a lad for trying! Well, I suppose you could, but it wouldn't change anything." He grinned and put an arm over her shoulders. She loved that she could simply be herself with Ian. She was not Samuel's daughter, or an inn wench; she was quite simply herself. She assisted Ian with his hawking, and in between waves of market goers; they caught each other up on what had happened during the previous week.

By the end of the day, after working at the inn, visiting friends, and simply enjoying the market, Mairead was exhausted. She made her way back from the village gate to the Inn and collapsed onto a bench against the wall. The sun had cast its last rays over the village, and now fires were being lit. Vendors bustled to close shop for the week, and cast made their way back to the Inn, their cars, or to tent city. Angus, also known as Brandon in the real world; had called for some of the stronger guys on cast to help him unload a whole pig on a spit to a platter. He had been doing cooking demonstrations all day for their Living History Center, utilizing the pig, baking fresh breads, and the like. Now that the faire day was over, the cast and staff that pitched in with money and food were able to reap the benefits.

About half of the cast, 25 people, gathered at the Inn. The atmosphere was cheery and almost magical. The fire that had been used to cook the pig was still glowing on one end of the yard, and another had been lit on the other side. Faerie lights had been turned on inside so that people could see as they loaded wooden plates with food. Laughter and happy conversation filled the air. After a little while, a friend brought out his lute and began to play. The evening was beginning to get cool, so people bundled up in cloaks or stood round the fires. Mairead sat on a bench near the fire and her friend Richard noticed her staring off into space. "Hey Gwen." He waited a moment, called her name again, and tapped her shoulder.

"Oh God,Richard, you scared the crap out of me!" she jumped at his touch.

"I called your name a couple of times, but you were spaced out I guess." He chuckled.

"That, and I answer to Mairead so much on the weekends, that apparently I forget my real name!"

"Hey, the struggle is real! You look cold. Want some cloak?"

"You know, that sounds great right about now!" She rubbed her arms as if to ward off the chill. He motioned for her to scoot forward on the bench, and straddled it behind her so that she leaned back against him, wrapping her up so they shared his cloak. They had been friends for some time and Sasha, his girlfriend, was one of the sweetest people she knew. There was never anything other than platonic friendship between Richard and Gwen. Sasha was just not that into Renaissance Faires, and on top of that, she had to work that night. "Much better! Thank you, Sheriff! You are like a freaking furnace! Sasha is a lucky girl in the winter! Having you around must cut down on heating bills!"

He shrugged. "Have to earn my keep somehow!"

Chapter One

Ten years later

Gwen couldn't wait for the Renaissance festival to start! She had been practicing her Scottish accent and getting her garb ready for weeks. It had been years since she had been to her home faire, and she was a bit nervous about it too. Many of her old friends were still there, and while she was excited to see them, it had been quite some time. Over that past decade she had changed. She was no longer the carefree Inn wench, and history nerd that they knew. Now she was an Air Force veteran with a good deal of emotional baggage, and much more worldly experience. She was still a geek though, and they had all inevitably changed as well. As the saying goes, the only constant is change.

One thing was for sure, her garb had upgraded since she last attended. She still wore the same burgundy skirt, but she had sewn a dangling beaded trim to the hem, which was shades of burgundy and green. Her bodice was a rich green brocade in the Elizabethan noble style that had back and side lacing. She wore the bodice over a lovely yellow bell sleeved chemise, finished with a black leather pirate hat with yellow feathers and deep red fabric roses. The final piece was a sash of bright yellow plaid, with black and red stripes of the MacLeod of Lewis. Chuckling to herself she thought of people calling it the "Loud Proud MacLeod " tartan for its vibrant color. Her rich chocolate brown hair was a bit shorter now and hung in wild curls just touching her bare shoulders. In preparation for the inevitably sunny and hot southern Louisiana late summer-early fall weather, she generously sprayed on some sunscreen on and hoped that it would last, and she wouldn't burn too terribly.

As she checked herself in the mirror at the hotel one last time before she set out to faire, she was overcome by a sense of melancholy. She pulled a curl straight to its full length, and it was still nowhere near as long as it had been last time she had been there. She had made a deal with Ian years ago. He had loved her long curls, and she had adored his long hair as well. She had told him all the time that women would kill for his hair, and he always laughed about it. One day he had mentioned that he was thinking about cutting his hair. She had immediately informed him that if he cut his hair, she would cut hers. He gasped and told her it would be criminal for her to cut her hair because he loved it so. "Ok, so you don't cut yours and I won't cut mine! Deal?!" she teased him.

"Okay, okay! I won't as long as you don't!" he relented. "Deal. I love you always!"

He had always ended every conversation that way. No matter what happened or how far apart they were. Their paths had diverged, but they still kept in touch and supported each other. When his number popped up on her phone, she knew she would hang up smiling. Before she joined the Air Force, she had been studying to be a teacher. Ian thought it was hysterical and was a true child of the eighties so he ran with the idea. What started with him teasingly presenting her with an apple, and singing the chorus of Hot For Teacher, led to apples popping up in odd places. He would sneak up behind her on occasion and sing the chorus; then abruptly wander off as if nothing at all had happened. Then, when she was assigned to a base overseas, he would leave voicemails letting her know he had heard the song on the radio and was thinking of her. Just short voicemails of him singing to her a verse, telling her he loved her, and hanging up. He had been her safe place. Even when things were at their worst, Ian could be counted on to lift her out of her worst moods. He had known that her step-father was abusive when she was younger and tried his best to be there for her even when she shut everyone else out.

The last time she had been to her home faire, they had a wonderful season together. However, that would not be the case this time. He was gone. He had committed suicide last year, after a fight with a friend. Every time she thought about it, it broke her heart a little more. She couldn't even listen to that song without bursting into tears.

Knuckling tears from her eyes before they could get too far, she took a deep breath. She left her hotel room and headed to the faire. Of course, she stopped for a Starbucks double tall peppermint mocha on the way. A fine faire morning should always start with a good strong and sweet coffee in her opinion.

The faire was well off the beaten path. After almost 40 minutes of driving on backroads, Gwen pulled into the field that served as a parking lot for the festival. A wave of nostalgia swept over her. It still looked the same. She was there early so that she could see the opening gate show. They were celebrating the reign of Queen Elizabeth this year, and it promised to be amusing from what she had heard.

Once 10:00 a.m. hit, there was a large crowd of patrons. The cast members were scattered throughout the courtyard for their opening gate bits. She did not know any of them. For the first time, she was able to see this opening gate from a patron's point of view. It was indeed fun, but she missed the inside jokes and asides with other cast members. At last, the cannon roared and belched smoke. The gates were open with the court jester standing atop the gate yelling for people to push, shove, and use small children as battering rams to get into the festival.

She need not have worried about seeing her friends again. One of them, who was now a queen's guard, had seen her from his position atop the gate. The moment she stepped through, she was greeted with countless hugs. She could not have been happier. She made her way around the lake, following the sounds of bagpipes and drums to a small stage where her friends were playing. Upon seeing her, they stopped the show and briefly introduced her to the gathered audience and welcomed her back. They even hopped over a bench or two to give her hugs, before returning to the stage and continuing their show. As she made her way about the faire, old friends on the cast or vendors would call out to her and she would stop and chat. At one point, she was pulled behind the scenes and was passed a cell phone to speak to one of her old friends who couldn't make it. All in all, it was a grand homecoming.

As the day was coming to a close, she was a bit drunk on mead and fine scotch; blissfully happy. She was stopped before she could leave the gates, and asked if she would like to join the cast for their traditional first weekend Saturday night dinner at a local eatery. She grinned and quickly agreed to meet them at Brady's. It was just like the old days. They were all still in their garb when they got to the restaurant, and while the wait staff was used to the odd and colorful display, the other diners were not. Most of them openly stared or made weird-remarks about how the rennies spoke or dressed. The cast was there to have a good time. On occasion they would respond to remarks from the other diners. When Gwen went to the bathroom at the back of the restaurant, she was accosted by a teenager who rudely asked her why the hell she was dressed like that. Gwen smiled sweetly "Och lass, I dress this way because tis proper for a lady tae wear clothing that covers her and is appropriate fer wear outside the keep. How could yer da have allowed ye out of the house as scantily clad as ye are!?" She motioned to the girl's short shorts and tank top. The girl turned beet red huffed in frustration and stormed back to her table while Gwen smiled and returned to her seat with a little wave to the angry girl, who in turn flipped her off.

Gwen's friends were surprised into laughter by the action. They ate, drank, and reminisced. They told stories of faires since Gwen had been gone, and laughed about memories of the faires for which she had been there. Perhaps they laughed or talked a bit too loud or got a bit too bawdy when talking about old jokes and places that lasses stored money, daggers, and the like; but they didn't care. It was as if no time had passed, certainly not 10 years. They stayed long into the evening until the wait staff informed them that Brady's was closing.

Once she was back at her hotel Gwen unlaced her bodice and took a massive gulp of air. While she loved wearing it, and would wear it any chance she got, that first deep breath of air unhindered by heavy fabric and steel boning was heavenly. Still in her chemise, she fell backwards onto the bed and then began to thumb through the pictures she had taken on her cellphone. It had been a wonderful day to be back at her home faire. Tomorrow would be her last day to visit until next year. She vowed that it would not be ten years before she got back here again.

The next morning, she rolled out of bed and began to put on her garb again. Another beautiful day to spend with her friends doing what she loved. She laced into her bodice and realized that her mind had been wandering. She still had not put on her striped socks that came over her knees to the edge of her bloomers, and boots. It would take her some serious work to get them on now that she had steel boning controlling her posture. After several minutes of bending awkwardly huffing and puffing, she was ready to go. Another stop for coffee, and then on to the faire. Again, she was early, but this time as the crowd gathered, her friends were among the cast woven in and they visited with her while waiting for the opening gate show. Today there was no concern or trepidation for Gwen, she was perfectly happy and content with where she was, and what she was doing. This morning, there was dancing before the gate show, and her friends pulled her into it. They held hands, spun, promenaded, and laughed as the music flowed around them. Upon the completion of the song they all stopped, clapped and bowed to their respective partners. Once they had cleared the way, the king of the festival approached and the show began.

For some reason today felt different. She wasn't sure why, but it was almost as if there was something heavy in the air. She took her time and meandered through the lanes, stopping to watch shows or look at the wares in booths. She stopped at one of the taverns and ordered a bee stinger which was a mixture of hard cider and mead. She produced her wooden mug for them to fill and then she continued around the festival as she sipped.

Chapter Two

Dunvegan Castle, Scotland, 1574

Donnchadh MacLeod lounged in a plush chair before a roaring fire in his chamber. One leg slung over the arm of his chair and a glass of scotch in his hand. He lifted the glass to eye level and peered at the fire through the amber liquid. He was most certainly drunk. The setting sun cast splashes of orange and red across the floor, filling his vision with shades of amber, gold, and red to match the fire in the hearth. He wished that the fire would warm him and drive away the ice that filled his heart now. He could not believe that Alasdair was gone. They had grown up together and fought side by side. He had even planned to marry Alasdair's sister.

Yesterday that all changed. Alasdair fell to a MacDonald dagger. The raid had gone wrong and the MacDonalds had been ready for the retaliation. Fergus MacDonald had reeved several sheep from the MacLeods and Donnchadh had gathered men to reclaim the cattle and retaliate. The battle had been quick but fierce. They had left in the pre-dawn hours of the morning hoping to avoid as much bloodshed as possible but old Fergus was a shrewd one. He had several warriors sitting watch near his flock. The men sat around a small fire and while the MacLeods had been as silent as possible, sheep were stubborn wee things. As luck would have it, Fergus's son Eogan was one of the men keeping watch. There had been ten MacDonalds to six MacLeods which Donnchadh thought might have been an unfair advantage since he and his men could easily take on three men a piece.

Just as the sun was rising, the MacDonalds raised their weapons and attacked when they heard the sheep startle. Early morning sun glinted off blades as they clashed and after only a few minutes, blood of the MacDonald's made the ground slippery. Sheep scattered as the men fought for the upper hand. With four of the MacDonalds gravely wounded and unable to fight any longer it seemed as if there might be a tentative truce. The MacLeods had only a few scratches and bruises amongst them. Eogan did not take kindly to this turn of events. He bellowed that he would kill Donnchadh if it were the last thing he did. "Now laddie, we just want our sheep back and I am sure tha there is a chance yer lads may survive. Dinna make this worse than it already is." Donnchadh rested the tip of his basket hilt sword on the ground before him. He turned to look at Ewan telling him to take Angus and gather up the sheep in question. At that moment he heard a shout and turned back just in time to see Alasdair taking a dagger to the stomach that was meant for him. "NAY!" He roared and charged Eogan with his blade upraised. Eogan was so startled by the reaction and speed of movement, that Donnchadh was able to avenge Alasdair swiftly. He cut Eogan down where he stood. As Eogan crumpled to the ground, Donnchadh rushed to Alasdair and sank to the ground beside him.

"Och Lad! Ye are goin tae be alright! We will get ye home and Molly will clean ya and sew ye up and ye will be fine." Donnchadh rested his friend's head in his lap.

"Listen Brathair. Look after me mam will ye and Cait too." Alasdair coughed up blood. "Dinna let the MacDonalds get away wi any more of our sheep, dinnae let them get the better of ye."

"I will look after them while ye recover and then we shall set those bastards aright. Fer sure Eogan is in worse shape than ye lad! I need ye as my second! Archie does nae understand what it takes tae carry the mantle we do."

"Ye are going tae do big things Donnchadh." another cough. "Wi or wi'out me." Blood continued to seep from his stomach as Donnchadh tried to use his plaid to staunch the flow.

"Ye are goin tae do them wi me! Ye can no mean tae tell me that after all of the adventures we hae had together and all the havoc we wrought that ye are givin up on me? Och, I thought ye kenned tha ye were stuck we me and tha one day we would face the d'eil together as old men." Donnchadh gave a watery laugh as tears streamed from his eyes.

Alasdair took a pained breath as his color became wan. "I'll beat ye there laddie. Finally, I do somethin before ye can. I mean tae take on the d'eil and beat him fore ye get there just tae spite ye." The last came out a whisper. "Tell me mam and Cait I am sorry. I let ye down laird. I am sorry…."

"Ye never let me down Dair!" Donnchadh shifted so that Alasdair could be more comfortable. "If ought, ye made me try harder tae be a better laird. Hell, I still can nae beat ya racing the coast when ye are ridin that beast stallion of yers!"

Alasdair gave a pained laugh that was more of a groan. "Aye well at least ye cannae now. One record I shall always hold......." and then he gave a final shuddering gasp and was gone.

Donnchadh had carried Alasdair's body back to Dunvegan over the saddle of his horse. Every step he took closer to home was more painful. Alasdair's mother and sister Cait would be devastated. Hell he was devastated. Alasdair had been like a brother to him. Archie, his younger brother, was different enough that it was surprising that they were actually related let alone brothers. He did not understand responsibility and would let everyone else take care of work for him. Now he had to deal with the boy on his own. He thought of his own mother and how she doted on Archie after their da passed. Donnchadh was the one that had to grow up over night at the tender age of 15 while Archie was spoiled and lazed about and was a general wastrel.

As he approached the gate, men flooded the court yard to greet the warriors. Donnchadh scanned the crowd looking for Maud and Cait. When he saw them, and they realized that Alasdair was not one of the mounted men they pushed through the crowd only to realize just what was draped over his saddle. Maud fell to her knees keening at the loss of her beloved son. Cait sobbed as she held on to her mother. He bent down to comfort them, but Cait stopped him with a questioning glance. "Wha happened tae him?"

Hanging his head, he took a deep breath and then met her eyes, sorrow written across his face. "The MacDonalds were ready for us. He took down two of them and then when we thought all was done, he took a dagger meant fer me. I would give anythin tae take his place so that he could be here instead."

She glared at him, tears pouring down her cheeks. "Aye he should be here! He should no have sacrificed himself for ye! He was all we had! What are we tae do now?" The crowd was dispersing and his men were taking their mounts to the stable, Leaving him there with his horse, Alasdair, Maud and Cait.

"I will take care of ye lass. I promised Dair I would. Ye shall be cared for and safe all yer life."

"And what is that supposed tae mean? Are ye goin to come help me mam wi the thatch when it rains or mend the fence in our garden, or sit wi us during bad storms because Dair did all that an more!"

"I will do my best lass. Dair had a softer touch than me bu I will do my best."

"Hah! As if you could!" Donnchadh accepted her anger, had expected it really, but it still tore at his heart. She grabbed the reins of his horse and helped her sobbing mother to her feet "Come Mam, lets take Dair home one last time."

"Let me help ye lass," he got up and offered to take the reins.

"Ye have done enough!" she spat and he watched as they walked away. He was not sure how long he stood there but it was nigh supper by the time he entered the hall. He looked over his gathered clan as they sat at trestle tables that ran the length of the large room. The fireplace was filled with a roaring fire and people were eating and talking. Normally it was a scene that he would welcome. But in that moment it was a stark reminder that he was on his own more so now than he had ever been. The table at which he and Alasdair normally sat with a few other family members and lads stood empty. He had no stomach for food or people, so he turned and ascended the stairs that lead to his chambers. The clan quieted for a moment when they realized his presence but resumed their conversations as soon as he was out of sight.

That was last night and a bottle and a half of scotch ago. His breakfast had been of the liquid variety and he planned on any other meals that day being the same. He had not left his chamber and had no plan to in the near future. He wanted to be left alone with his sorrow. He heard the sounds of a busy castle and clan but took no interest in anything other than finding the bottom of his glass. He heard a pair of boots stomping down the hall to his chamber, and a moment later his door was flung open.

"If I kenned tha ye were about my favorite past time I would ha joined ye brother!" Archie strolled into the room. His hair was a bright red, and his frame lean. "Have no seen ye since ye returned wi the sheep. Saw Cait all serious at the market at the nooning and expected ye and Alasdair tae be wi her. So I got curious"

"Leave off ye numpty! Get out of my chamber and leave me be!" Donnchadh snarled over the rim of his glass. "I ken ye follow gossip like a wee village lass, so I ken ye damn well know what has happened. Ye seek tae needle me fer yer own amusement. Sae go back to yer gossips and share tha, Aye I am in my cups as I have ne'er been afore. The Laird is a drunken arse!" He downed the whiskey and lurched to his feet to pour another glass. The bottle sat on a desk against the wall. For the life of him, he could not figure out why he had left the damned thing there instead of bringing it to the chair with him last time. He swayed and almost stumbled as he made his way across the room. He grabbed the back of the chair at his desk to steady himself for a moment.

Archie crowed with laughter, "Oho this is grand! My self-righteous elder brother is sae far gone he canna walk straight! Ye berate me endlessly fer my drinkin yet here ye are worse off than me!"

"Aye, well ye dinna lose the best friend ye ever had who ye grew up with. So piss off lad!" Donnchadh stumbled and would have fallen had he not landed as if to sit on a chest that was pushed up against the wall.

"Oh Aye brother mine! Dinna mind me, keep drinkin! Pickle yerself as ye have mocked me for. Just means I will take over as laird all the sooner!" with that Archie left and slammed the door. Donnchadh knew that the entire clan would know of his state by the time evening meal rolled around. Christ, he thought to himself, he could not let Archie run the clan! He would surely drive it into the ground.

With that he sat down his scotch and attempted to stand again. He was slightly steadier this time. Alasdair would be appalled at his current state were he here. He slowly made his way across the room to a mirror he had. His long dark slightly sun bleached hair hung in a disarray of tangles past his shoulders, his shirt was dirty and stained where he had spilled drops of whiskey here and there, and his trews were stained with blood. He shook himself; he was laird and could not afford to wallow. He could hear the muffled yells of Archie demanding that a wench bring him ale immediately. Alasdair would understand and would have been angry with him for letting himself get to this point. He realized that the best way to honor his friend and brother in arms, was to succeed and make the

MacLeods the strongest clan there was. "Aye lad, I ken ye would kick my arse all the way across the bailey if ye saw me like this." He spoke as if Alasdair was there with him. He peeled off his clothes and tossed them in the fire. He had no desire to try and salvage them only to remember what happened when he wore them. He leaned over a small basin and poured a pitcher of cold water over his head. It was a shock to his system and served to sober him up a bit, well at least enough to stand without swaying and walk without falling. He withdrew a fresh tunic and trews from his wardrobe and donned them. He then wrapped a length of plaid across his chest. No way would he let Archie think he had the upper hand.

One Year Later

The games had just started. Men of the clan, surrounding villages, and other clansmen from neighboring ally clans were signing up for competitions like the caber toss, tug of war, and shifting stones. The skirl of the pipes lent a vibrant feel to the early morning, as if to promise that today would be one full of laughter and pride. Fog was lifting and blue sky was peeking through. Donnchadh watched as a few women practiced jigs near the piper. There would be a dancing competition as well as piping competitions later. Everyone seemed to be in grand spirits. It was as if the cloud that had hung over the clan for the last year was lifting. It had been the worst year of his life. Not only had he lost his best friend, but 6 months ago he had proposed to Cait. He cared deeply for her and had planned on marrying her before they lost Dair, and it had only seemed fitting that he continue on that path especially since he had been tasked with caring for her and her mother.

Cait had been shocked when he asked. Tears spilled from her eyes as she shook her head. "I have been keeping my distance for a reason, Donnchadh. I can't marry ye."

"Och lass tell me what I can do."

"Can ye bring back my brother?" She looked sharply at him. When he sighed and his shoulders sagged, she continued ruthlessly. "Aye! I thought not! Every time I look at ye I see his face, his eyes staring sightlessly as we laid him tae rest. I hear me mam's wailing as we buried him. I can barely stand tae look at ye wi'out crying for him or being angry wi ye."

"Cait, I canno tell ye how sorry I am and how much my heart aches for ye and Maud. I think on Dair every day and he still figures in my actions. If there is ought I am unsure of, I ask myself what he would hae done. I wish tae God I could bring him back for ye, for all of us!" He reached out to clasp her hands in his. "I care for ye deeply lass and on top of that he asked that I take care of ye and yer mam. Let me do tha. Let us try tae make each other happy. I vow, I will spend every day doin all I can to make yer life grand and see that ye want for naught."

She yanked her hands from his grasp. "No way I will ere allow that tae happen. Ye could ne'er make me happy now. It is because of ye that my family is broken, that me mam cries most days and my heart breaks every time I look at the chair at our table he will-no longer occupies. Now get thee gone. I cannae even bear tae look at ye any longer!" she stormed off.

As Donnchadh watched her leave, his heart broke a little more. Here he thought he no longer had a heart. Surely, this would be the last of it. If that were the case he was glad of it since that meant, he would no longer hurt. He took his time about the village. He had no desire to return to the castle sooner than he had to. He stopped and spoke with crofters and watched the shaggy sheep thinking about the shearing season to come. Suddenly there was a great commotion down the road. He heard screams coming from the direction of Cait's home. He ran back there scared of what he might find. Her mother was collapsed just outside the door with Elsie trying to comfort her. When he entered the small croft, he saw her and his heart stopped. Cait had hung herself with a length of Dair's plaid. He ran to her, and lifted her enough that he could loosen the plaid, and free her. As he laid her on her bed, he realized that she was not breathing and he could find no sign of life. He was too late.

She had been laid to rest next to her brother and clan life continued on. He had moved Maud into the keep so that he could see to her safety. She rarely talked or did much more than look out over the sea. At least he consoled himself that he was able to see to her comfort.

He mentally shook himself and continued on his way to see what people were selling at the makeshift market that popped up during the games. People would sell and trade all sorts of wares. He hoped that it would keep his mind busy. He didn't want to think right now. He only wanted to drink some ale and listen to the pipes. Dunvegan was known for having the best pipers in all of Scotland. The Mcrimmons were deservedly touted as the best pipers in the land, and people would come from all over Scotland to learn to play the pipes from them. Most of the time it was pleasant to hear the sound of pipes throughout the village or castle, unless they got a particularly green lad. Then it was so much discordant honking that it was enough to drive people daft or even wake the dead. He stopped at a small tent that promised pasties and ale. He took a mug and sat at a small wooden table that overlooked the field where lads were practicing and warming up. He missed the days when he and Dair would compete in tossing sheaves of wheat or tug of war. Dair had never beaten him. He came close but that was it. Horse racing was another thing, Dair always won then. People walking past called out greetings to him or doffed their caps out of respect as he sat nursing his ale.

It was becoming more crowded and the energy was picking up. Donnchadh could not help but enjoy watching the caber toss competition. He loved the feats of strength that he and the men of his clan prided themselves in. So far MacLeods had been the winners of every competition in spite of other clans sending their best men to compete. He took great pride in that. They were strong, he was strong!

When the caber toss was complete, with another MacLeod the winner, it was time for the mid day meal. People milled about, some talking and catching up with friends they had not seen since the last games and others went in search of food. As he walked among the people and looked at the booths a sound caught his attention. There was music played on a lute. He did not recall any musicians other than pipers, drummers, and the occasional fiddler. He wandered trying to find the source of the lovely tune. Just when he thought he was getting close it would fade away as if it was moving.

Chapter Three

Gwen sank easily into character again and now, it was as if there was no Gwen, only Mairead MacLeod, a lass returning home. She feasted on scotch eggs and mead with her friend Chastity Cockamamie who was an inn wench. While they ate, they stood at an old wooden cable spool that served as a table and catcalled men in kilts that were passing by. Chastity was not shy about offering kilt checks. Some of the men passing by laughed while others could not get away quickly enough. There were even some whose girlfriends or significant others would comment on the status of what was under their kilt much to the amusement of everyone around. It was good fun for all…. well, most involved. Once they were sated, Chastity had to go back to the Inn for a living history demonstration on games and entertainment in the Renaissance.

Mairead made her way to the other side of the lake to listen to the newest addition to the musical acts at the faire. He was a lutenist and was quite talented. She leaned up against a tree in the shade to watch for a bit. He played several tunes, each sweet and beautiful. Then he was playing "She Moved Through The Faire". He played and sang it beautifully. While he played, she stepped across the lane to refill her mug with some bloody knight, a mixture of mead and sweet red wine. Once she had done that, she pulled a few dollars from the pouch at her waist and put them in his tip box. A grin split his well-groomed beard, and he nodded his thanks to her as he continued to play. She listened a moment more and began to wander to the back of the faire toward the joust field. They had moved it since she had visited last and there were new vendors she had yet to explore. She could still hear the music as she sipped from her wooden mug while she took her time looking at the booths.

This was part of what she loved about her home festival. It was like a time out of mind. It was far enough removed from civilization that all you would hear aside from the sounds of the faire itself, was the wildlife. One could almost imagine that they really were at a little festival in an obscure village in Scotland. The back of the faire was not as heavily populated unless the joust was in full swing so it was rather peaceful for the time being. She looked around and realized that she could not see the back fence of the festival and some of the booths looked more primitive than she remembered. Perhaps they were trying for period accuracy and the festival was in the active process of expanding. She did not think much about it.

*   *   *

DONNCHADH followed to music to the far edge of the market and caught sight of a lass decked in red green and yellow wearing an odd hat. He found her lovely and watched as she examined the wares of the booths. Beyond her he could barely make out what he thought was a joust field fading into a fog bank but thought perhaps his eyes were playing tricks on him. The song was fading on the breeze, but he caught the last few words "And fondly I watched her move here and move there...." She stopped between booths as the pipes began to play and closed her eyes. She smiled, her face upturned and looked utterly at peace, when she opened her eyes she seemed startled as she looked around. She turned to look behind her and just stood there a moment. The people near her as well as vendors were beginning to stare, at not only her odd behavior but her manner of dress as well.

*   *   *

SHE was looking at a knife booth when she heard the pipes. They sounded so sweet and mournful that she closed her eyes and swayed to the music for a moment. She loved the bagpipe music much to the chagrin of any of her friends and family that did not attend renaissance festivals.

A cool breeze ruffled her hair. She stilled for a moment. It was southern Louisiana in the late summer. There was nothing cool about anything in southern Louisiana in late summer, not even the coolers meant to hold water for the cast. At best, the water was slightly cooler than the outside air. She opened her eyes and could not believe what she saw. There was a castle overlooking a loch. What's more the castle didn't look like a ruin, it looked rather busy with people going to and fro and a market nearby as well as thatched cottages. She spun around to look at the joust field that was right behind her, or at least it had been a moment ago. It was gone. All she could see was green countryside and mountains. There were NO mountains in Louisiana. Monkey Hill in the Audubon Park had been the highest point in New Orleans, and when she had been there as a child it was not much more than a pile of dirt. She turned to look at the castle again and her eyes were caught by what had to be the most attractive man she had ever seen. He put romance novel covers to shame with his long wind-blown hair and great kilt wrapped around massive shoulders.

Heat stroke! That was it, she was suffering from heatstroke and passed out and was imagining this beautiful place and handsome man. She made a choked sound that might have been a laugh, she had to hand it to her imagination, it was good! If only a guy like that really existed. Before her thoughts could process much more he was approaching her, his kilt swinging as he strode in a purposeful manner.

Her mouth went dry as he stopped before her. "Is aught amiss lass? Are ye alright?" His voice was deep and his brogue was thick. She peered up into his blue eyes as he towered over her. For a moment she could not speak.

She took a sip from her mug and cleared her throat. "Aye! I mean Nay. I mean I am well sir. Thank ye." She blushed.

He chuckled and she wanted to melt. "Ye dinnae sound so sure about tha. Is there anythin I can assist ye with? Ye looked a bit lost a moment ago."

She shook her head "Um..no. I was just caught off guard is all. Must have taken a turn wi'out paying attention." Her mind spun as she fought to take in everything she was seeing.

He cocked his head and raised an eyebrow at her. "Is tha so lass?" He sounded disbelieving. "I see ye are a MacLeod of Lewis. Perhaps I can take ye back tae yer family?"

She was shocked for a moment and didn't know what to say so she opted for the truth. "I am no here wi family. I was visitin friends." She offered no more.

Donnchadh had to admit the lass was strange. She was lovely to be sure but odd. "I can help ye find yer friends then if ye like. What's yer name lass?" he offered her his arm.

"I am Mairead MacLeod. And who be ye sir?" She hesitated to take his arm.

"I am Donnchadh MacLeod, Laird of clan MacLeod." He gave a small half bow from his waist.

She searched her mind. She was a history buff and loved Scottish history. She read all she could on the Clan MacLeod not only because of her character but because she loved the legends and the beauty of the place. There was no Donnchadh that was laird at present. She was sure that the current Laird was named John. She did not understand what was going on. Then she looked at the village and the castle again and everything clicked sickeningly into place. That was Castle Dunvegan. She was somehow on the Isle of Skye and the castle looked oddly rough, almost unfinished or at least not as polished as she remembered. Suddenly she could not get enough air. She was not in Louisiana anymore. Somehow, she had ended up in Scotland long before Castle Dunvegan had received its last renovations. This was not possible. She had to be dreaming. Perhaps she was in a coma and this was the culmination of all the Scottish history books and historical romances she read.

Her sudden change in pallor worried him and he moved just in time to catch her as her knees gave out and she lost consciousness. He scooped her up in his arms as if she weighed nothing and quickly took her back to the keep where he would have Molly check on her before he reunited her with her friends. People were quick to move out of his way as he strode through the gate. His clansmen openly gawked as he passed. He bellowed for Molly as he entered the keep and proceeded to take Mairead to a chamber next to his. The wee woman scurried from the kitchens and followed him. Her faded tartan skirt and a tan bodice over a chemise with her sleeves rolled back gave her a bit of a shabby appearance, and her graying auburn hair peeked out from under the cap she wore. "Aye laird. What be the matter? Is the lass injured?" Molly knew a bit about herbs and healing. Some claimed that she was a witch with her pale blue almost white eyes. Some of the more superstitious lads even made the sign of the cross when they crossed paths with her. Donnchadh on the other hand adored the woman. She had been more of a mother to him than his own. Not to mention her gift for healing had come in handy many times. He hoped that she would be able to help the lass, Mairead. She seemed sweet and well spoken. Perhaps she had a malady that made her weak and fragile, or mayhap she was ill, or injured in some way he could not see. He shook his head in an attempt to stop his thoughts from going down a dark path. He surprised himself then, why should he care so much if she were well or not. Then he reasoned that he would be just as concerned about any clansman or woman that fainted like that. Not that a man would faint like that but that was not the point. He explained to Molly what had happened. Leaving out the part about the music no one else seemed to hear.

"Well let me take a look then laddie. Tis almost like when ye were a wee lad forever bringing me some injured creature or another." She chuckled softly as she examined the girl. "At least this one will no try tae eat us out of house and home like that goat ye rescued years ago."

He smiled at the memory. "Aye, I think she may be better mannered. What do ye think is wrong with her Moll?

"Perhaps just a shock. I cannot find any other signs of illness. Ye said ye caught her afore she could hit the ground aye?"

"Aye. Just so." He leaned over the bed and looked at the lass as Molly made her way to the door.

"I will bring some herbal tea and a cool damp compress for her head. Once she wakes ye need tae make sure she drinks all the tea, every last drop." She pointed a bony finger at him.

"Indeed I shall Moll. I promise. I have always followed yer directions to the letter....at least when it comes to healin issues." He winked as the old woman turned and hurried down the hall. Who was this lass? He knew her name but that was all. She seemed genuinely confused when he told her his name. It was odd to say the least. He studied her while she lay there. She was a fine lass indeed. She had lovely curves that he might even call buxom. She had felt lush in his arms. It had been a long time since he carried a woman like that. He could not help but compare her to Cait, who had been slim and petite rather than curvaceous. She had been fair where this lass was dark. They seemed as different as day and night.

Molly returned and shooed him out of the room so that she could get the lass out of her tight bodice and tend to her. Once she had finished she allowed Donnchadh to return. He had been leaning against the door and nearly fell when she swung it open. "Ye can come in Laird. The lass seems tae be resting. The compress should help. Moreover, remember ALL of the tea when she wakes.

He smiled and nodded while he pulled a plush chair next to the bed and sat in it propping his booted feet on the mattress. Mairead lay there as if dead. Were he unable to see the rise and fall of her chest he could think just that. Molly had removed her bodice and skirt as well as her boots leaving the lass in her chemise and stockings tucked under the covers in the large four-poster bed. She looked so small laying there; it tugged at his heartstrings. He got up from the chair to examine her clothing that was laid on the chest at the foot of the bed. The fabric of her bodice was as fine as any he had seen at court and the stitching was precise and perfect. Her skirt was a heavy almost utilitarian fabric in comparison to the bodice but the beading at the hem indicated that perhaps it was not as much for utilitarian use as one might think. The colors of her clothing were rich and saturated. The metal grommets of her bodice were faultless. Overall it spoke of wealth. Someone had to be missing her, looking for her. He turned back to her just in time to see her eyelids flutter open.

When she opened her eyes all she saw was the Macleod of Harris tartan high above her. It took her a moment to realize that she was lying in a large plush bed. She also realized that she was only wearing her chemise and socks now. The last thing she remembered was seeing the castle and then everything went dark. She felt like there was something she should remember, it just kept escaping her. She reached up and removed a damp rag from her forehead. She heard a rustle of fabric and sat up to see what was going on. As soon as she sat up, she locked eyes with him. Her romance novel cover guy. They stared at each other for a long moment. She opened her mouth as if to speak and then closed it again. Donnchadh stepped to the bed beside her "How are ye feelin lass?"

She looked at him as if confused for a moment. She bit her lip as she now remembered the events that led up to her loss of consciousness, including the fact that she had introduced herself to him as Mairead MacLeod instead of Gwen Pierce. She had thought she was still at the festival and acted accordingly. She had never dropped character at a renaissance festival and this time it seemed she would have to carry it a bit farther. She was sure it would seem suspect if she all of a sudden didn't have an accent and her name was totally different. Yeah totally trustworthy, not an English spy at all. She had seen enough shows and read enough books to know that was not a pleasant way to go. Nothing to see here she thought to herself, except a crazy girl who put her foot in her mouth. "I feel a bit better thank ye." She finally responded in her broad scots accent.

"Let's get ye comfortable then so that ye can drink this tea Molly left for ye." He helped her scoot back in the bed and fluffed pillows up behind her. His hands were big and callused. Even through her chemise, she could feel the warmth of them. He was so gentle for such a large man. "Now here ye are." He handed her the teacup and sat back. "Be a good lass and drink it all, then we can discuss gettin ye back tae yer friends."

She gave a wan half smile as she accepted the cup with both hands and began to sip. She took a moment to look around the room. The walls and floor were stone. Tapestries filled with Celtic knot work hung on the walls. The wall across from her contained a fireplace which had a wing back chair and ornate table in front of it sitting atop a sheepskin rug. After a few sips she turned to him. "Where am I?   Last I recall I was talkin wi ye in one of the lanes and then I woke up here."

"Ye are in my home, Castle Dunvegan. Ye fainted so I brought ye here for my healer Molly to take a look at ye. And so ye dinna worry, she was the one tha undressed ye down tae yer chemise. She chased me from the chamber while she tended ye, and only allowed me tae return once she was done and ye were tucked safe in tae bed."

She took another long sip and smiled at him briefly. "Aye tha's a relief!" She finished the tea and handed him the cup. He sat it on a small nightstand next to the bed and then sat on the edge of the bed facing her, his back to the fire.

"Sae tell me Mairead where are yer friends and wha can I do tae help ye get back tae them." He took her left hand in both of his. His hands swallowed hers.

She had to think a moment. If she had really traveled back in time as crazy as that sounded, she was at his mercy. She had to watch everything she said and everything she did lest she betray herself. She took a deep breath and stayed as close to the truth as she possibly could and not be called a witch or crazy. "Well I dinna think there is aught ye can do at the moment. I passed out because I dinna see the tent that belonged tae my friends nor the horse cart we arrived tae the market in. It scared me tae think tha they just left me and I was alone again."

His brow furrowed as she spoke to him, "Alone again? Wha do ye mean?"

She had slipped. She hadn't meant to say that last part. There was no way to explain that she had been to Germany much less as a woman alone. In addition, she couldn't even fathom explaining that she had been in the military. She had to think quickly. "Me ma and da...are nae alive" It wasn't a lie really. If what she thought were true, they in fact were not alive and would not be so for several hundred more years.

"Christ lass! They dinna seem like friends tae me if they are able tae leave ye like tha." He stroked his thumb over the back of her hand. "Perhaps after the evenin meal I can take ye to the village tae look for them or find ye lodging for the night.

Good God the man was putting her through mental Olympics! Good thing she loved to research Scottish history and excelled at improv with her friends at the renaissance faire. She just had to make sure she kept everything in order in her mind and try to keep a step ahead of him. She looked down to where he held her hand and sighed, "I dinna think tha will work. I have no seen them since early this morn when they left sae her husband could sign up for the games. They left terribly early and I dinna think much of then. Later I dinna see him compete in any of the games he had mentioned and I thought it a bit odd but I thought perhaps I had just looked away and missed his turn. When I dinna see the tent or cart earlier I knew they left me. We had nae seen each other in a long while. Neither of us was the person we were when we last knew each other. We had an argument last eve and I can only assume tha is why they left me. Wha's more, all I had wi me was in that tent. All the money I had, everythin. " She peeked up at him from under her lashes.

He growled low in his throat. "Och dinnae worry lass. Ye can remain here o the now, until we can get this resolved for ye." He could not abide people like her supposed friends. Something told him that he needed to take care of her, to protect her. She breathed a sigh of relief. "In the meantime if ye are feelin up tae it, would ye like tae join me watching the games and dancing?"

"I think tha would be grand. T'would take my mind off the horrid turn of events today. Give me bu a minute tae get dressed. Um, might I leave a few things in here if I am to be staying or is there another place I will be?"

"Of course ye may! This is yer room as long as ye need it! Dinna worry about tha. I shall be waiting in the hall for ye." He smiled almost nervously and ducked out of the room as quickly as he could.

Good lord the man was hot! Thankfully, this time when she was getting dressed she remembered to put her boots on before her bodice. It made the whole process much easier than it had been...was it just that morning? Once she had her skirt and bodice on she decided to leave her hat behind and to remove her tail from her belt as well as her skirt hikes. She put her mug back on its strap and checked her pouch one last time and opened the door to the hallway. Donnchadh was leaning deceptively lazily against the opposite wall using his sgain dubh, a small dagger he kept tucked in his sock, to clean his nails. He straightened immediately and ran a hand through his wild hair to pull it back from his face. His eyes warmed at the sight of her as he looked her over. "Ye look lovely mistress! Tis glad I am tha ye are joining me for the afternoon." He took her hand and wrapped it around his arm. For some reason it felt good to have her touching him. It made no sense to him but he was not going to question it now. That would be for later.

Mairead shaded her eyes as they made their way out of the castle to the field where the games were in full swing. The wind blew her hair in her face but she figured if that were the worst of her worries then she would be alright. Donnchadh noticed her fidgeting with her hair and realized she had nothing to secure it with and thanks to her supposed friends she had no money. He knew just what to do. As they made their way through the market on the way to the games, he saw what he was looking for. It was a booth selling all sorts of fabric and ribbon. He glanced over at her as she let go of his arm and became absorbed in studying the fabrics and baubles that were on display. She was not even aware when he purchased a beautiful green ribbon shot through with blue and gold. He could have watched her there all day. Her face was alight with wonder like a child. Perhaps she had not seen such fabrics or ribbons or buttons before, but her clothes were finely made. He shrugged it off. "Come here lass. Ye look as if yer hair has been vexin ye."

She turned to look at him surprised that he was holding a gorgeous green velvet ribbon out to her. "Och I cannae accept that m'laird. Its very kind of ye though and I thank ye for the thought."

"Tis already purchased lass and t'would be an insult tae yer laird tae turn it down. Now be a good lass and turn back tae me so I can take care of yer problem for ye." He spun his finger about motioning for her to turn around. She liked the sound of him offering to take care of her problem more than she should and said no more as she turned around.

His warm fingers swept across the back of her neck as he gathered her hair sending shivers down her spine. He was so close she could almost feel the heat radiating from him. She could smell the pine, wool, leather, and man sent of him and it was not at all unpleasant. His fingers seemed to linger on her flesh a moment more that was necessary, and she inhaled as he deftly pulled her hair into a low braid and secured it with the ribbon.

He thought her hair oddly short for a lass but it was wonderfully soft and curly. Now that he was close, he could see that it was a rich chocolate brown with strands of red and blonde here and there. Her skin was soft where his fingers touched her neck, just as her hands had been. A wild part of him wondered if she would be soft all over. He pulled himself from his inappropriate thoughts and tied the ribbon in a bow at the end of the braid. "It looks very bonny on ye lass. Matches yer bodice and yer eyes."

She turned back to face him and ran a hand down her braid and gently stroked the soft ribbon. She blushed and looked away for a moment. "I canna thank ye enough m'laird. Ye are far tae kind." This time she took his arm before it was offered and they continued on their way. "So I was nae exacly focused when we met earlier so I hope ye can forgive me. But do I recall correctly that ye said yer name was Donnchadh?"

"Aye ye have the right of it lass."

"Seriously...Donnchadh MacLeod?!" She arched her eyebrows disbelievingly at him.

"Aye lass. Why would I jest about my name?" He questioned her, puzzled as to her response.

She was trying hard not to giggle. "Ye mean yer name translates to Duncan MacLeod...of the Clan MacLeod?" Oh this was too rich. Whatever force sent her here had a twisted sense of humor. The Highlander was her all-time favorite tv show and movie series.

He was truly confused now and perhaps getting a bit irritated. "Aye lass, though most dinna call me Duncan. Why is this a surprise or an amusement tae ye?"

She did her best to look apologetic, "Och I am sorry if I have offended ye m'laird. I am just curious if ye have a cousin named Connor who was born on the shores of Loch Shiel and died in yer grandfather's time." She bit back a smile as she waited his response. Her favorite part of The Highlander was the very first episode of the series where the hero Duncan MacLeod introduced the hero of the original movie, Connor MacLeod using a similar line and she was practically giddy at being able to use it now with Donnchadh.

Perhaps there was something more wrong with the lass. Perhaps the loss of her friends had unhinged her a bit. "I ken nae such person Mairead. Are ye sure ye are aright? Should I take ye back tae yer chamber tae rest?"

"Please forgive me m'laird. I fear I am overwrought and nae at my best. The fresh air off the Loch will do me well. I realize I have no thanked ye yet. Ye caught me afore I could fall and hurt myself. Thank ye for saving me and now being here for me takin my mind off of my loss today. Ye are my hero."

"Ye need no thank me lass. I am just glad I got tae ye when I did."

He was stiff and formal. She nodded quietly and turned to watch the field as they approached. Men were lifting great stones above their heads and hurling them as far as they could. 'Will ye be competing at all?" She looked up at his stern profile.

His continued to watch the competitors not looking down to meet her eyes. "Aye. As laird of the MacLeods it is expected of me, at least in the tug of war. Today I will be competing in the sheaf toss as well and tomorrow the sword dance."

"Oh my It has been sometime since I have seen the games up close. Last time I saw a friend compete and he tossed the sheaf so hard that it hit and bent the pole he was tae throw it over." She smiled at the memory as she watched the field. Donnchadh looked at her while she was unaware and was struck by the beauty and wistfulness he saw there. She was not like any one he had ever met. He had known her but a few hours and already she baffled him with her mentality and openness to him.

"Have ye been tae games often?" now he hoped she would look up at him. He felt like a green lad, his guts in knots and unsure of just what he really wanted.

"I used tae go regularly. I had friends that competed and some that played the pipes. So my friends and I, true friends, would go to the events and support them. We drank scotch, ate haggis, danced, sang, and more often than no finished the day off sitting around a fire." She looked so happy as she told him about her experience with highland games. Her eyes lit with joy at remembering the good times she had. He found he wanted to see more of that. He craved it like a balm. It struck him as rain on parched dry soil.

"It sounds as if ye had good friends and kenned how tae enjoy yerselves. I am curious though, did ye actually drink aqua vitae?"

His question surprised her and made her laugh. "Aye laddie. I like mine a bit sweeter. I love a well-aged single malt."

"No many women drink scotch it just surprised me."

"Aye well, I am just full of surprises now aren't I?" she winked at him and tugged his hand. "Come on, I want tae get closer. The crier just announced tha the sheaf toss was the next event. Should ye go get ready and where should I wait for ye? Where can I stand tae best see ye compete?"

Her exuberance amused him. Her enjoyment of the event was childlike and contagious. He escorted her to the side of the field closest to the sheaf toss "Aye, tis. Aye I should, and ye can wait for me over here where there is an opening in the crowd by the field. I will be back shortly lass." He winked at her and turned to join his clansmen. As he approached, they looked askance at him. Aside from Cait he had never been overly attentive to women. And even with Cait it had not been as public. They had not held hands and she attended the games with her brother so she was never there just for Donnchadh as this woman seemed to be. The problem was that no one recognized her. She was not a clanswoman and didn't belong to any of the families present. Gossip had spread like wildfire when Archie saw his brother catch the odd lass as she fell unconscious. Moreover, since they had emerged from the keep he had smiled at her several times. He had not smiled that much since Alasdair died.

Brogan slapped Donnchadh on the back as he adjusted his tartan so it would not be in the way of his toss. "Bonny lass ye have there laird!" he jutted his chin to where she stood. "What's her name then?"

"Her name is Mairead." Donnchadh told him offering nothing more. He looked around sizing up his competition. Cameron was the one that was closest to him in height and breadthand was just an inch or so shy of his own 6 foot 7 inches. There was also Brogan who was a good bit shorter and barrel chested but he was all muscle. When it came his turn, he did his best to keep his attention on the sheaf as he approached his mark and not look at her in the crowd. When he was given the signal, he grasped the pitchfork and hurled the burlap sack cleanly over the bar. All but two of the 9 competitors did so as well. Between his turns he watched her. Sometimes she was engrossed in the games and sometimes she would catch him watching her and smile and blush. Finally, he, Brogan, and Rabbie Macrimmon were left. Rabbie's toss did not clear the bar. He was out. Donnchadh took a deep breath and hurled it for all he was worth and it just barely cleared the bar. Normally he would not have minded so much if Brogan took first place while he took second. They were well matched and often passed winning titles back and forth. Today was not like that though. He wanted to win so badly he could taste it. He wanted to impress Mairead. She cheered for him each time he stepped to the mark and it did something to him. He had never wanted to impress Cait like this. He looked over to her and she looked to be on edge as much as he was, waiting for Brogan to toss his sheaf. She was adorable there, hands clenched before her chest and eyes wide. She looked as if she was even holding her breath.

Finally, after what felt like ages, Brogan tossed and the sheaf sailed through the air. He held his breath as he watched it. It looked as if it might be close but it struck the bar and fell. Everyone cheered for him and Brogan shook his hand with good sportsmanship while they exchanged pleasantries. She caught his eye again and he excused himself from the growing throng that was gathering to congratulate him on his win.

She was grinning as he approached. "Well done m'laird!' she leaned up on tiptoe and kissed his cheek. "Ye were very braw!"

He startled and pulled back from her. He had not expected her response. No lass had ever greeted him like that when he left the field after winning a game. Granted he had been kissed many times by lassies in dark corners and on a rare occasion by Cait, but there was a sweetness in this kiss he had never expected.

Mairead noticed his response and stepped back embarrassed. "Forgive me m'laird," she said downcast, "I dinna mean tae cross any boundaries. I was far tae forward and I am sorry."

It took Donnchadh a moment to process her response, which only made her feel more awkward. She turned back to look at the field to watch dancers prepare for their competitions to give him time to compose himself. She could have kicked herself. This was not her renaissance festival and she was not in her time. "I am the one who should be sorry lass. I dinnae mean tae offend wi my reaction. Merely caught me off guard." He addressed her and hoped she would look at him, meet his eyes and see that he appreciated her response to his win. She did look up to him briefly and flashed him a smile that was clearly placating and not genuine before turning back to the dancers. He did not like that smile. He did not like that she was humoring him when he tried to apologize. He did not understand this woman. He did not understand why he even cared what she thought or how she reacted. Cait had been easy. His relationship with her had been comfortable. Why couldn't all women be like that, easy to understand and get along with? He sighed and addressed her again. "Come lass, the day is waning and the dancers are on stage now. Let us go sit on that grassy area there." He pointed to a spot within clear view of the stage that was not overcrowded.

"Aye tha would be nice. My feet are fair sore." She began to walk toward the spot he indicated without waiting for him. He had not meant for her to do that. He wanted her to take his arm again. Instead, he was left to catch up. When he came abreast of her, he watched her for a moment. She was a confusing one. One moment warm and sweet and the next a distant stranger. Granted it was his fault for reacting the way he did to that peck on the cheek, but that did not mean he had to like it. They sat and watched the dancers. When the pipers played a particularly poignant song, she closed her eyes and swayed to the music and a tear rolled down her cheek. He could not take his eyes off her. He wiped the tear from her cheek with the pad of his thumb. Her eyes snapped open and bored into his. They were over bright with unshed tears. He wanted to ask her why she cried but he could not form words. After a few moments she broke eye contact. The music picked up again and was far livelier this time. Mairead sat there in contemplation of what had just happened. She saw something in his eyes that confused her. The dancers on the stage spun and jumped as if they were spring-loaded toys. Their elegance and power of movement was amazing. She told herself that she had to figure out where she stood here. Yes Donnchadh was beyond handsome and incredibly sweet sometimes, he was not for her. Surely a laird like him had some sort of arranged marriage planned to strengthen the clan. Even if she were to stay instead of finding a way home, she could bring nothing to a relationship and that was a scary thought in a time and place where a woman's safety and well-being virtually relied on a man. Hell, she was putting the cart waayyy before the house. He might not even like her. She realized he was staring at her instead of watching the stage. Surely his whole clan would notice them sitting in the middle of the field surrounded by other groups and families. "I was out of line earlier..." she began.

He shook his head and spoke over her. "Nay lass. ye were nay. Tha was the sweetest congratulations I ever received. It caught me off guard. I liked it and dinna ken how tae react." She blushed at his statement. He continued, "It has been some time since I was in feminine company, especially company so fine. A kiss from a pretty lass shocked me. I dinna expect it but I welcomed it. I just could no get the word out." It was his turn to blush.

Now she smiled at him, a genuine smile, one that he liked. "Well perhaps I shall have to congratulate ye again some time." He smiled back at her; he would welcome her method of congratulations any time.

"So wha made ye cry a moment ago lass? Was it me, my behavior when ye kissed my cheek?"

She laughed softly and shook her head. She looked at the piper that was playing, but it was not him she was seeing, not really, it was images of her friends she saw. "Nay m'laird t'was no ye. I was simply remeberin a time long ago. I was going away from my closest friends. Moving someplace new. And a group of my friends got together and surprised me. They put together a picnic at a park on a rivers edge near where we lived. I had a beloved friend who played the pipes and his wife played the bodhran. They played a selection of songs for me in honor of my departure. That was one of the songs they played and it always brings tears tae my eyes. Reminds me of them and the wonderful friendships and adventures I had."

The sun was setting and the purple hour was upon them. He continued to listen to her, enraptured. Fires were being lit and the dancers were done. The pipers switched to celebratory music as the day came to an end. He could not have cared less. She told stories like a true scots woman, with her whole heart and soul and it showed. It was as if she were giving a piece of herself to the listener. After a moment he realized she had gone silent and was looking at him questioningly.

He looked around then and realized what was going on. "Come lass. Tis time for dinner. Let us go eat and ye can tell me more of yer friends and adventures if ye like." He got up from where they sat and offered her his hand to help her up as well. She took it and once she was on her feet, he did not relinquish her hand, he simply kept hold of it and wrapped it around his arm, keeping his hand atop hers. She smiled up at him as they went back to the castle. "Ye shall sit wi me at the head table."

She looked at him surprised, "I have never dined in a great hall let alone at a head table. It seems like a great honor of which I am no deserving. I am not part of yer clan."

"Ye are plenty deserving lass. Besides ye dinna have a choice in the matter. As laird I command it." He arched a haughty eyebrow at her. She giggled and acquiesced.

When they entered the hall, all heads turned and the roar of the clan dropped to a dull whisper and rustle of those about the tables.

Mairead was sure that she was a thousand shades of red and Donnchadh led her to the empty table. It was one thing to have the attention of an audience when performing a bit, it was another to have an entire clan stare at her because she was an outsider with their laird. She had no idea that he had not dined there since Alasdair died and rarely even joined the clan for meals since Cait died. His clansmen were wary to say the least.

He pulled out a chair to his left for her. The chair to his right had been reserved for Alasdair and he still held that sacred. Maids brought out trenchers and set them on the table before them. Mairead's eyes lit up. She was at an actual renaissance feast in an actual castle eating real renaissance food. It was a history geek's dream! Then she spied what was on the platter before her, Haggis. She could barely contain herself. The clan faded into the background as the hum of people talking and eating resumed. She had read about feasts in great halls and the foods they served. She had even helped Brandon put together reasonable facsimiles of renaissance recipes for the living history center. She never in her wildest dreams thought she would enjoy the real thing.

Donnchadh was happy to see her enjoyment. He was proud of his home and his people and to share it with a beautiful lass was a pleasure he hadn't really had before. Cait was just part of the clan, she never reacted with this kind of naked joy and wonderment. It made him wonder again where she came from. With the fine weave of her clothes, one would think she was from a noble house and had experienced such a meal. He shrugged and decided it would be another question for later. He took her plate and served her some haggis with neeps and tatties. She grinned at him and thanked him as he placed it back in front of her. She leaned over her plate, inhaled the aromas of the food, and softly moaned in pleasure. Donnchadh barely heard the sound and it was possibly the most erotic thing he had ever heard. She paid him no mind and daintily picked up her fork and tasted her haggis. Her eyes closed and she moaned again and murmured "Sooo good!" before opening her eyes and taking a bite of neeps and tatties. Dear God he had just met the woman earlier that day and now he had a terrible cock stand just because she was enjoying her meal. What was wrong with him? He was not a lad of 16 to be unable to control himself! She was lovely, aye, but he barely knew her! He shifted uncomfortably in an attempt to make sure that she was not aware of his current issue. He roughly cleared his throat, "So ye like the food lass?

She glanced at him and with a mouth full of haggis and covered her mouth as she tried not to laugh and finished the bite. "Aye, I do! It is the best haggis I have ever had! Everything is delicious and so well-seasoned!"

"Our cook is a fine woman and Molly helps her with the seasoning. She has a way with herbs. They are putting their best foot forward for the celebration of the games but even our regular meals are outstanding."

"My compliments to the cook then! I don't know that I could ever cook neeps and tatties like this let alone haggis!"

"Do ye cook?"

"Aye. A bit of this and a bit of tha. I like tae try new recipes and edit them just a bit wi spice. A while back I made a rabbit tenderloin wi tasso and parmesan grits cake and a cream sauce. It came out so nicely. Next time I think I will add a bit more garlic."

"Sounds grand and fancy! I am no sure about the tasso and grits cake though. Never heard of those."

"Shit!", she thought to herself. She had gotten complacent and slipped. At least these were easy enough to explain. "Tasso is a type of smoked ham and a grits cake is kind of like oats mixed wi a lot of cheese to thicken them then cut in tae circles and baked until they have a nice golden-brown crust tae them. Takes some time and a bit o work but it is worth it." She shook her head. "I never got any complaints at least."

"So was tha yer job lass? Tae cook for nobility?"

She leaned back from the table and laughed for a moment. "Nay, I cooked for my family and friends on occasion simply because I enjoyed it and liked seeing them enjoy my cooking. It was rather gratifying"

His laugh was delightful and genuine. "Och I see now. If ye are wi us for a bit, might I ask ye tae cook for me some time?"

She glanced at him from the corner of her eye while she took a sip of wine. "For the whole clan or just ye?"

"If yer cooking is as grand as it sounds, I could nay imagine sharing! Just a meal for ye and me."

She beamed at him then. "Aye. I think I can manage tha some time. I noticed that ye have a plethora of sheep. I happen tae know a rather pleasant recipe for lamb shank with vegetables and an au jus tha I would be happy tae make for ye."

"Och my mouth is fair watering already at the thought of it!" She continued to amaze him. As people finished their meals, the tables were pushed back and a piper as well as a drummer with a bodhran entered the hall. They struck up a lively tune and the assembled clan danced. Donnchadh pushed his chair back, got up from the table, and offered Mairead his hand. "Will ye dance wi me lass?"

She looked up at him and shook her head. "I dinna dance much and I dinna ken these dances. I would trample all over yer feet and if ye have no noticed I am nay exactly a small lass."

"Aye. I have noticed." He grasped the back of her chair and leaned down so only she could hear. "Ye have curves in all the places I like them. I have tae admit that I am eager tae get ye on the dance floor just tae have an excuse tae touch more than yer arm or hand or tae wipe a wayward tear from yer cheek. Dinna worry I will lead ye through the steps and I am a braw lad, ye canna hurt me by steppin on my toes during a reel. Ye may no be a waif but ye are hardly capable of causin that kind of injury. If that is wha does me damage I am no fit tae be laird. So…will ye dance wi me now?" He hoped he had not offended her this time. Perhaps he had gone to far. He had not meant to tell her that he longed to touch her but it was true and it had been so long since he had the urge to dance. His heart was lighter than it had been in the past year and he longed to make the most of it.

She had looked down at her hands in her lap while he spoke softly to her. If she closed her eyes she could imagine they were the only two people in the room. When he asked her again to dance with him she looked up and met his eyes. They shined with mirth and a genuine happiness. She hesitated but a moment more and then took his offered hand. He led her around the table to the floor and placing his left hand on her waist and taking his right hand in hers, led her through a jig. During the next song the dancers separated into lines. Mairead realized she knew this one. Just this morning she had danced it with friends outside the faire gates. This time was different though, more exciting. She smiled at Donnchadh as she got into the rhythm of the dance. He arched an eyebrow at her in surprise that she seemed to dance this one with such ease. During the dance, there were stolen touches and heated looks as they came together and then were swept apart by the music time and again. For a time, everyone present forgot about any outside problems and simply enjoyed the celebration.

More than several dances later Mairead was exhausted. She didn't think she had ever danced that much at one event. Donnchadh was not far from her side talking with a few of his clansmen. She took advantage of the moment to slide down into a chair that had been pushed out of the way against a wall. She closed her eyes for a moment thinking about all that had happened that day. It had been wild and felt more like it had been a week rather than a single day. She was still not sure how she ended up here or how to get home for that matter. How much longer could she keep this up? Her thoughts spun.

"Come lass. Let's get ye tae yer chamber for the night." Donnchadh's voice had a sharp quality to it that roused her from her reverie in a jarring manner.

"Are ye alright m'laird?' She asked as she got up. He did not offer her his hand this time, merely began walking to the stairs. She almost had to run to catch up.

"Fine." He practically barked at her. He seemed like a different man from the one she had been dancing, laughing, and flirting with not all that long ago.

She reached out and grabbed his arm as they walked down the hall to her chamber. He stopped and rounded on her. "What do ye want mistress?" there was that formality again.

She took a step back at the anger she saw on his face. "What happened m'laird? One moment we were laughing and having a fine time, and the next ye are barking at me as if I have wronged ye terribly in some way. What did I miss?"

He took a fortifying breath and pinched the bridge of his nose. Christ he was making a fankle of this, of everything. He could not afford to let his guard down right now especially with all of the clans gathered. The MacLeods needed him at his best and strongest. She was a distraction, admittedly a welcome one, and perhaps had she shown up at any other time, one he would have readily embraced. Now was not the time however.

Murtagh and Brogan had reminded him of that once the dancing concluded while Mairead sat nearby looking so peaceful. But he was a laird who had shut himself off for a year and now his clan needed him desperately. He had no time for his own wants. He was theirs, his life was theirs and he would give all he had to protect and take care of his clan.

"Tis naught but my own folly. Ye have done naught." He did not offer anything more than that and simply turned once again to lead her to her door. He opened it for her and stepped out of the way to allow her to enter. "I had Molly bring ye a basin wi some water tae wash up a bit in. I also had her fetch ye a clean set of clothes." Gone was the softness she had heard in his voice earlier. She was wary of him now.

"Thank ye m'laird. Good night tae ye." She slid past him into her chamber and set about situating her belongings so that she would not have to look at him.

"Good night mistress." With that, he shut the door and left. She looked up when she heard the soft click of the door closing. What the hell had happened? Why was he treating her like this all of a sudden? She removed her bodice and skirt. She changed into the fresh chemise and crawled into bed. As she lay there, she remembered what she loved about romance novels that at the same time made her kind of nuts. It was the "Insta-love". The hero and heroine would take one look at each other and fall madly in love or at least be drawn to each other inexplicably. The hero didn't do random one hundred eighty degree turns in his attitude and she certainly was not a romance novel leading lady even if her host looked like he belonged on the cover of a bodice ripper. So knowing that, why did that exchange outside her door hurt so much? She shouldn't care about it so much. She finally drifted off to a restless sleep.

Donnchadh had a terrible night after he left Mairead's room getting only a few hours' sleep. He knew it was better that they not get any closer but it had cut him to the quick when she had flinched and stepped back from his angry outburst. He kept telling himself she was a distraction. He rose early. It was the last day of the games. He plaited a braid into the hair at his temples and readied himself for the day. As he left his chamber to go to the games he stopped in front of her door. He could hear her humming and moving about the chamber. His heart clenched. He raised his hand to knock and then dropped it, changing his mind. His clan needed his full focus today.

Mairead had been up for some time. She took her time dressing and was trying to figure out what to do with her hair when she heard boots that she assumed belonged to Donnchadh approach her door and stop for a moment. She held her breath hoping that he would knock, but after a moment the boots continued on down the hall. Her shoulders sagged and she gave up on her hair and decided to pull it back into a simple ponytail at the base of her neck. She ran a finger over the green ribbon he had given her wistfully, and then used it to secure her wild curls. She had nothing else to use. She was sure she was as ready as she was going to get. She could hear the castle waking up around her and could see the village and market beginning the day as well. For all her frustration, she was still awed by the thought that she was in fact at real highland games and enjoying a stay in a real castle with all that came with it. She was even dressed in actual historic clothing! She should be on cloud nine right now, and she was close just not quite there. She looked down and smoothed the soft blue skirt and burgundy bodice, which she wore over a simple cream chemise. This bodice laced in the front and she was tickled to find out that it was stiffened with whale bone. She was not hungry so she skirted the great hall and made her way out to the market. Molly flagged her down as she was about to step out of the castle gates.

"Och tis glad I am I caught ye lass Donnchadh asked me tae see ye got this." She handed Mairead a small pouch. "I hope ye enjoy the games and the market today!" she was already hurrying away before Mairead was even fully aware of what was happening. "Thank ye!" she yelled at Molly's retreating back. She opened the pouch and found several coins. She was confused for a moment and then remembered that she had told Donnchadh that all her money had been taken yesterday. She didn't want to take his money but she would need to eat and drink during the day. Bearing that in mind she decided that she would return the remains of the money to him that evening when and if she saw him. She was not holding her breath if last night and this morning were any indication.

She would be lying if she said she was not looking for Donnchadh in the crowd, but she did not see him and she was not sure why that concerned her so. She decided that she would think no more of it for the time being and instead gave herself over to the experience of being at what was essentially an actual festival in what might have been the renaissance era. She did not know the exact year, but it certainly had to be around that time judging by the modes of dress and behavior. She meandered aimlessly for some time. It was usual Scottish weather with a fine mist and clouds scudding across the sky, but that did not seem to dampen anyone's spirits. She stopped and watched dancers and eventually decided that she needed a drink. She should probably eat something too but she was not as concerned about that as her thirst. She found a booth Donnchadh had taken her to yesterday and ordered some mead. She emptied the mug they provided her into her own mug and proceeded to continue her explorations. Perhaps if she went back to the area she had been in when she first realized there was a problem, she could get home. Or maybe she could find some clue as to what happened or why she was here.

Alas there was nothing there aside from the same few vendors and she did not notice anything odd. She heaved a sigh and walked back to the main field of the games. She noticed that there was a large crowd gathered and she could hear a rollicking tune coming from bagpipes. As she neared, she saw that men in kilts were dancing over swords that lay crossed on the ground. She remembered that Donnchadh told her he would be taking part in this. She glanced around the dancers with their arms upraised and their feet flew in patterns around the swords. She finally spotted him off to one side. All of his focus was given to the dance. One by one men left the field as their feet touched the blades as they danced. It was down to just a few men now. Donnchadh had not seemed to notice her yet and she was glad of that. It gave her a moment to study him. He was indeed strong and handsome, and ridiculously tall, but she reminded herself that he was not for her and she was being foolish in even entertaining any thought of anything at all, much less romance with him. She watched long enough to see that Donnchadh won and quickly turned and lost herself in the crowd. She was glad for him, really. She wandered a bit longer and found herself a quiet patch of heather covered hillside where she could sit and enjoy the mug of ale and the scotch egg she procured while out of the hustle and bustle of the market but still able to hear the skirl of the pipes. This reminded her of the times she had attended renaissance festivals alone and where she knew no one. She still loved them but they could make you painfully aware of just how alone you were. The scenery here was like nothing she had ever seen. It was breathtaking. Fishing boats dotted the loch and the area surrounding the castle was a riot of color. And the castle itself stood above it all like a proud king surveying his domain.

Donnchadh was exhilarated after the sword dance. Of course, he had won. He loved it. He could have sworn he saw Mairead in the audience at one point and he was glad she was there to see him do something he loved so much. But when all was said and done and he had accepted his accolades he looked to where he saw her last and she was not there. There would be no congratulatory kiss on the cheek this time. He had no right to even desire such a thing, but it made his heart a little heavy that she had not stayed for his win. He just met her yesterday. There was no way she should have such a pull on his emotions. Still he kept an eye out for her as he traversed the market. His clansmen were much more at ease with him today than they had been last eve, which made things easier, but he hated the reason for it. He realized that he had no idea what she was wearing. He had not seen what Molly had dropped off for her the night before. Occasionally he would catch a small vibrant flash of green and hoped that it was the green ribbon he had given her woven into her hair. That had not been the case so far. Where in damnation had she gone? The games were not that large, in fact they were rather small in comparison to some of the others. Towards midday something seized his attention. There was a lass sitting on the hillside alone. He could not be sure, but he thought the hair was the same rich brown of Mairead's. He had to check.

Mairead finally admitted, if just to herself, that she was grateful for this vantage point. Every now and then, she could see Donnchadh head and shoulders above most of the crowd. He would stop, converse, and then continue on his way. He seemed to be looking for something. She sat there, chin resting upon her knees and her arms around her legs trying not to feel sorry for herself. She looked off to the left at the beauty and majesty of the Loch and drank it in. When she turned to look back at the games and market, Donnchadh was gone. She figured it was probably for the best, the reality was that she was just torturing herself with him. She shifted where she sat and this time rested her forehead on her knees and closed her eyes. She just needed to clear her head. She had been like that for a while when she heard someone approaching. She didn't bother to look up.

As Donnchadh got closer, he could tell that it was indeed Mairead and he was relieved to have found her. When he drew near, he cleared his throat and addressed her. "Are ye alright lass? Might I join ye?"

She lifted her head and he hoped to see her smile there. Instead, he was greeted with an impassive face that might as well have declared him a stranger to her. "I am fine m'laird. And ye can sit anywhere ye like as this is yer land and ye are laird." there was no malice in her tone, it was just flat. That was almost worse than her upset.

He nodded and settled down beside her, close to her but not so close that he was touching her. "How long have ye been up here Mairead?"

"Why does it matter? I have been here long enough to enjoy the view and eat." She said nothing more.

He gave a bitter sort of a laugh. "Ye are nae going tae make this easy are ye lass?"

Her head jerked sharply to look at him. "I am no making this easy?! Just wha am I no makin easy?? Is it troubling ye tha I am no swooning over ye and falling all over meself just because ye deigned tae seat yer lairdly arse on the same hillside as me? So tell me m'laird just what am I no makin easy for ye?"

Her vitriol surprised him for a moment; perhaps she was not as unaffected as he thought. "I wanted tae apologize for last night. I just had to come to a difficult realization and I was no exactly...."

"And that gives ye the right tae snap at me as ye did? Granted I am no one of yer clansmen but I dinna deserve tae be treated like a bug under yer boot heel." She withdrew the pouch Molly had given her. She saw his look of confusion as she withdrew a coin and then hurled the bag at him. "I hope for yer clan's sake ye dinna have tae make any more difficult decisions. I will be leaving so it does nae matter that ye take it out on me as much, but yer clansmen cannot leave and will appreciate yer temperament even less I am sure! So take yer coins and yer difficult decision and shove it!" She shot up off the ground, dusted the grass and heather from her skirts and began a brisk walk down the hill back to the booth selling mead. She ordered another mug.

Donnchadh sat there for a minute wondering what the hell had just happened. He meant to ask her forgiveness yet she was mad at him now. He did not understand. He watched her leave with a sense of de ja veux. He looked over the field and noticed that they were setting up for the final event, the tug of war. He ambled down the hill and saw Mairead at the ale tent ordering a drink. He was unsure what to make of it.

She downed her mead in short order while she watched the tug of war. This time Donnchadh was aware of her and glanced at her on occasion. She went back to get another mug of mead. He watched her with a concerned expression. She noticed and gave him a mocking salute with her mug.

The MacLeods carried the day. The games ended and now people were packing up their belongings and tearing down booths. Again, he looked for her in the retreating crowd of people making their way back to the keep. In the looming dusk, he could just make her out. She was not as steady on her feet as he would have liked. He began to head after but James intercepted him. He clapped Donnchadh on the back as he shook his hand. Fine showing m'laird! Tis glad I am tha we have ye back! For so long ye cloistered yerself in the keep and we worried about ye."

"I am glad tae be back James, Now if ye would excuse me." He patted the man on the back in return and then went around him. He scanned the people walking down the lane to the castle and saw her just in time to see her stop just on the side of the road, drain her mead, stand there for a moment and then resume her walk with her mug dangling from her fingers. Christ he thought to himself, the lass was plastered. He tried to get to her quickly but she was too far ahead of him and the lane too packed with people. By the time he reached the castle, she was gone. He ran up the stairs and down the hall to her room. Before he could open the door, he heard her singing. Her voice sounded different. He stopped and listened to her.

"Wherever I may roam, by land or sea or foam, you can hear me singing this song; Show me the way to go home!" she paused and then there was another outburst "Fuck! Please just show me the damned way already. This sucks!"

He tapped on her door and heard what sounded like a furious scramble and then silence. Just when he thought he might have to break the door down to check up on her, she none too steadily opened the door. "Och Donnchadh! Wha are ye doin here laddie buck?! No come to tell me of any difficult decisions I hope"

He looked sternly down at her. "Lass ye are knackered. I wanted to make sure ye were alright."

"I am a big girl m'laird and can hold my liquor just fine. Been drinking stronger shite than tha mead for years so dinna worry yer pretty little head about the likes of little old me." Then she tried to close the door on him but he stopped it with his boot. Apparently, she did not realize his part in it because she tried to close the door again, and again he stopped it. This happened a few more times before she gave up, tossed her arms up in the air and ambled over to one of the chairs by the fire and collapsed bonelessly into it. He would have been laughing at her repeated attempts if he had not been so irked about how she spoke to him and treated him.

He followed her and sat in the chair across from her. "Lass I am so sorry for the way I treated ye. Ye have the right of it, ye did no deserve my ire. But I hardly think that warrants getting plastered and ill-treating me."

She gave a snort that sounded like a laugh. "Sucks don't it, tae be treated like so much shite. I have no gotten drunk like this in years." She laughed outright this time. "If only Michaels could see me now.

The lass's moods changed so fast they gave him whiplash. He did not understand all of what she was saying but it seemed that she was, if not accepting, at least acknowledging his apology. "Who is Michaels lass?" he leaned forward with his elbows on his knees.

"A drunken friend. Saved his arse many a time. Used tae tell me 'Next time we go out to drink I'll stay sober and let you drink since you always end up taking care of us drunks.' Problem is," her voice lowered to a conspiratorial whisper, "It takes me a hell of a lot tae get drunk and I have a nasty habit of soberin more quickly than my friends so tha never happened. It was more of the same. Friends go out, friends drink, friends realize the person designated to stay sober is 4 shots deep. Mairead is the only one cognizant enough tae stop drinking so she can make sure that everyone got home safe. Always the same. 'Hey Mairead, lets treat ye tae drinks this time!....oops sorry we had tae much and ye seem like yer sober, can ye get us home?'"

Donnchadh was not sure how to handle her outburst. He decided that he would try to let her know she was safe with him and there was no one else she need worry about. "I cannae imagine how frustrating that must ha been. Well if ere ye feel like having a drink here, dinna worry that anyone else will need ye tae take care of them. I will take care of ye as they should have. I just worry about the hangover ye will have in the morn." He winked at her.

She laughed hard for a moment and then sighed, shaking her head and looked at him, trying not to giggle, "Thank ye Donnchadh. And I dinna get hangovers so I am just fine. Dinnna worry over me!" Another giggle escaped her. He had to admit she was quite amusing like this. He had never known someone that did not get hangovers before. Perhaps she was just telling him that to make him feel better. He noticed that she was getting up out of her chair. She was swaying as she tried to make it over to the bed.

"Think it is time fer bed fer me." She mumbled as she fell onto it. He got up and went to her side to help her. She was already half asleep when he scooped her up so that he could place her properly in the bed instead of hanging half off it. "Mmmmm I like yer big muscles Duncan. Ye smell good too." She mumbled against his chest. He froze momentarily. Indeed, he had been called Duncan on occasion but no one had ever said it like that, as if his name was hers alone to say as if she claimed ownership of it. Once he laid her down, he realized that there was a slight problem. She was now snoring gently and still in her bodice and skirt. The maids were most likely down at the Ceilidh so there was no one to help her, except him. He swallowed hard pulled at the string that laced the bodice together down the front of her chest. As the bodice loosened, she drew a deep breath and shifted in her sleep. When she did that, he accidentally grazed her breast with his knuckles while trying to finish unlacing her. God she was so soft and warm. Even with her chemise between them, it practically shocked his fingers whenever he touched her. It was not altogether unpleasant. Several times, he had to stop and take a breath. She had him so turned on and there was nothing he could do about it. She was so soft and pliant in her sleep. When he finally removed the offending clothing and she was just down to her chemise and stockings, he drew the covers up over he, kissed her forehead and left the room. Once he was out in the hallway, he leaned his head against the door and groaned in frustration.

"Surely it can no be as bad as all that eh lad?" he almost jumped out of his skin when he heard Molly speak up behind him. He whirled around guiltily to look at her. He knew how this must look. Leaving a lassie's room this late in the eve.

"Och nae tis no Molly. Just a long day." He did his best to keep his voice even.

She nodded and squinted her eyes at him "Hmm" she grunted and then spoke "Ye take care of that lass ye hear? She is a good one and will mean more tae ye than ye ken. She has a soft heart and does no deserve any of yer blustering. Never mind what the other lads say. She is important, for the clan as well as ye. Ye had best heed me in this Donnchadh lad."

Donnchadh had never been so confused in his life. "Aye Molly, I will take care of the lass. But what do ye mean that she will be important tae me and the clan? What are ye talking about?"

Molly crooked a finger for him to lean down to her. Once she could look him in the eye, she patted him on the cheek. "Dinna worry yer pretty little head about tha." With that she turned and left the way she came. He shook his head as he watched her. She had said the same thing to him that Mairead had earlier and he thought it rankled but now he was not sure. The woman was vexing as well as daft. But Molly had not steered him wrong yet. Tomorrow after Mairead recovered, he resolved to apologize again and make up for treating her the way he had.

Chapter Four

M airead stretched and realized the light streaming in through the narrow window had woken her. She sat up in bed and surveyed the carnage around her. The bed was a rumpled mess, her bodice and skirt from yesterday were in a pile on the floor and the chairs in front of the fireplace sat at haphazard angles with pillows strewn across the floor. Slowly she remembered the night before. She had a fair amount to drink on what amounted to an empty stomach and made an ass of herself. She remembered the exchange on the hillside and drinking still more while she watched him at the tug of war. She also recalled telling him about some of her drinking adventures. Thankfully she had not let anything incriminating slip. The one thing she could not remember was how she got out of her clothes and into bed. Thankfully she was still immune to hangovers otherwise she was sure she would be in a very bad place right now. She heaved herself out of bed and padded over to the wardrobe. She pulled out a soft butter yellow dress and selected a narrow-sleeved chemise to wear underneath. She used a comb that lay by the basin to brush out her curls and then dunked her hands in the water and ran them through her hair to re-curl it. She then tied the ribbon around her head like a headband and made her way to the great hall for breakfast. She was surprised at the number of people breaking fast. She had expected more of them to be recovering from the previous night's celebrations. Donnchadh saw her the moment she entered the room and motioned her over to his table. The lass looked positively glowing in the soft yellow dress. The color was lovely on her and hugged her curves almost sinfully. 'Good mornin Mairead. How fare ye?" He asked gently.

She laughed softly as she approached and ran her hand across his shoulders as she passed behind his chair. "I told ye last eve that I am fine. I dinna get hangovers. Tis just another morn for me." She scooped some kippers on to the trencher in front of her and sipped the small beer the maid poured for her.

"Hmm ye truly dinna suffer after a night of drinking." He was surprised to say the least. To see the lass one would never think she had been out of her head with drink last night.

She took a bite of the kippers with a piece of fresh baked bread and shrugged. "Just lucky I guess. I am sorry for my behavior last night. I have no drank quite like that in years. I always try tae have some food on my stomach tae balance it. I had only a scotch egg sometime around mid-day and a good quantity of mead before and obviously after."

"I am the one who needs tae apologize lass. I treated ye terribly the other night and was not much better yesterday. I should not have. Ye are more deserving of respect than my blustering as Molly calls it." He gave her a half smile. "How much do ye remember about last eve?"

She glanced sidelong at him and tore off a hunk of the bread. "I remember most all of it. Made a right arse of meself as

I recall." She tore off a small piece of the bread and popped it into her mouth.

"Nay lass ye did no. Ye were fine, quite a friendly drunk as it happens."

She snorted quietly and then looked at him again. "There is one thing tha puzzles me. I dinna remember removing my skirt and bodice and getting in tae bed."

Donnchadh swallowed hard. "Aye well ye were fair gone at that point. I picked ye up and laid ye in bed so that ye dinna fall."

"Ah. Makes sense. Thank ye. That still does not explain my clothing."

"I had tae remove it for ye. The maids were all at the Celidh. I promise ye I was a gentleman and did no take advantage."

She sat there blinking down at her trencher for a moment. Some of the memories slowly came back to her. He had scooped her up as if she was light as a feather. She had told him she liked his muscles! She had called him Duncan and nuzzled his chest! What the hell was wrong with her!? If that all happened then had he really kissed her on her forehead before he left the room? He hadn't said anything about it so she pushed that aside as a dream. Her face felt like it was flaming with embarrassment now. She could barely meet his gaze. "I promise ye, I dinna drink like that normally. I was far tae forward when ye assisted me tae bed." She practically whispered the last part. Thankfully those gathered were engrossed in their breakfasts and had nary a care for what the laird's guest might or might not be saying.

He tilted her face toward him with a finger under her chin. His heartbeat sped up at the memory of her nestled in his arms and what she said. "Ye were no tae forward." He spoke low enough that only she would hear. "Ye were adorable and charming." He was quiet for a moment and then began again. "In fact if ye would like ye may call me Duncan when we are in private."– He knew he should not suggest it as it seemed far too intimate.

She stared unblinking for several heart beats. "Aye, I would like." She smiled up at him. Donnchadh was sure he would have kissed her had they not been interrupted by someone clearing their throat. He dropped his hand and turned to address the interloper. It was Brogan.

"M'Laird some of the crofters beg yer indulgence. Mistress Lottie's thatch is leaking and wi her husband gone and a wee bairn she canna see to it herself. Angus is asking about building a fence tae pen his sheep so his neighbor Donald canna claim them. Seems they had another falling out. And of course it looks as if there might be a storm brewing so the upper pasture needs to be checked and fencing secure so we dinna give the bloody MacDonalds an opening."

"I shall join ye presently Brogan, and ride out tae see tae the matters. Tell the stable lads tae saddle Loach for me." He sighed and turned back to Mairead once Brogan was making his way out of the hall. "Such is the life of a laird. I shall be gone most if not all of the day." She looked crestfallen at that. "Can ye ride?"

"Aye, I can. I love tae ride and have some skill at it."

"Would ye like tae join me then lass?" He was hopeful but held his breath.

"Indeed, I would m'laird! I would very much like tha! I promise tae stay out o the way."

He grasped her hand and pulled her from her seat not caring that people stared. He bellowed for the stable lads to saddle Realta as well. She almost had to run to keep up with him. Once the horses were saddled and the men were ready, Molly emerged from the kitchen with two saddlebags laden with food for all of the lads. She winked conspiratorially at Mairead. "I packed ye a wee surprise tae share wit the laird later. Ye will ken it." Donnchadh took the saddlebags from her, loading one up on his horse and handing another to a clansman named Cameron. He gave Molly a quick kiss on the cheek and turned to Mairead to assist her into her saddle. She had insisted that it not be a sidesaddle and he was interested to see how she would handle the young horse. Realta was a spirited chestnut filly with a blaze on her forehead and two white socks on her front legs and another small white marking on her rump. Before he could reach her, Mairead hiked up her skirt, planted a foot in one stirrup and hoisted herself deftly into the saddle. This truly would prove to be an interesting day he though as he watched her adjust the reins and make sure her skirts covered as much of her legs as possible. She caught him staring and shook her head laughingly. "Dinna we have a good bit tae see tae this day? We willna get aught done with ye standing there gawping." She gave a gentle nudge to her horse and made a clicking sound with her mouth. Realta responded immediately and eagerly swung around and headed toward the gate. Donnchadh and his clansmen were left to stare after the lass. After a long moment of stunned silence, Donnchadh slapped Brogan's horse on its withers as he passed him to get to his horse.

"Ye lot heard the lass, lets go!" He swung up into his saddle and kicked Loach into a trot to catch up with Mairead. The lass may have had no idea where they were going, but she was a brave one, he would give her that. Cameron and Brogan rode just behind him. Cameron pushed shaggy black hair out of his eyes and watched as Donnchadh pulled abreast of Mairead. More and more he liked the lass. The fact that she did not wait for Donnchadh's help and was even eager to be about their business for the day was in her favor. He also had to admit that the lass had a good seat. Brogan was not so comfortable about her yet. He felt she was an unwelcome distraction. Donnchadh was coming out of the morass he had been in and did not need the lass clouding his judgement. The clan needed their Laird not a besotted swain. He snarled and kicked his mount into a trot to catch up to Donnchadh.

"M'laird, do ye think it necessary for the lass tae come wi us? We attend personal clan business today and she is an outsider after all." He addressed Donnchadh as he rode up beside him.

"I understand yer concern Brogan, I do. However, I have made my decision. I am laird and if I say the lass goes wi' us, she indeed goes wi' us." He looked sharply at Brogan. Granted he had no love for outsiders but Brogan had never been this outspoken about one before. It gave him a brief pause and then he remembered what Molly had told him about the Mairead. She was important.

"If my presence is a cause for concern or may discomfort yer crofters, I can go back. I dinna want tae cause any upset." Mairead offered to placate Brogan. She did not want to cause any strife amongst the men. Had she thought it would cause an issue, she would have declined.

Donnchadh gave Brogan another hard look and then turned back to Mairead. "Nay lass. Ye are goin out wi' us. The decision has already been made. Yer presence is no cause for upset. Brogan oversteps his bounds in this. That aside, I think my crofters will like ye." He gave her a broad smile as Brogan fell back to his place by Cameron. "Ye look as if ye are comfortable on Realta."

She smiled at him and leaned over to stroke the filly's neck. "Aye! She has a lovely gait and her temperament is wonderful." Donnchadh wished she would stroke him like that. The thought struck him and while it did not surprise him, it annoyed him. Yes, Molly said he needed to take care of Mairead, but that did not mean to act like a lecher over her. He should not be thinking of her thusly. She was not a village doxy. "I will be honest wi' ye. I have tae wonder what it would be like tae fly over the fields wi' her. Several years ago, I visited a lovely beach and was able to ride a wonderfully spirited paint pony named Cheena down the beach. Och she was amazing. All I had wanted tae do for years before that was tae fly down the beach on horseback enjoying the surf and the sand. She was a spirited one. Could no stand to have someone ahead of her. The lass who was our guide getting tae the beach warned me once we got started she would nae stop until there was no one close tae keeping up wi her. Most of our group stayed close tae the trailhead while the guide and I kicked our mounts into a trot and then a gallop. She was right. The second her mount slightly edged further than Cheena, she took off like a bat out of hell. We rode hell bent for leather down that beach for a while. Eventually the guide fell away and it was just Cheena and me racing down the beach. It was an amazing feeling, her powerful hooves pounding the sand below me, the breeze off the ocean and the gulls flying overhead and naught else." She closed her eyes for a moment, reliving the memory.

Donnchadh was transfixed. She had so much passion. He found himself wanting some of that for himself. "Perhaps later we can put the wee beastie through her paces later and see just how the twa of ye get along and find out if she can take on this old war horse of mine. Be warned, he is a stubborn one. Does nae like tae lose, much like his master."

She opened her eyes and turned to him with a smile. "I like the sound of that m'laird!" she leaned low over Realta's neck. "What do ye think Realta?" The horse's ears flicked back at her as if to catch what she was saying. "Can we take on these lads and show them that we are not tae be taken lightly?" Realta tossed her head, whickered as if she understood Mairead, and agreed. The men, aside from Brogan laughed at that.

The party stopped at a small croft and a woman with a baby in her arms emerged. "Och m'laird! I cannae thank ye enough for coming tae look at my roof. Since my Johnny passed last winter I have no been able to see to it with wee Kenna needing my attention."

He approached the woman and ran a gentle hand over the bairn's head. "Worry not mistress. We shall see ye taken care of. Come lads! Let's see what we are working with. Mairead, would ye mind spending some time wi mistress Lottie and wee Kenna while the lads and I see tae the roof?"

"T'would be my pleasure." She smiled at Lottie and then dismounted before he could come her aid. It was most impressive but also frustrating. He wanted an excuse to touch her. He nodded and turned back to the croft as he saw her introduce herself to Lottie.

Lottie was a sweet plump woman with straight blond hair pulled back into a braid, a soft voice, and gentle demeanor. Mairead liked her almost instantly. The two of them sat on a bench at the edge of the garden and talked while the men worked. At one point Donnchadh looked up to see the two of them laughing and Mairead holding Kenna on her lap. He thought it a beautiful sight. A moment later Cameron jabbed him in the side. "Eyes forward Laird. Much tae do. Would no want ye fallin off the roof because of a buxom wee lass now."

Donnchadh snorted with amusement, "Ye cheeky bastard."

Once the roof was repaired the men mounted up. This time Donnchadh did not offer to help Mairead mount. She was atop her horse as quickly as the lads. He turned to Lottie, "Now if aught else happens ye come tae the castle and we'll see ye taken care of." She bobbed a quick curtsey and agreed. "Johnny was a good lad and would no want tae see ye do wi'out. And perhaps ye can join us for meals in the great hall on occasion." He saw how well the two women got along and wanted Mairead to have someone to talk to that was not one of his clansmen. Perhaps he was a bit jealous. It was a new feeling for him.

Next, they made their way to Angus's home. The old man had seen them coming and was waiting on the roadside as they approached. He did not even wait for them to dismount before launching into a tirade about his neighbor stealing his sheep. Mairead didn't pay much attention to the outburst as she dismounted. The croft they were at now was on the outskirts of the village. It was beautiful. Blue sky was peeking through the clouds and a breeze blew across the field. A hawk soared overhead and she watched it for a moment. She looked back at Donnchadh to see him and his men listening intently to Angus. He stood there arms across his chest and stance wide. There was no way he could be mistaken for anything but the leader of these men. A man that looked to be of an age with Angus emerged from a home just down the road and marched over to the group and added to the cacophony that was Angus. She figured that must have been Donald, the sheep thief of a neighbor. She heard enough to understand that two of Angus's lambs had gone missing and Donald had to be the thief. While the men continued to debate and discuss the situation, she decided to look around. She rounded the stone croft and saw the aforementioned flock. The land was beautiful here. A stream ran behind the house and tree branches dipped low enough that they almost touched the water. She noticed two ewes staying closer to the stream than the rest of the flock and decided to investigate. The rushing water was a bit noisy, but she could hear something on the other side. It seemed to be coming from a small copse of trees. She got closer to the stream and bent down. She caught a glimpse of white between the leaves. She stepped closer still and was able to see that there was a lamb hiding there Surely the two ewes nearby were trying to look out for their young.

She looked around for a bridge or even some rocks to cross the stream by, but she could see none and it was just a bit too wide to make it over in one jump. That settled it for her; she would wade across and carry the lambs back with her. She removed her shoes and hiked up her skirt. She dipped one foot in the water and gasped. It was freezing cold, like ice water cold. She thought for a moment about getting Donnchadh's attention and letting him carry the lambs across but he was still engrossed in dealing with Angus and Donald and she was here now. She took a deep breath and stepped again out into the water. The stream was deeper than she thought. It came almost to her knee, with the water was rushing around her soaked her skirt. A few more steps and she was on the other bank. She slowly approached the lamb's hiding place. She saw that there were indeed two of them. She wondered if these might be the two stolen lambs. She gently picked up one and was halfway across the stream when she heard Donnchadh yelling for her. "Mairead lass! Where are ye??" He was just coming around the croft when he spotted her in the middle of the stream with a lamb in her arms. He startled her and she slipped a bit. "Och Christ! I am coming lass!"

He ran across the yard toward her, his men following with Angus and Donald bringing up the rear. "I am fine!" She tried to reassure them as she regained her footing and took another careful step. She was near enough to the bank that Donnchadh was able to reach down and grab her by the arms to pull her from the stream. "What in the bloody hell do ye think ye are doin lass?! Tha water is deep enough and moving fast enough that it could hae swept ye away and us none the wiser!" His voice was raised and he gestured to the stream.

"I told ye, I am fine. I was looking around when I noticed the two ewes away from the rest of the flock and standing by the river. I got closer and I could hear bleating. Sure enough, I spied the two lambs. Ye were busy, and there was no bridge or any other way across, so I took matters into my own hands." She set the lamb down and it bounded over to its mother. "Now, if ye would be so kind as to assist me, there is another lamb still over there, or I can go across again and get it." She turned back toward the stream.

Donnhadh grabbed her arm and spun her around before she could get far. "Ye will be the death of me lass." He looked down at her for a moment and then stepped around her toward the stream and crossed it in two steps, grabbed the other lamb and brought it back across. The freezing water soaked his boots. Once he sat the lamb down and watched it make its way to its mother he turned and addressed Angus. "Might these be yer missing lambs?" The man had the grace to look ashamed.

"Aye they are. I was sore mistaken. I dinna think tae look across the stream. It swelled the other day and I dinna think any of my flock were on the other side. I am sorry Donald."

"Just be sure ye check there afore ye accuse me of anything ever again." Donald huffed and made his way back to his croft.

"Thank ye m'lady, m'laird! I dinna ken how I dinna see them there."

Donnchadh nodded and smiled at the man. He looked to Mairead then and he could see her shivering. She was putting her shoes back on and squeezing the water out of her dress. He scooped her up in his arms and carried her back to the horses. "Cameron, Brogan, can ye take the other two lads and see to the pastures and fencing?" Brogan looked as if he had just bitten something sour and was about to say something but Cameron interrupted him.

"Wi' out a doubt m'laird. We have it covered. Go take care of yer lassie". He shoved Brogan toward his horse. He then turned and emptied part of the food in one of Donnchadh's saddlebags into his. Once mounted, Cameron motioned for the men to follow him and they headed down the lane, Angus waved them off, said his goodbyes to his laird and then ambled back to his sheep. That left Donnchadh and Mairead standing between Loach and Realta.

"Come. Let me show ye sommat and get ye warmed up." He offered. She turned to mount Realta but was stopped by his hands on her waist. "Ye are ridin wi' me lass. Yer freezing from the water and I will no have ye shivering so hard ye fall off yer horse." He was relieved when she simply turned around to him and did not argue as he fastened Realta's reins to the back of his saddle. Once that was done, he swung up to his saddle and reached down for her. She put a foot in the offered stirrup for leverage and he pulled her up to sit across his lap.

He nudged Loach into action and Mairead wrapped her arms around his waist and leaned against his chest. She seemed to burrow into him. "Mmmm, ye are so warm!"

He wrapped an arm around her and adjusted her so that hopefully she would not notice how hard he had become. "Hmm, well chasing a lass across a field tae rescue sheep will do that to a lad."

"Thank ye Donnchadh."

"We are alone lass." She looked up at him in surprise and then a sweet smile spread across her face.

"Thank ye Duncan." She put her head on his chest again as he kicked Loach into a trot with Realta following suit. She fit perfectly in his arms and grasped him tighter at the sudden change of speed, which inordinately pleased him. A short time later, they crested a small hill. He turned Loach about so that he could show her the view of Dunvegan.

She gasped, struck by the awesomeness of the view, the castle, the loch, the village, all of it. He shifted, dismounted, and then raised his hands to grasp her waist and pull her from the saddle. Once she had both feet on the ground, he kept one hand on her waist while he dug into his saddlebag with the other. He pulled out a length of plaid and wrapped it around her shoulders. "There ye go lass, we will get ye nice and warmed up." She watched him as he proceeded to unload the rest of the items in the saddlebags. He spread another plaid on the ground nearby and there was also a bottle of mead. He motioned for her to join him sitting on the plaid. He uncorked the bottle of mead and offered it to her. "I would imagine this is what Molly was speaking of this morn." He chuckled

She took it from him and since they had no mugs or glasses. She took a sip from the bottle. It was heavenly on her tongue. The sweet honey flavor mixed with a bit of spice was perfect. She handed him the bottle and he took a gulp from it and set it aside within reach. She pulled her legs up under the plaid he had wrapped her in. "Are yer legs still cold lass?" He was a paradox. He was this large, strong, and admittedly handsome man who led an entire clan, and then he could be so gentle with her. Hands that swung a sword gently brushed a wayward curl from her cheek, and sharp blue eyes softened as he gazed at her.

"A bit, but it is no tae bad now. My feet and calves are a bit cold where my dress is still damp. I should be fine ere we make it home this evening." She assured him.

"Och, tis nae acceptable. Dinnae do that again lass. Call for me should something like that ever happen again. I promise ye I will come running. " He swiftly reached over and yanked her legs across her lap and set about removing her soft leather shoes.

"Donnchadh, I" He cut her off with a sharp glance and a raised eyebrow. She cleared her throat and began again watching him for approval. "Duncan I am fine. I promise. I am no made of glass."

He nodded appreciatively of her correction of his name. "I dinna say ye were, but Molly would skelp me if ye caught a chill because ye came out wi' me. She is fond of ye lass. And If ye tell anyone, I shall deny it, but the wee woman terrifies me betimes when she is angry. She wields a wooden spoon like a sword. I cannae tell ye how many bruised knuckles I suffered as a young lad." She had no stockings on today so there was nothing between her soft skin and his fingers. Her skin was indeed chilled so he began to rub his hands over her feet and calves. He drank in the sight of her as she leaned back on her elbows and let her head fall back

"Tha feels amazing! Thank ye Duncan!" She could not believe that she was sitting here with a Scottish lord rubbing her feet overlooking a castle in the Highlands of Scotland. She raised her head again and looked at him. His hair was a riotous mass of dark browns that seemed almost black in places, to light brown, auburn, and some burnished gold. His jaw was covered with a well-trimmed beard that was a similar mix of colors. His features were hard in a way that would make women stare. Combine that hair and face with the tall chiseled body, and she could swear she had just died and gone to Scottish heaven.

"Ye are welcome lass. I ken it is no exactly proper for a man tae touch a lady's feet and calves like this but extreme times call for extreme measures" Now he was massaging her feet more than rubbing them to restore warmth. She felt so dainty in his hands. He wondered why she risked her fool neck for those sheep. She did save him some major trouble between Angus and Donald though and spared him what was sure to have been a massive headache.

"Proper or improper has naught tae do wi it lad! T 'would be improper if ye stopped o the now." She laughed and tapped his leg with her free foot.

"Och we cannae abide that kind of impropriety!" as he said that his fingers lightly danced across the sole of her foot. She laughed and tried to yank from his hold but his grip was stronger. "Hmmm a bit ticklish are ye?" He lightly traced her foot in the same manner. She laughed more and renewed her attempts to escape him.

"Aye! Aye ya beast I am! Leave off!" She pushed at him with her other foot in an attempt to free herself. She could hardly catch her breath from laughing as his assault was almost continuous now. He grabbed her other foot and yanked it into his lap as well tickling each foot in turn. "Stop! Ple...plea...Dear God please stop." She could barely get a word out for laughing so hard. She tried to sit up and push at him but he was like a great stone. Solid and immovable. He just laughed and tickled her feet more.

"Do I hear ye beggin for mercy?" He stopped for a moment and leaned as if to hear her better.

"Aye! Mercy! Please!" She begged gasping.

He tickled her again and she shrieked with laughter "Och I thought ye said Nay Mercy!" he pretended bemusement after a few moments and loosened his grip on her feet. She sat up abruptly her eyes still sparkling with laughter. Neither of them realized just how close they had been. Laugher died in her throat. He closed the small distance that separated them and pressed his lips to hers in a gentle kiss. She stilled, surprised and then melted into the kiss. She slid a hand up his chest and around his neck. He groaned as he kissed her and then speared his fingers through her hair. They fed at each other's mouths as if they were starving. When he pulled back, they were both breathing heavily.

"I swear tae God if ye apologize and do no do that again we will have problems." She exclaimed before he could even think to do such a thing. So he just smiled, adjusted their position to a slightly more comfortable one where she sat in his lap yet again.

He leaned into her again and was millimeters away, "Would nae dream of it lass!" He closed the gap and kissed her again. His tongue traced the seam of her lips and she opened to him with a sigh. He groaned and devoured her. She tasted divine, like the spiced mead she liked so well. Her hands explored his chest and shoulders while one of his stayed anchored in her hair. The other explored the curve of her hip and her luscious ass. As if of his own accord, his hand began to travel down the length of her leg, down her thigh to her calf, stopping at the hem of her dress and sliding his hand under it. Their kiss grew more heated as his hand began to make its way up her leg, this time unhindered by a layer of fabric between them.

Mairead's head was spinning. He felt so wonderful, tasted so wonderful. His mouth did amazing things to her. She shifted in his lap, trying to get closer to him. She was startled when his hand began creeping up under the hem of her skirt but she could not bring herself to stop him. It all felt far too good. His hand was almost to her bare hip before he stopped himself. They were both gasping for air.

"While I will no apologize for this, because it would be a lie, I will say that we should no go any further just now. T'would not be right and I am sure Molly is wondering where we are right about now." He traced her cheek with his fingers and leaned forward to kiss her nose. "But I do crave more of ye lass. Make no mistake about tha!"

She watched him as he got up and began to repack the saddlebags. It took her some time to catch her breath. When she did, she walked up behind him while he stowed the remaining bread and cheese. When she was close enough, she wrapped her arms around his waist and laid her cheek against his back. "Thank ye Duncan, t'would be a lie as well if I apologized. It has been a lovely day. And ye are a lovely man." She placed a quick kiss against the same expanse of back she had hugged, and then stepped away to untie Realta's reins from his saddle.

He stood stock still, unsure of what to make of what just happened. No woman had ever been as intimate with him as she just had. Granted he had been with a village wench or two and perhaps a doxy in Edinburgh, but that had only been some slap and tickle. With Cait it was different. She had been a sweet lass, and he knew her all her life, but it was never exactly what he would call intimate. This however, was by far the most intimate thing he had ever experienced. It seemed like most things were new or bigger or better than they had been where she was involved. Once he was done, he turned back to look for the bottle of mead. He did not see it on the ground where he left it so he turned a bit farther just in time to see her upend the bottle and take a long drink. When she brought the bottle down again she handed it to him. "Let us head back tae the castle. Come ride wi me again." He offered.

She had other plans. She winked at him and swung herself up into her saddle while he was still fumbling with the bottle. "Sounds like a fine idea Duncan. But ye will have tae catch me first!" She blew him a kiss, spun Realta around, and tore down the hill toward Dunvegan.

Chapter Five

The woman continued to astound him. He gave up on trying to recork the bottle, instead he lifted it to his lips and drained it before haphazardly stuffing it back in the saddlebag. He vaulted onto Loach and took off after her. He had no idea a woman could ride as she did. She and her little filly were making his old man work for it. Loach's gait ate up the ground drawing closer to her. Every now and then she would look back over her shoulder and grin at him before leaning back down over Realta's neck and coaxing her onward. The filly would put on a burst of speed then that amazed him. Perhaps she was meant to be a racer rather than a lady's mount. He urged Loach forward again and gave him free rein. Finally he drew even with her but it was only as they approached the castle and had to slow to a canter and then a trot into the bailey. She fell forward over Realta's neck and Donnchadh thought there might be something wrong. He jumped off Loach, tossing his reins to Cameron as he approached. She did not respond when he called her name. When he came around the front of her, he saw that she had her arm's found the filly's neck and was whispering to her. Realta's ears twitched as she stood there calmly while

Mairead alternated between stroking her mane and hugging her neck. "Come, we need tae get ye upstairs so that ye can clean up for dinner."

He held his hands out for her as he stood beside Realta. She turned to him, her eyes gleaming, "Aye m'laird". She swung one leg across the saddle and then slid off into his waiting hands. He kept his hands on her waist while he called for a stable lad to take Realta and see to her. He didn't notice Archie and Brogan off to the side of the yard watching their every move. Donnchadh had not thought about his meddlesome brother since Mairead had arrived, and he was not upset by that. Once he walked with Mairead to her room, he left her and headed to his chamber next door. His heart was the lightest it had been since he lost Dair and for the first time in the year since his death, he did not feel guilty for his happiness. He knew that Alasdair would have approved of Mairead. Her stubborn streak would have amused him to no end and he was sure that had Dair still been around, the two of them would have ganged up on him to either get their way or tease him. He could not imagine either of them being malicious about it.

About an hour later he was washed and bathed and assumed she would at least be close to ready herself. He tapped on her door and she called for him to enter. She took his breath away, she sat there before her vanity, with one of the maids assisting her with her hair, piling it in artful curls at the crown of her head with sapphire blue ribbon woven through them with tendrils falling around her face. This evening she wore a sapphire blue gown with delicate silver trim. "Oh Donnchadh, I am just about ready. Jenny was just finishing my hair. She is amazing!" The maid blushed and bobbed a cutesy as she bolted out the door.

"Ye are stunning Mairead! Ye look beautiful!"

She blushed and thanked him. He offered her his arm and they descended to the great hall. Again, all were hushed as they entered. Donnchadh led her to his table and she noticed several people already sitting at it. There was a man with copper hair and pinched sour features, a well-dressed and very haughty woman and another woman who dressed in black and seemed to fold in on herself. Donnchadh cursed under his breath and she glanced sharply at him. "Are ye alright m'laird?" she asked.

He glanced down at her and gave her a tight smile, "Aye it will be. Just follow my lead and dinna pay any mind tae what my brother Archie says tae ye." He covered her hand with his where she clasped his arm. She nodded mutely as they reached the table. This time she sat down on Donnchadh's right, which drew a gasp from people nearby. She did not understand it, but she had no choice since the man who must be Archie sat in the seat she occupied last night. Donnchadh glared at the people that gasped and shook his head. She didn't understand what was going on here. Clearly she had missed something significant. "So big brother, this is your lovely lassie?" Archie leaned across Donnchadh in an attempt to get a better look at Mairead. When Donnchadh moved to block his view, he tried another tactic. "Och Maud, dinna ye think Mairead is a fine lass? Perhaps no as good a match as yer Cait was, but she will do aye?"

Mairead watched the woman Archie had addressed sit up and blink a few times. Her eyes focused on Donnchadh and then flitted to Mairead. Donnchadh tensed, unsure what to expect from her. She had been mostly silent for the past 6 months and had avoided him like the plague, so it had surprised him to see her in the dining hall. Archie had to be playing some kind of game, and he liked it not. "Och Donnchadh, ye are a good lad." Maud began slowly and softly. "But ye and everyone else here ken it should be my daughter Cait who sits at your right. Not some wench ye picked up off the streets during the games. Tis all well and good tae dip yer wick, but I thought ye would have more respect for my wee Catie." Maud glared at Mairead for a moment more and then looked at her trencher and sunk in on herself again as if all of her energy had been spent on that one exclamation.

Donnchadh had no idea how to react to that. He did respect Cait and aye, at one time she would have sat beside him but that time had passed. "I do respect yer Catie" he said softly to her. "She always has a part of my heart, but she cannae be by my side now, even if I wished for it. Mairead is a good lass and doesnae deserve yer venom."

Maud pushed away from the table and left the great hall. Mairead was at a loss. Clearly this Cait, whoever she was, was very special. So why was she not here, what was going on? Nothing made sense at the moment. Donnchadh stared sadly after the woman. Mairead touched his arm to draw his attention. "M'Laird, Donnchadh, Are ye alright? Is there aught I can do? I am here if ye need me." She offered even though he did not look at her. He pulled his arm from her hand, sliced some fish, and put it on his trencher along with some carrots and potatoes. She stared at him in confusion, knowing that he was upset but unsure of how to proceed. He did not set anything on her trencher as he had before and for some reason it hurt. It was as if he had taken a little piece of affection for her and hid it away as if it had never been. She sighed and mentally shook herself. This hot and cold with the flip of a switch was getting old. Even if she did care for Donnchadh, was it worth the vicious mood swings? Yes, he had stood up for her briefly and then immediately shut down. Meanwhile Archie was quite pleased with the outcome of the evening so far. He was eager to drive a wedge between Donnchadh and Mairead. Mairead's influence on Donnchadh was far too positive for his liking. If he just kept putting pressure like this on Donnchadh, perhaps the laird would crack, and Archie would have it all as his mother said he should. Finola had not told him why she did not support Donnchadh, her first born. He just figured it was because he was her favorite.

He took a breath and sucked his teeth for a moment. It was time to finish off this meal with flair. He felt the need for an explosion. "So will ye no properly introduce us brother?" When Donnchadh only grunted at him he continued, "Tis very rude indeed to not introduce people with in yer household."

Donnchadh cut his eyes at him and forcefully set down his fork. Archie could have danced with glee, here it came, his big brother was about to blow, and he had the whole clan to witness. "I will nae introduce ye because it does nae matter! She is no part of my household and ne'er will be. So let it go brother!" Mairead watched the exchange silently listening to every word and inflection. "She will no be here long enough to make it worthwhile in any case."

"Is that so brother dear?" Archie glanced briefly at Mairead and saw that her expression was shuttered. He pressed on. "So I suppose she does not compare to your Cait?

Donnchadh shook his head, looking down at his plate but not really paying attention to it, "Nay, they are as different as night and day there is no comparison." Mairead was not sure why it hurt to hear those responses from him.

"Aye, Cait was a one though. Wi' her fine long blonde hair and slender frame. She was like a delicate flower." Archie again glanced over at Mairead and was glad to see that she was beginning to internalize what he was saying with the comparison between the two women. She blinked rapidly and had even stopped pushing her food around her plate in an attempt to look like she was eating. She just sat watching, growing colder with each statement.

Donnchadh chuckled, "Aye she was a one." Mairead could not take any more. Between Maud, Archie, and Donnchadh, it had been made clear she was not wanted here. Earlier today Donnchadh had been so tender and passionate. It made no sense, but then it clicked. She was a poor substitute for the beautiful women they spoke of. That had to be why Donnchadh was so eager to touch her even when it was not proper. She was merely there as a toy. She did not really matter. He was content to play with Mairead because he needed an outlet but nothing more. She remembered one of the fathers of a football player at her high school defending his son after he assaulted a girl and tried to get away with it. "Boys will be boys" he had said. Thankfully the punk did not get away with it. Well, she guessed that it must be the same in Scotland in this time. She gave up on her meal and quietly pushed her chair back in an attempt not to draw attention to herself.

Archie was the only one watching her as she exited the hall. She heard the final comment he made, "Dair would not approve of this and ye ken it."

"For once brother ye are right. He would not have approved of this mess"

Mairead was glad that at least she knew where she stood here. She had to find a way home because clearly she had stepped into the middle of something she always avoided, drama. She made her way back to her door once inside she bolted it. She quickly stripped out of her gown and put on her yellow chemise and bloomers. She wanted her own clothes right now, her comfort. A short time later she heard boots coming down the hall. She sat before the fire and held her breath. She hoped he did not knock on her door. She did not want to deal with anyone right now, let alone him. But apparently that peace had been too much to hope for because he did knock. She sighed and got up to open the door a crack. It was not Donnchadh, but Archie who stood there. She tried for polite but knew she failed miserably, "What do you want?"

"Just tae check on ye lass. Ye seemed as if ye could not leave the hall quickly enough"

"I'm quite fine. Thank ye." She responded curtly and he began to turn away, "Wait, what did ye mean by "Dair would no approve?"

He grinned while his back was to her, she took the bait! He sobered as he turned back to her. "T'is merely that Dair was his best friend and Cait was his sister. I merely meant that Dair would not approve of the situation at the table, wi' ye to Donnchadh's right and his mam being upset." With that explanation being enough to plant a seed of doubt in her mind, he turned again and as she closed the door behind him and leaned her head against it. He had agreed with his brother about it.

Some time had passed since she came to her room and Donnchadh had not come after her. Surely that meant something. She gave a bitter laugh at the direction of her thoughts. Yet again she reminded herself that she was not in a romance novel and by no means a romantic heroine and she had no desire to be involved with that gorgeous, sexy, drool worthy man.

Chapter Six

It had taken Donnchadh a moment to realize that Mairead left the table. He had not heard her go but her chair was askew and her food mostly untouched. He rose to go after but his mother placed a hand on his arm. "Donnchadh, we need to talk." She motioned for him to sit. He did so warily, he wanted nothing more than to go after Mairead and find out what had happened. Perhaps the lass was feeling ill after the chill of the stream.

"But a moment Mother. I must needs check on Mairead."

"Very well my son. I shall speak plainly then. We have all watched ye mourn this past year and I think it is time tae move on." She petted his arm as if he were a lap dog. Donnchadh hated it, but it was the only human contact he ever got from his mother so he quietly accepted it. Archie had made his way around to Donnchadh's other side and sat in the chair Mairead had vacated. In Dair's chair, where he should not be. He began to tell him to move but his mother drew his attention again. "We, yer family, need ye strong. Yer clan needs ye strong. And tae that end, ye need tae surround yerself wi the right men. I think it is time ye give my wee Archie more power. He needs a respectable standing among the clan."

Donnchadh was gobsmacked. How dare she ask this of him. Archie did nothing! He never fought to protect the clan, never even so much as looked at a weapon, let alone picked one up and trained with one. His hands were as soft as a maids and he gossiped like one too. He was weak and soft with a snake behind his eyes. He turned to look at Archie and saw him peering at his drink. He narrowed his eyes at Archie, snatched up his mug and downed his heather ale. Archie got up and shrugged. "Let me ken brother where and when ye want me tae take over." With that he got up and left his mother to try to talk Donnchadh into elevating his status.

"I love and respect ye mother, but ye are daft if ye think I will let Archie run anything!" his head was feeling fuzzy and he was starting to slur his words "I have betters thins tae atten...aten...see tae. Blast woman le me up!" She placed a hand on his shoulder and exerted just enough pressure to let him know she meant business.

"I would be remiss if I let ye go upstairs in yer state lad. Yer brother has retired and I am not strong enough tae support ye. Best ye stay here and I will send someone tae see tae ye." He nodded obediently. "There's a good lad." She returned to her chamber and readied herself for bed. She instructed her maid, Brigit, to see to Donnchadh in any way that he needed, she just needed to make sure that he did not go to his chamber or the one next to his. The woman eyed her for a moment. She had always fancied the Laird. "In ANY way at all?" She clarified and when his mother nodded, she all but ran down the stairs.

She found Donnchadh still in his chair at the table and slowly approached, hips swaying seductively. M'laird, might I at least help ye tae a chair by the fire? T'would be more comfortable."

He nodded, mute, and allowed her to lead him to the chair. Once he sat down, she sat across his lap and wiggled her bottom as she wrapped her arms around his neck. "Mmm, Donnchadh ye are so big an strong!" She ran a hand down his chest to his kilt.

Donnchadh was not totally aware of what was happening. He knew he needed to be doing something but he couldn't clear his mind to think of it, and the wench on his lap felt really nice there. Reminded him of something else, he just could not put a finger on it. The lass kissed him then and took the lead in the kiss. She drove her tongue in to his mouth until he responded. Pleasure sparked in him and he ran a hand up her back and grasped one of her breasts with the other. She moaned and squirmed. Her moan was not right. He couldn't shake the feeling that something was not as it should be. The lass changed position so that she straddled his lap and pulled his head to her breasts. He kissed them in turn and drew them from their bodice to lave them with his tongue. She ground her hips against him and he gave a throaty growl. She giggled and squirmed closer.

*   *   *

IT had been some time since dinner. Mairead was sure that plates would have been cleared so she figured that she could pilfer enough for a sandwich from the kitchen. She wished they had fries or spicy chips here but it would be some time until they were invented. As she approached the great hall on her way to the kitchen, she heard something. She thought it was moaning but she couldn't be sure. She quietly moved closer. She accidentally kicked a chair.

*   *   *

BRIDGIT was sure she heard something and stopped her ministrations looking around for a moment. When no one appeared, she returned her attention to her laird. He was hard for her. She had let his kilt slip when she was startled and worked to lift it again. She would have him this night. She kissed his neck and and made him moan.

Mairead was shocked at what she was seeing. She really was just a bit of fun to him. He had already moved on to another woman. For a moment she considered going back and saying nothing but then changed her mind. She wouldn't be here much longer so she may as well give him a piece of her mind. "Donnchadh I demand an explanation now! I dinna care who ye have on yer lap.

"Oh God Mairead! Lass!" He moaned again. Brigit squirmed on top of him, trying desperately to keep control of him and the situation.

She realized that the shadow of the fire obscured her face. Perhaps she could salvage some of this after all. "MMMM M'laird. Aye that was grand." She kissed him and moved to get off his lap.

"Mairead dinna go. Stay wi me..." He was not seeing her and if she was honest, it made her angry. She looked over at the woman who had interrupted and glared at her and then stormed out of the room. "Mairead?? Lass?"

"I am over here Donnchadh." She said dully from the other side of the room.

"Wait, how??? Ye were just on my lap and doing the most wonderful naughty things tae me. How are ye over there so quickly and so put together?"

A tear rolled down her cheek. "Because that was not me Donnchadh. It was someone else. I was in my chamber until I came down a minute ago and found ye two. I will let ye be then. Good night Donnchadh." She turned to go. He got up and stumbled unsteadily attempting to follow her. He tripped and fell into some chairs causing a racket. Mairead turned back to check on him out of concern. He stood doubled over, his head resting on his arm across the back of a chair. Before she could say or do anything more, he was violently spilling the contents of his stomach. She hurried back to check on him. He sounded awful. "Oh my God Duncan! Are you ok?" She placed one hand on his back and swept back some of his hair with the other.

Donnchadh could not catch his breath between heaves. He was glad she came back but confused as well. Her voice sounded different again; like that time she was drunk. He did not have much time to think on it. He had never been this ill before. Neither his stomach nor his body had ever felt like this. While his body rebelled, she stayed by his side, pulling his hair back and talking softly to him, attempting to soothe him. After his stomach was emptied repeatedly, he slumped down into a chair that he had knocked out of place and looked at her for a moment. Once the spinning stilled he could see that her face was filled with concern for him. "You are so pale. What happened sweetie?" She stroked a hand across his forehead.

"I dinna ken....ye....ye sound different I think..." he tried to focus on her.

"Yeah well it looks like that is the least of our problems because you don't look so hot. Come on big guy, let's get you comfortable and taken care of and then we can have a talk, which it looks like we are both in need of." She gave up her accent. She decided it was not worth it right now. He already heard how she really sounded and she was too focused on worrying about him. "Let's get you upstairs to bed and then I will find Molly."

He peered at her for a moment trying to make sense of everything as she tried to help him up. He finally realized she was trying to help. decided to do so. For such a small lass she was strong he thought. She wrapped one of his arms over her shoulder and supported him with an arm around his waist with her hand clutching his belt. She helped him make his way up the stairs. They had to stop a few times along the way for him to throw up. "Good God man! How do you have anything left in you by now? We are almost there. Just down the hall and you can get off your feet and rest."

By the time they were to her door, she was winded. Donnchadh was a heavy man and as impaired as he was, most of the forward motion had been her doing. She laughed ruefully at this turn of events. It took her back to her early days in Ramstein, being the most sober of the group and hauling drunken friends back to their dorms. Granted none of them had been as big as Donnchadh, but trying to herd two unruly drunken airmen back across base, one practically draped across her back, had to count for something. She decided to cut her losses and just take him into her room instead of trying to make it further down the hall to his.

By the time she got Donnchadh into the bed and his boots removed, Molly was hurrying in. "Och God's eyes! What happened lassie?!" She rushed to the bedside to check on Donnchadh.

Mairead composed herself. "Thank God ye are here! I was just about tae go in search of ye. I am trying tae figure that out as well. Dinner was passable, but odd tae say the least. I went downstairs a little while ago tae get something from the kitchen since I dinna eat…..much, when I saw Donnchadh wi' a wench on his lap goin at it. I confronted them, he got up, tried tae follow me but stumbled, and then he was vomiting. He has been doing so ever since." She looked down and reached out to smooth the hair from his brow when she noticed him staring at her as if she was crazy. Molly tsked and looked him over while Mairead was talking. Mairead pressed her lips together; she knew what would be coming from Donnchadh when they were alone.

"I am going tae prepare a draft and some tea that should help settle his stomach. He does nae seem fevered. Keep him calm and a bucket nearby just in case. I shall be back presently." With that, she disappeared down the hall.

Donnchadh groaned and tried to sit up. His whole body ached. He cleared his throat and began to speak. "So lass. What is going on? Who are ye really? Ye sounded like a different person."

Mairead snorted and briefly looked away. When she looked at him, again her eyes were resigned and almost seemed a little sad. "Figures ye would be coherent enough tae ask that of me."

"Tell me true. T'is no the first time I heard ye sound different. That night ye were drunk singing about going home."

Mairead lost it and started giggling. "Of course you would hear me making a fool of myself like that."

He looked sharply at her and all but barked "Out wi' it lass!"

She sighed, her shoulders slumped, and her head dropped. "Here goes nothing." She looked back up at him. He was not sure what to make of her now. "I am not exactly who I led you to believe. My name is Gwen Peirce and I play the part of Mairead MacLeod. I do renaissance festivals back home. It is much like a play in some respects. Everyone on cast has their character and part to play. I was an inn wench with one hell of a convoluted back story." She gave a sad little half smile. Donnchadh wanted to touch her, stroke her cheek, hold her hands, but he dared not because he did not even know the little he thought he did about this woman. She had appeared out of the mists and music one day. No friends or family, no clansmen to claim her, just a strange lass alone. All he had was her word and that was becoming increasingly suspect by the moment. "I have played Mairead MacLeod for over thirteen years now and she is like a part of me. Slipping into her character is like putting on a well-worn coat. It just fits. I had not been back to my home faire in over 10 years and it was my first time going back. Something felt different but I don't know what. Next thing I knew I was looking at you and your castle."

Donnchadh did not respond right away as Molly entered the room with the draft and the tea. "It seems ye were poisoned or drugged laddie. Now drink this draft. It will help combat any of that nasty stuff that may be left and then drink all of the tea. It will calm yer stomach. I had the maids start cleaning up. I will bid ye good night. If ye need me ye know where tae find me." She kissed him on the forehead and turned to leave. Before she reached the door she turned back to him for a moment, "Be kind tae the lass. She needs ye and she is a good one. Dinna doubt yer instincts lad. They have served ye well thus far. And fer crying out loud, hold the lassie's hands. She is shaking like a leaf. She will rattle her bones loose if she keeps it up!" Having said her piece, she disappeared down the dark hallway. Molly had never been like that, never kissed his forehead. She had never really been harsh with him but she was never overly demonstrative toward him. Occasionally she would sneak him an extra pasty on or when he was a lad, she did not yell at him as harshly as other lads, but she had never been loving. He pulled himself out of his thoughts and looked at Mairead....no Gwen. She was looking in the direction Molly had left. She was indeed shivering. Her hands were folded in her lap one clasping the other to the point her knuckles were white. He reached over and laid a hand atop hers drawing her attention to him. He lifted her hands then and enveloped them in his as he shifted to his side.

"You owe me nothing. I know that. I have only been here a few days. I also know that everything I said and will say is now suspect. However, I never meant any harm. I did not think I would be here long enough for it to matter. I hoped to find my way home and be long gone by now. But clearly I am not. I like you Donnchadh. You are a good man and I am sorry if you feel ill used by me. I only ask that you let me stay one more night and lend me a few pounds so that I may procure lodging in the village." She tried to pull her hands from his. However, he would not let her. She looked up, met his eyes, and was unsure of what she saw there.

"Nay lass. I will no do that." He all but growled. Her heart sank. She had hoped he at least felt some kindness toward her. "Ye dinna need tae leave until ye are ready and if ye need aught, I shall see tae it. I like ye as well and I understand a bit of yer reasoning. We still have much tae speak on though."

She gave him a small watery smile. "Thank you Donnchadh."

"We are alone ... Gwen." He arched an eyebrow at her. He suddenly craved hearing her voice caress the name she claimed.

"Thank you Duncan. And I am sorry for down in the great hall. I know you have your life and I am only here but a short while." She did pull away from him this time.

Donnchadh loved how his name sounded upon her lips. Then with dawning horror, he realized what had happened down in the hall. No wonder she did not want him to touch her. She had said she was not the woman on his lap, but he could have sworn she was! Then how would she have gotten off his lap and across the room so quickly. "Lass I swear I thought it was ye. I dinna ken what happened. One moment ye were on my lap doing some delightful things and the next ye were across the room."

"I have no claim on you Duncan. Whoever you choose to tup is your business."

"NAY! I dinna mean tae or want tae tup anyone but ye!" He stopped and blushed furiously.

"Is that so?!" Gwen laughed nervously. "Look I know that things were hard with the loss of your best friend and that he was and still is very important to you. I understand that you were going to marry his sister, and if she was the one on your lap, I get it. This is not my home and you need to stop telling me things like you just did."

Donnchadh could not understand for a moment. How did she know about Dair? Or his sister for that matter? Moreover, why did she assume that whoever the wench on his lap was, that it would be Cait? "Why do ye say that lass?"

"Archie came up shortly after I left the hall. He told me that Alasdair was your best friend, and that he died a year ago and you were to marry his sister. He said that Dair would not have approved of the situation in the hall or his mother's upset, among other things"

Donnchadh tried to recall the meal. He remembered bits and pieces. She had been sitting by him; Maud had been upset and then left. Then he recalled Archie saying something and then Mairead, or rather Gwen, had been gone. His mother had stopped him from going after her. "Damn and Blast! That bloody little weasel!" he roared loud enough that Gwen flinched a bit. He was horrified that she would draw away from him like that. "Och lass. I am sorry about tha. Come here." He patted the bed beside him. "Let me tell ye the truth of it. I ken now that ye are no who I thought ye were, but I still like ye fine."

She studied him warily for a moment and then crawled up on to the bed next to him. "Ok. Just one thing. Promise me no more yelling for now."

"Aye lass. I can promise ye that." He pulled her close to him and then gulped down the tea and set the cup on the bedside table. "Now, Aye Dair was my truest and best friend. More like a brother tae me than Archie, my own. We grew up together. Did everything thing together. Sometimes his sister Cait would tag along. As we grew up together it was just a forgone conclusion that Cait and I would wed and Dair would be my second, my war chief. Last year all of that changed. In an ambush gone wrong Dair took a dagger meant for me. He bled out and died in my arms on MacDonald land. I lost my brother that day. I have nae been the same since. So I brought him home tae Maud and Cait. It was the hardest thing I had ere done. Seeing him draped over my saddle like tha and them sobbing. Maud collapsed and Cait tried tae comfort her as best she could. They took him home tae clean and bury him. I was there at the burial. On the outskirts. They were mad at me. I canna say as I blamed them. Their son and brother was dead because of me. With his last breath Dair asked me tae watch over his mother and sister. Tae tha end 6 months ago I asked Cait tae marry me." He stopped and took a breath. He was unaware of the tears rolling down his cheeks until Gwen gently wiped one away. He took another fortifying breath and kept eye contact with her as he continued. "I asked her and she said that every time she looked at me all she could see was her brother's face. She told me she would never even consider marrying me. So we parted. She went home and I wandered down the street unsure of what tae do with myself. I was a ways down the street when I heard a scream. I ran back and saw Maud sobbing outside and when I went inside, I found Cait hanging there. Apparently my proposal pushed her over the edge."

"Oh my God! Duncan no! I am so sorry! I can not even imagine..." he placed a finger over her lips.

"I dinna tell ye that tae make ye feel sorry. I told ye that tae let ye ken me better and so that ye would know the lass on my lap surely was no Cait. I dinna truly ken who she was. Molly told me tae follow my instincts and I shall. I kenned that there was something different about ye since the moment I saw ye listening tae the bagpipes. Ye have made me feel more alive than I have since I lost Dair and that means a lot tae me. Is there aught else I need tae ken? Aught else I need tae know that was nae true?"

She nodded listening to him. "No. There is nothing else that has been a lie other than my accent and name. Everything else I shared with you was true. I hate that you have suffered with this for so long and if I offered you a bit of respite from the sorrow, I am glad. That still leaves the question of who the woman in your lap was."

"Ye are the only lass I want on my lap." He winked at her and then sobered. "I dinna ken who she was, but I intend tae find out. I feel a bit steadier now. I should get out of this soiled kilt. Would ye mind if I stayed here? I dinna fancy being alone o the now. Tae many dark thoughts and I still feel a bit off."

"You can stay if you like. I can't even imagine how you must be feeling now." She patted his chest and got up to blow out candles while Donnchadh got up and dropped his kilt. His saffron shirt hung well down his thighs so all was covered. He situated himself in bed and pulled the covers over him. Had he been in his right mind he would have left her chamber then and there, but he was not and the lure of her cuddled against him was too much for him to turn down.

"On the morrow I will address Archie and find out why the devil he was talking tae ye about things he had nae business sharing. Something is nae right here. But that is for the morn. Come lass and whisper my name and tell me good night so that this warrior may sleep peacefully."

Gwen crawled across the bed to him. She was glad that her chemise was so long and the neck was gathered so that he could not see anything inappropriate. She settled down near him and found his hand. Clasping it in hers, she did as he bid. "Good night my Duncan. Sleep well."

He pulled his hand from her grasp and then repositioned himself and adjusted her so that she was wedged under his arm cuddled against his chest. He let out a sigh. "Mmmmm, yer Duncan. I like that more than I should." He gave her a quick kiss and was soon snoring softly. Gwen lay awake for quite a while thinking about what had just happened. He accepted her as herself and did not demand she be tossed in the dungeon as a traitor. He had opened up to her and flirted with her. She was pleased as she drifted off to sleep.

The next morning Donnchadh awoke peacefully and realized the source of his contentment. Gwen was sprawled atop him. Her nightgown rucked up just above her knees with one leg thrown across his and one hand resting on his arm, while she nuzzled his chest sleepily. The wee thing was beautiful in the early morning light. The chamber was a bit cool and he was startled when a maid entered with a coal bucket. She gasped in shock when she saw him there and then backed out of the room quickly and slammed the door. Hell and damnation! The gossip would spread quickly. He knew he had no choice in what would happen next. This was not how he planned on his life turning out. "Come lass. T'is time tae rise. Apparently we have more tae discuss this morn."

Gwen mumbled in her sleep that she was too cozy to get up and that she needed five more minutes. She was surprised when her pillow chuckled and squeezed her in its arms. She looked up and realized what was going on and then gave him a blinding smile. At that moment they were both startled by the door bursting open and subsequently being slammed. "Och ye daftie! What hae ye done?! Nay dinna answer that! I can see fer meself!" Molly barged in and was gesturing to the two of them; she hurriedly made her way across the room to the teacup on the bedside table. She scooped it up and examined it, "Hmmm just as I thought. This is nae as much trouble as I expected." Donnchadh looked at Molly curiously. "Aye very good. But no that. Hmmm that will need some work." Finally, she turned to the two of them. "So how long will we be waiting for the wedding?" she asked as she set down the cup.

Gwen blinked at her repeatedly, unsure if she had really understood Molly. Donnchadh dropped his head back and groaned. "Och lass I am so sorry! But Molly has the right of it. We have tae wed now or yer reputation will be in tatters. A few moments ago, a maid came in and saw us together and surely, she has shared that bit of gossip far and wide by now."

"Wait wait wait. So I am expected to marry you now?! Nothing happened! We talked! That was it!" Gwen blushed furiously. "I have never even....been with a man that way! There is nothing wrong with my reputation!" She hesitated and then mumbled, "I am still a virgin."

"Tis no how it appears lass. Yer bed is a mess and both of yer bare legs are showing and there is the matter of the soiled kilt on the floor as well," Molly reasoned.

Gwen pushed up from Donnchadh and looked over the edge of the bed at the offending piece of wool fabric. "No! I swear nothing happened! Isn't that good enough? I will even sign a sworn statement to that as well!"

Donnchadh blushed as she pointed out what should have been obvious. His memories of the previous night were hazy and his head was pounding. He sat up. "Aye we ken that lass, but it does nae make a difference." His mother chose that moment to insert herself into the situation along with Archie. They barged into the chamber. They looked as if they had bitten into something rotten. "Aye mother dear?" Donnchadh asked sarcastically as he got up and stood between his mother and the bed where Gwen sat.

"Donnchadh, how could ye let down yer clan like this? Ye needed an advantageous marriage now that your Cait is gone and ye are out of mourning." Her voice was shrill.

He pinched the bridge of his nose and shook his head slowly. "Dinna pretend my life matters tae ye now mother."

"But ye have let yourself become distracted by this whore!" Archie spat from behind his mother.

Donnchadh growled low in his throat. "Lad I suggest ye leave this room of yer own volition now or I shall remove ye by force and with great prejudice. Ye are speaking of my lady and I will no tolerate it!" The only thing keeping them separated was their mother who tried to interrupt Donnchadh in vain. "Get out of here, the both of ye. What's done is done. No taking it back, thank God."

Gwen sat in a daze watching everything around her. It was almost as if she was watching a tv show or a play happening around her. She didn't feel like she was really there. She looked to her left and Molly had set down the teacup and was digging through a pocket on her apron. To her right Donnchadh was fuming at his mother and brother. Donnchadh saw her dazedness. "Alright everyone out! I need tae speak wi' my lass!" He shooed them all out of her chamber. He sat on the bed facing her. "Are ye alright Gwen?"

She focused on him after a moment, bemused. "I am not sure honestly. I don't know how I got here, or why I am here, or how to get home. I like you but I don't know how long I might be here and I don't know about marrying someone I have just known for a couple of days."

"This is not what I expected either lass, as ye ken," he watched the panic and upset pass over her face as she realized what he meant but he stopped her from saying anything with his fingers over her lips. "That aside lass. I like ye and it seems ye like me. If we walk out of here no in accord over a marriage, ye will be branded the lowest whore. Ye do no deserve that. And in reality marriages have been built on less. I would much rather marry a buxom lass I like than some whey faced lass chosen by me clan or mother. I would hope that perhaps we could grow tae love each other one day."

She absorbed what he was saying. She felt terrible for being so thoughtless about his situation. "I suppose you are right. And yes I do like you. I guess when it comes down to it I am scared and unsure." She cocked her head and just sat there looking at him for a while. Finally when he was just about to break and demand she say something, she spoke. She took his hands in hers this time. "Yes Duncan I will marry you. But I ask one thing. I would marry you privately as Gwen Pierce."

His heart pounded. She said yes. But would the clan accept that? He had to think quickly. "The clan will demand a public display and I can no naysay them." Her shoulders drooped at that, "However what if we have private ceremony just ye and me wi' Molly for a witness. I trust her wi' my life and would trust her wi' yers as well. Then the day following we will have a grand clan wedding for the laird Donnchadh MacLeod and his Lady Mairead MacLeod. What do ye think?"

She did not say a word but leaned forward to kiss him. His lips were warm and gentle against hers. She brought her hands to his chest and applied a bit of pressure, surprising Donnchadh, and pushed him on to his back. She straddled him and kissed him for all she was worth. Once his surprise passed, he was an active and eager participant in the kiss. Their tongues stroked each other and passion grew. He fisted his hands at her hips trying not to pull up her chemise and complete what they had already been accused of. Suddenly there was a fierce pounding on the door. Gwen shrieked and tried desperately to get off him, but he only held her tighter and whispered. "Shhh lass. I will take care of this and ye. Dinna fash." Then louder to whoever was on the other side of the door. "Bloody Hell, give yer laird some peace. Piss off!" The knocking came again, this time he heard Molly begging entry. Defeated he lay back and closed his eyes, not even thinking to let go of Gwen. "Good God woman go ahead and enter."

"Oh my dear lad there is something I need tae be telling ye that is long overdue. I dinna think I would ever need tae share it as I was sworn tae secrecy years ago. And yer life looked tae be turning out grand in spite of it all. I see now that things have shifted. I cannae remain silent anymore and yer Da is long passed so I recon I am free of that oath."

"What are ye talking about Molly? I have been more confused than ever lately and I have had enough."

"Aye, well then lad, I will cut tae the chase. Yer lady mother is no really yer mother. She has always treated Archie different because he is really her son." She pressed on as Donnchadh was shaking his head. "I had a sister, Iona. She was 3 years younger than me and she and yer da fell in love. They dinna marry because they thought that the clan would object as she was a servant. Yer mam died in childbirth, but she loved ye so lad! She could not wait to be yer mam. She held ye before she died and named ye. Donnchadh, her wee dark warrior born in the darkest hour of the night. She thought ye were beautiful."

He sat up once she had begun talking. He could not believe what he was hearing. How could this be? Why was he never told if this was so? He had been unaware of Gwen for a moment and was startled when she wrapped her arms around his shoulders from behind. He placed his hand over where hers were clasped at his neck and bade Molly to continue. He felt grounded enough to hear the rest. Molly nodded, noticing his need for comfort. "Yer da had been forced in tae an arranged marriage that happened shortly before yer birth. Yer da insisted on recognizing ye as his heir. He loved yer mother so much he could no fathom anything else. Ye reminded him of her and he adored ye for tha. The woman ye ken as yer mother was forced tae accept ye as her son. She resented ye. It was some time until she had Archie and once she did, she was jealous of how he treated ye instead of Archie. I had visited the castle on occasion when yer mam was alive, but once ye were born and I saw the neglect she inflicted on ye, I kenned that I had tae stay for ye. She could nae handle another woman in the household and threatened yer da until I was relegated tae a servant if I wished tae stay. The reality of it is that I am yer aunt lad."

Donnchadh had no idea how to react. He stared at Molly for a time. The poor woman was wringing her hands. Eventually he reached a hand out to her. She placed a shaking hand in his. "So I am a bastard then?" He waited her response, she nodded mute. "But a recognized and legitimized one. My claim tae the MacLeod seat is no in question?" She shook her head this time. "And ye, ye are my auntie?" Her eyes welled with tears as she nodded. At that, Donnchadh surged off the bed and wrapped the woman in his arms. "Och Christ Auntie! Why dinna ye tell me sooner?" He did not let her answer that time. "Ye will no longer work wi' the servants. Moreover, ye damn well will no stay in the servant's quarters. Ye will have a chamber on this floor near yer family and be well taken care of!" His voice was thick with unshed tears. "And be damned tae anyone who may object!"

Molly pulled back and wiped her tear on her sleeve. "There is one more thing lad. I am sure both yer mam and yer da would want ye tae have this." She pulled a delicate knotwork silver ring set with a beautiful sapphire. "Yer da gave it tae Iona when he found out she was pregnant wi ye." I hid it afore he remarried. I thought ye might have need of it one day when ye decided tae marry."

Donnchadh made no move to take the ring from her, merely looking at it sitting in her hand. There was so much of his life that had been a lie. His chest felt tight and the world spun on its axis for a moment. He swallowed hard and shook his head.

He shoved away from the bed and walked to the fireplace bracing a forearm on the mantle, his other hand on his hip and staring into the embers for a moment. He stood there silent, contemplative, trying desperately to accept everything he was hearing. While it was everything he had hoped for at one time when he was younger, it was difficult to process in light of the life he had led to this point. After a few minutes he squared his shoulders and stood straight. When he turned back to face Molly and Gwen, his eyes were clearer and he his inner turmoil seemed to have ebbed. Now he knew that he had remembered correctly, that his Da had loved him and realized that he had been right that Molly treated him as if he was special. He had an auntie who loved him in ways his mother, well the woman he thought was his mother, never could. He looked at Gwen then. She sat on the bed where he had left her, silently smiling through tears. He knew she was happy for him. He took the ring from Molly and went to the other side of the bed nearest Gwen. He dropped to one knee and offered her the ring. "I ken we have already been through this lass, but this seems right o the now. Will ye marry me, Gwen Pierce?" She slid to the floor in front of him and offered him her hand so that he might put the ring on her finger.

"Aye my Duncan!" Once he pressed the ring on to her finger, she wrapped her arms around his neck and melted into him. He silently stroked her back as they knelt on the floor. Molly looked questioningly at him and he shook his head indicating that now was not the time for the answers she sought. After a time, he helped Gwen to stand and bellowed down the hall for a maid. Once the girl drew near, he asked that she have the green chamber prepared for his Auntie and directed that her things be moved there from the servant's quarters. The girl bobbed a curtsey and ran down the hall.

"Och now ye have caused a stir nephew. All the tongues will be wagging. In a lassie's chamber with ye both barely clad and subsequently engaged, and now raising ye auntie up from a servant. Busy morn even for a laird like ye."

"Aye. Well, someone has tae keep everyone on their feet. That aside Auntie, I need tae ask ye a favor. Mairead wants a private wedding using...her middle name, Gwen, and we need a witness. Of course, the following day she and I will wed before the clan as is tradition."

Molly arched an eyebrow at them and considered it. Gwen was concerned she would either have more questions or deny Donnchadh request. "Aye laddie. Just tell me the when and the where and I will be there for ye as I always have been. I have a request as well. For the time being, I would like tae maintain control of the maids and assist in the running of the house hold."

"Ye dinna have tae ask that. This is yer home. Ye are welcome tae do aught ye please here. And I suspect that my lassie is nae in a hurry tae take over the running of the household." He winked down at her and she smiled. "Now if ye dinna mind, would ye assist Mairead in dressing? I am better at removing a lassie's clothes than putting them on." He winked roguishly at Gwen. "We will need tae make an appearance at breakfast or the tongues will be wagging right out of people's heads."

Molly nodded and was all business again. "Right ye are lad! Now out. Ye twa are nae married yet so ye should no see her in such a state of undress." She shooed him out the door. "Now

lassie, let's get yer war paint on." Then she whispered, "Oh and I
ken well yer name is Gwen and why ye want a ceremony using
that name instead of Mairead. Ye dinna need tae worry though. I
will not say anything. I just want my wee Donnchadh happy and
ye make him so. That is all that matters tae me."

Gwen could not say anything for a moment. How should
she respond to that? How much did Molly really know? Did it
even matter if she said nothing? Clearly, the woman could keep
secrets. She decided then to trust Molly. "Thank you
Molly. That means a lot. Donnchadh and I may not know each
other well, but I know him enough to know he is a good man and
you are a wonderful woman. I am glad to become a part of this
family."

Molly nodded and set about digging through the
wardrobe and found a beautiful overskirt made of MacLeod
plaid and a blue bodice to match. Once Molly helped her dress,
she tied Gwen's hair up with the green ribbon. They were almost
finished when there was a knock at the door. Molly answered it
while Gwen checked herself one last time in the mirror. "Och
lass ye look grand indeed! I have never been happier tae see a lass
in my clan tartan!" He came across the room to her and reached
for her hands. "Let us go to the great hall for breakfast
m'dear. We shall sit at the head table, ye tae my right and my
auntie tae my left. Tis how our little family shall dine from now
on." Gwen beamed at him.

"As you wish m'laird!"

"One thing I think we should be aware of is that ye are
still Mairead tae the clan. Tis best that way I think." She nodded
in agreement with his statement. "Aside from that, I would keep
Gwen for meself. I dinna want tae hear anyone else speak that

name. Tis mine alone tae call ye. Just as I am yer Duncan, ye shall be my Gwen." He had forgotten that Molly was there but then realized he had nothing to worry about from her. "Come m'ladies. Let us descend in grand fashion!" Molly took his left arm and Gwen his right. They made their way downstairs and there was an audible gasp from the clansmen gathered. His stepmother and brother already sat at the table. As they approached the table, he could see them trying to figure out what was going on. Once they stood behind the table, Donnchadh cleared his throat. "Archie ye need tae move tae a more appropriate seat. My betrothed shall be seated there and my Auntie tae my left so hie yerself to the end of the table or another entirely if ye dinna like that."

Archie and his mother gaped at the goings on. "What is the meaning of this? I demand an explanation! Yer father would be furious!" Finola, the woman he has thought was his mother, cried

Donnchadh rounded on her in a fury. "Aye he would be! Ye have treated my auntie horribly and me like so much refuse. He would not have accepted this. I ken the truth. Ye are no really my mother. Molly's sister Iona was. He loved her so much he legitimized me, much tae yer chagrin. So when yer bairn came along he was not the immediate successor. Here is the part that should concern ye. Now ye are here by my allowance. Should I decide that ye dinna deserve tae be here, there is no one that can nay say me or would even dare."

Finola stood up. "Yer a bastard! Born to a lowly whore who dinna deserve the attention she got. Yer father was a fool!"

"Aye, by definition I am a bastard. But my da recognized me, legitimized me. So the status of my birth does no affect my leadership of the clan." He crossed his arms over his chest as he addressed her. "Now my family and I wish tae enjoy our meal. So, kindly remove yerselves from the seats ye dinna deserve." As the two of them took their time moving Donnchadh summoned some servants to move their plates and lay new trenchers. He pulled out the chair for Molly and then for Gwen. As she sat down, he stroked her shoulder and then leaned over to kiss her cheek. A flurry of whispers overtook the hall as she smiled up at him and placed her hand over his on her shoulder. He raised his voice and spoke again, to the gathered clan. "I wish tae present tae ye all my betrothed, Mairead MacLeod. Soon she will be Lady MacLeod and I ask that ye treat her with the same respect ye treat me." A tentative cheer went up from those gathered. He took his seat next to her and served her a choice piece of salmon and some bread with jam. Once he had served himself some salmon he reached for the mug that sat between them. It was filled with the mead she liked. He took a sip, savored it, and then passed it to her so that she might taste.

"Are we sharing Donnchadh?" She teased him as she took the mug from him and sipped. She moaned in delight. "Tis the most amazing mead! I like it better than any I have had at home."

He leaned toward her "Aye lass. We share. I will take care of ye."

She raised a hand to his cheek and gently stroked it. "Hmmm I like sharing wi ye. Just remember that I am no from here and I am an independent woman. Been on my own for some time." She then kissed his cheek and then turned to her trencher and began to eat.

He was unsure what to make of that. She had certainly proven her independence on their ride, proven that she did not need help from him. However, he was used to protecting women within the clan. Moreover, he liked the idea of protecting and taking care of her. He decided that they would need to discuss this further when they were alone next.

The hall calmed down while everyone ate. Donnchadh thoroughly enjoyed the time, having his betrothed on one side and his auntie on the other. The experience was new. Dair would have been shocked by the revelation, but he would have celebrated the outcome with him. Had any of his clansmen had further concerns about the turn of events, they were laid to rest by the laughter and animated conversation of their laird. As far as they were concerned, they had him back and if it was because of an outsider lass and a serving woman who was actually family, so be it, it did not matter how it came to be. Once the meal was over Donnchadh offered to show his auntie to her new chamber but she politely declined and told him that his time was better spent getting to know his bride to be.

Gwen blushed at that. She was sure she would get used to the idea of marrying a Scottish laird in the renaissance, but it would take some time. For now, she was happy with him, and realized it could be worse. She could have ended up in the clutches of someone like Archie. She shuddered in revulsion. "Come my lovely, let us go to yer chamber." He offered as he led her up stairs. She wrapped both of her arms around his left arm and leaned her head against his upper arm. "Mmm ye feel nice beside me like that lass." She did not respond verbally, just squeezed his arm and leaned into him a bit more. When they made it to her chamber, he opened the door for her and then seated himself in one of the comfortable chairs before the fire and gestured for her to sit on his lap. Once she was on his lap they both settled comfortably. "I think ye will agree we have much tae discuss."

"Yes, we do." She nodded.

"I ken this is all moving at incomprehensible speed lass, but tis best this way honestly. I am coming tae care for ye and this way I can protect ye without raising any questions that none of us need."

She studied him with a critical eye. Her scrutiny was so intense that it became uncomfortable for him. She searched his features and studied him as if she was trying to read his mind. When she spoke again it was without her accent, "There is a lot to unpack here. So I just need you to listen for a minute sweetie. You are a good man, I like you, and honestly, I am coming to care for you as well. I won't lie, that scares me. We barely know each other. I mean we have only known each other a hand full of days and the kind of attachment we ha...," she stopped and took a movement to breath, "the kind of attachment I feel growing, wanted or not is not something I have ever felt before. We are vastly different. We come from entirely different places with different cultures and beliefs. I have been raised to be very independent, while women here are raised to rely on and serve their men. That is not me by any means. I want a partner who will be by my side," Donnchadh started to speak and this time she stopped him with a finger to his lips, "and sometimes protect me when I need, let me be myself, but also let me be there for them when they need support. As we talked about before, I don't know why I am here or how I got here. The biggest and scariest question for me is how long I will be here. What's more,

I am less sure what would upset me more. Staying here and never seeing people I love again, or leaving and never seeing a man I am coming to adore ever again. Long story short, I know why it is best we marry, and obviously we agreed on it already, but I need you to be patient and understanding with me when it comes to your expectations of women verses my reality."

He acknowledged that what she was saying was painfully true. He had no idea how long she would be with him, but he was willing to marry her. Thinking about it that way sounded insane. However, insane or not, it made him happy, she made him happy. He had to fight to suppress a grin when she said she was beginning to adore him. "Och Gwen, ye have but tae ask and I will do all I can tae see that it happens. While I canno say that I will not slip, I give ye my word that I will take all of that and all of ye in to consideration always. And no, our marriage may no be one of convention, I would hope though, that it will be one filled with caring and room for growth. And when it comes tae yer situation here, I would rather enjoy what time I have wi' ye than wonder what if after ye are gone. I want a true marriage wi' ye lass but I can be patient as we are still learning each other."

She looked away and he wondered if he had said something wrong. She did not look back to him when she spoke again. She stared into the fire. "I decided earlier to stop fighting whatever is growing between us. I decided to take things as they come. And while it is frightening at some points, it is also reassuring. When I told you of my requirement about a private wedding between you and me as Duncan and Gwen, it was because I wanted whatever is between us to be real. While Mairead MacLeod is part of me, she is not a real person. I want you for real. I want us for real for as long as I can be with you."

His heart stopped as he studied her profile, the flames casting them both in a soft orange glow. He turned her to face him with a finger under her chin. "It will no be easy dearest. There are those of my clan who will object or allies that will no understand but we will face them together and be stronger for it. Dinna let anyone give ye cause for doubt. Come tae me if there is aught for concern and we will work it out together, aye?"

"Aye sweetheart." She laid her head against his shoulder and he stroked her hair.

"We shall be married in the Kirk this Sunday before the clan. I ken it is soon but wi' all that has happened and the discovery of us by the maids, time is of the essence." She tensed in his arms for a moment. He nuzzled her neck then, "And I do not know if I can wait much longer tae have my way wi' ye." He kissed a spot on the side of her neck and she all but purred.

"Oh Duncan." She said on a sigh. "Sunday is fine. So does that mean that Saturday evening you and I will have our private marriage?"

"Indeed it does lass. Ye shall be my lady then, Gwen MacLeod, wife of the laird. I like the thought of ye as my wife, my bonny lass." He resituated her on his lap, grabbed her backside with both hands, and squeezed a bit. "God ye drive me tae distraction. On second thought, I think Saturday eve is tae long tae wait!"

Chapter Seven

The next three days passed in a blur for Gwen. She spent the majority of her time with Molly. She insisted on helping Gwen with embellishing a dress for her two weddings. She wholeheartedly approved of her nephew's bride, but she wished she had more time to help them prepare. When they were not working on the dress, they were in the kitchens. Gwen insisted on cooking a special meal for Donnchadh and herself Saturday evening. She planned on roast leg of lamb with carrots and potatoes in a pan sauce. She didn't have the kitchen tools she was used to, so she had to learn to use what she did have. Molly even helped her bake some loaves of bread and some shortbread that Donnchadh had loved since he was a lad.

For Donnchadh the days dragged on. He caught glimpses of Gwen about the castle but had very little actual time with her to himself. His clan even seemed to take some amusement in his frustration. It had become a regular occurrence now that someone would invariably stop him every time he spied Gwen and tried to make his way toward her. Meanwhile someone else would catch her attention and draw her away. They had both caught on quickly and she usually winked at him when she was being diverted in another direction. Apparently since he was smiling now, that meant he was at their mercy. Everyone seemed to be in on it except his stepmother, brother and Brogan. The three of them sulked around the castle as if it was the end of days. Cameron seemed to be leading the diversion effort and while he was deeply frustrated, Donnchadh was amused and glad that his people seemed to accept Gwen enough to tease the both of them like this.

Saturday dawned beautiful and clear. Gwen dressed simply in the yellow dress she had worn before and met Donnchadh in the great hall at their dining table. "M'laird, tis good tae see ye." She leaned over and kissed his cheek. "Looks tae be a lovely day"

He smiled wolfishly at her. All the time she seemed more beautiful to him. He could not wait until that night, until she was his. The last real kiss they shared had been the day they agreed to marry. "Aye that it does. And it looks like it is promising tae be a grand evening." He leaned over and kissed her cheek in return. Molly sat down on his other side and cleared her throat.

"I hope ye two are behaving! Ye are no married yet!" she shook a teasing finger at them.

"Och I am the Laird woman! I behave as I wish!" He said with exaggerated frustration and then pulled Gwen into his lap to kiss her soundly. The clansmen and women laughed and clapped. His men cheered him on. Molly snorted, pretending irritation but was doing a poor job of concealing her smile. Once they broke the kiss, Gwen buried her face against Donnchadh's neck while she caught her breath. It was a mistake on her part because she caught a whiff of his fresh woodsy masculine scent and just wanted to burrow in deeper and never leave his lap. Donnchadh reveled in her kiss, his happiness, and the amusement of those around him. It felt as if all was as it should be. He made no move to dislodge Gwen from his lap. He was quite content at that moment. He turned his head to look at her and his heart swelled. Sometimes she seemed so strong and independent, and sometimes, like now, she looked so soft in his arms. "Are ye hungry lass?"

She leaned back to look at him. "Perhaps a bit, but not for food." She replied softly.

His eyes went wide for a moment and he groaned and then leaned his forehead against hers. "Christ! I want ye so bad I can taste it. And knowing that ye want me as well…tis like tae drive me mad all day! I may be daft afore this evening." They were both smiling when Cameron interrupted.

"My laird, we have some things tae attend this morn. I ken ye have yer hands full at the moment, but tis important." Cameron smirked.

"Aye. I will be there in a moment." Donnchadh waved the man away. He wrapped his arms tightly around Gwen and simply held her for a moment. "I look forward tae this evening lass. If I ken anything about Cameron, tis that he is up tae something and I doubt I shall see ye till then. He seems to relish his little game of frustrating me and keeping us apart as much as possible till tomorrow morn."

Gwen smiled at him, pushed his hair back off his face, and then pulled him to her for another kiss. The passion of it seared him. He was hot and hard and wanted more. When she leaned back, he almost whimpered at the loss of her lips. "Hopefully that will hold you over sweetheart." She got up out of his lap and he let her go. He stared after her as she left the table and waited for Molly to join her.

Donnchadh found Cameron outside in the bailey. "So I am unclear as to what takes precedence over a man enjoying his bride tae be the day afore he is tae wed."

Cameron laughed at him and winked. "Och ye sound like an old man Donnchadh! The kind that takes us out hunting for the feast tomorrow! The kind that means we, yer clansmen have some time tae warn ye about getting married and the perils of married life!" he winked.

"Ye idiot! Ye have more wenches than any man could ever need! What do ye ken of married life?" Donnchadh arched an eyebrow at him, and some of the other lads nodded in agreement with the assessment.

"Och I have heard tales lad! Why do ye think I have no settled down?" They all had a good laugh.

Molly and Gwen had heard the ruckus in the castle yard as they headed to the garden and decided to take a look at what was going on. They got there just in time to see the men mounting up and checking their bows, arrows, and assorted weaponry. They were all laughing and in good spirits. When all was settled, Cameon gave the sign and they all turned their mounts and headed out of the yard. Donnchadh looked back over his shoulder and spotted her. She blew him a kiss, which he pretended to catch and place in his sporran. Cameron saw the exchange and shoved him hard enough that he almost fell out of his saddle, at which point Donnchadh pushed him back. It degenerated into what looked like an intense argument and the two ended up in a headlong race down the road. She and Molly laughed and shook their heads and returned to their task. She needed herbs for the lamb.

Gwen was exhausted by the time the baking and cooking were done. She had not eaten noonday meal in the hall opting instead to fix herself a quick sandwich out of some of the fresh bread and lamb. She was practically shaking by the time Molly came to help her with her bath and preparations. Lottie had come to the castle that afternoon so she could be here for the celebration the next day and was eager to help and chat with Gwen. She welcomed the distraction. Finally, just before sunset she was ready. She wore a sage green gown with delicate gold details that she and Molly had sewn about the neckline and hem. She also had a circlet of ivy and heather about her brow. The dinner she prepared was laid out on a table in Donnchadh's room. All she needed now was her groom. She and Molly waited in the library. She could not help but wonder if he had gotten cold feet. It was a quick wedding after all. She heard the clatter of hooves in the yard. She looked out the window and saw a lone rider in the falling dusk. She held her breath wondering if it was Donnchadh or if something had happened to the hunting party. Then after a few minutes more she heard him bellowing for Molly. Molly hurriedly left the library to intercept him and direct him to the bath and clothes waiting for him in Gwen's room. Then she returned to tell her what was happening.

"So he is fine then?"

"Of course lass. Dinna fash. He is a tough one." In short order they heard the rest of the hunting party clatter into the yard. There was much yelling and cheering and the occasional curse as the men unloaded the deer, rabbit and grouse from their mounts and took them to the kitchen. A short while later Donnchadh entered the library. He had bathed quickly and thoroughly and dressed in his best great kilt and shirt. There was a bit of lace at the cuffs and jabot, and a dark blue jacket. He had combed his still damp hair out of his face, put a small braid at each temple and then pulled it all back into a queue at the nape of his neck. He wore his basket hilt sword and his favorite sgian dubh with a robins egg sapphire on the hilt tucked into his boot. He wanted honor to his wife to be. When he caught sight of her it was as if the breath was knocked out of him. She looked stunning in her gown. The gold trim caught the firelight and sparkled just a bit. She wore a sapphire necklace that matched the ring she wore and her hair fell in soft curls beneath the heather crown. Her cheeks were slightly flushed and her eyes shone.

"Och lass! I am struck dumb! Ye are the most beautiful woman I have ere seen!" he approached her with his hands out. She stepped into his embrace. Her soft feminine scent mixed with the heather was a heady combination for him. He bent to hiss her but Molly stopped him.

"Donnchadh! Be patient lad. Wait till the vows are spoken then ye can paw the lass tae yer heart's content."

They both laughed a bit and stepped apart. He dug through his sporran and withdrew a strip of tartan with a trefoil embroidered on it. "Come Gwen, give my yer right hand." He clasped her hand and passed Molly the fabric so that she could bind their hands.

"Where is the priest?" Gwen asked. She was unsure of what was going on. She was familiar with hand fasting but that was usually just for a year and a day, and he had said nothing about that. Handfasting was meant as a trial marriage. It gave the couple a year and a day to live as man and wife, and if things did not work out the parted ways as if nothing had happened and there was no shame or stigma to the separation. It also assured that any children born of the union during that time were legitimate. But she had thought that was all irrelevant. She assumed that this was a forever thing,

"Tis just us and Molly lass. We are doing a hand fast. But ye do no get the year and a day option." He squeezed her hand and winked, "This is forever, and the vows will be worded accordingly. Tae me this is more important than the marriage before the clan. This is a marriage of souls, a choice made by two people tae become one heart and soul. This is for us in our hearts. No matter what happens, we are always joined by this." He used his left hand to brush a curl back from her cheek and looked at her tenderly. "I shall start and say the vows and then ye repeat them to me. Ready?" he arched an eyebrow at her. She took a deep breath and nodded.

"Ye canno possess me for I belong tae meself. But as long as I live, I give ye that which is mine tae give. Ye canno command me for I am a free person, but I shall serve ye in all the ways ye require. I pledge tae ye that yours will be the name I cry aloud in the night and the eyes into which I smile into every morn." His gaze burned with the sincerity and passion of what he was saying to her. Gwen repeated the vows to him with a sincerity that surprised even her. She realized that she truly wanted this union to be genuine, not just a safeguard to her reputation. She loved how his eyes bore into hers when she said the vows.

Donnchadh could wait no longer, hands still bound; he pulled her toward him and kissed her with more passion than he had ever felt. Molly stood silently, watched for a moment, and then spoke. "One more thing...." They both started a bit guiltily and looked at her. "I ken ye will want this part of the vows lassie considering the reason ye requested this privacy. Donnchadh Maxwell Callum MacLeod, Do ye take this woman tae be yer wife?"

He smiled sheepishly when he realized what she was about. "Aye, I Duncan Maxwell Callum MacLeod take this woman tae be my wife."

"And Gwen Pierce, do ye take this man fer yer husband?

"Yes, I Gwendoline Alice Pierce take this man to be my husband."

"Now ye may kiss yer bride lad! Congratulations tae ye both!" Molly gave them each a peck on the cheek and left the room.

"Ye are no longer Gwen Pierce. Ye are now my wife Gwen MacLeod! And I could nae be happier!" He beamed with pride.

"Hmmm it sounds so noble. I like it and I like the man attached to the name even more!" She stood on her tiptoes to kiss him. Neither had thought to unbind their hands so it was a bit awkward but neither of them cared.

Eventually Donnchadh unbound their hands and tucked the strip of tartan into his sporran. "I am sorry lass, we have missed dinner. Perhaps we can sneak sommat from the kitchen."

Gwen giggled at him. "Don't worry my dear husband. I think we will be all right. Let's retire to your chamber." He was confused by her reaction but he took her hand and followed her. He figured that he could go to the kitchen later if they needed anything. When they approached the door to his room, he scooped her up in his arms and carried her across the threshold. He sat her down and stared at the surprise she had prepared for him. After waiting a few moments for his response, Gwen stepped to the table and began to prepare a plate of lamb and vegetables for him. "You asked me to cook for you some time and I figured this would be the perfect time to do it. There is even some of the heather ale you like and a surprise for dessert." She realized she was rambling out of nervousness. Once his plate was prepared, she took his hand and led him to the table to sit. "I hope you like it sweetheart." She kissed his cheek and then turned to fix herself a plate.

He quickly grabbed her wrist stopping her mid motion and drew her attention back to him. He said nothing at first, only continued to stare at her, his eyes searching. He pulled her closer while he sat, and wrapped his arms around her waist and leaned his head against her stomach. "I canna thank ye enough for being so thoughtful and sweet! I am the one who takes care of everyone else and aside from Molly, no one really reciprocates. But that does nae upset me. Tis just the life of a laird. But now tae have a wife who goes out of her way to do things like this just for me, tis almost overwhelming." He leaned his head back to look at her face. She had stroked his hair while he held her and now she framed his face with her hands. "Thank ye Gwen! I promise tae do everything I can tae make ye happy!"

She bent down and kissed him sweetly then. "Then go ahead and eat sweetheart. That would make me happy right now and then you can make me even happier after."

He squeezed her again quickly and turned to the plate she had prepared. It didn't look real, it was almost too perfect. The lamb was cooked to perfection, the aroma with the herbs it had been roasted with was heavenly, and the carrots and potatoes had been finished with the pan sauce. He could not believe his little lady wife had cooked this. He took a bite of the lamb and was delighted at the rich flavor. He leaned back in his chair and moaned. Gwen laughed at his response. Next, he took a bite of the vegetables in the sauce and yet more pleasure spread through him. This put the castle cook to shame. He decided then and there that he would tell no one of this. This was his alone. He did not want her cooking for anyone else. He could not imagine sharing this pleasure with anyone else. "Good God lass! This is amazing. I have ne'er tasted lamb like this! If I had kenned this is what ye were talking about, I would have married ye immediately. As it stands, it looks as if I am going tae have tae train twice as hard so that I dinna get fat from eating yer cooking. At least I mean tae say, I hope ye will cook for me again!"

"Of course I will! I am so relieved you like it! I was worried. I hadn't made it in years. And there is still dessert."

"Ye had naught tae worry about! I imagine this could rival any fine chef of any noble house anywhere. I would no be surprised if this was better than what they serve at court."

"All of your flattery will give me a big head Duncan. All that matters is that you enjoy it."

"I enjoy it more than I can tell ye! I recall ye told he ye did things like this afore for friends and family, and by the by, I want tae try that rabbit dish sometime now that I ken how ye cook, but why did ye learn things like this?"

Gwen was beyond flattered at his response to her cooking. He was the prime example of why she loved to do it. "Where I grew up, food is love. The kitchen is the heart of the home. You always have something for company in the way of food and drinks and when you have company for dinner, you go out of your way to make it enjoyable. I knew the basics of cooking because that was how I grew up. Quite often, the women would be in the kitchen talking and drinking wine or something like that while the men were in the living room or outside in the yard and the closer to the meal, the more people would gather in the kitchen until everyone was there or in the dining room. Unless there was a cook out or seafood boil. Then most of the time the men of the family drank beer and cooked those outside while the women relaxed once everything was prepped for cooking. So I took classes to learn more ways to cook and how to get creative. It became more and more fun."

Chapter Eight

Donnchadh ate most of the lamb while they sat and talked. They spoke of everything and nothing. She shared stories of her cooking and how she grew up. He told of the adventures he and Dair had as children. The fire was burning low by the time their meal was done. Gwen got up and grabbed a covered dish from where it sat on one of the chests. "I hope you saved some room for dessert!"

"Aye! If that dessert is ye!" He leered and pulled her to him so that she fell into his lap. He playfully nipped at her neck making her laugh. She squirmed in his arms and reached for the plate she grabbed a piece of shortbread and offered it to him. "Och a lad couild get spoiled! Not only does his beautiful wife cook for him, she feeds him from her own hand!" He took a bite of the cookie and leaned his head back closing his eyes. She smiled at his enjoyment. "That is my favorite! Only ever made for special occasions! I have no had it in a long time!"

"Molly mentioned that. She figured that today counted as a special occasion."

He looked back to her and sobered, "Aye it is. And I cannae imagine a better start tae a marriage than we have had this eve. I do think that we should retire tae bed now that we have eaten our fill." His hand stroked her arm gently causing her to shiver. "Are ye nervous lass?"

She bit her lip and was quiet for a moment. "I am a little." She said no more. He lifted her as he stood.

"Is there aught I can do tae ease yer nerves?" his eyes were filled with concern.

She looked up at him shyly, "Kiss me." That was all the prompting he needed. He had been waiting for this since he had been discovered in her chamber. He captured her lips with his and she melted against him. He loved it when she gave herself over to him like that. He ran his tongue over her lower lip and she opened for him. She grabbed the collar of his shirt in an attempt to get closer to him. He groaned and ran a hand down her back to settle on her ass. He drew her against his body, and she could feel the hot ridge of his desire pressed against her. While they kissed, he removed her flower crown and tossed it across the room. She tugged at the lapels of his jacket wanting closer contact with him. He shed his jacket hurriedly and broke the kiss for a moment to untie his cravat. Gwen ran her hands over his chest as he did so, the fine lawn of his shirt separating her hands from his skin. He caressed her shoulders, turned her around, and began to unlace the bodice of her dress while he kissed her neck. She leaned back into him, soaking up his every touch. He traced the shell of her ear with his tongue and she gasped and shivered. "Och lass! Ye are so responsive! The slightest thing seems tae elicit so much pleasure." He gently bit the spot where her neck met her shoulder and her knees gave out. He caught her and chuckled darkly. He was sure he would enjoy this. Before he continued, he slipped her dress from her shoulders so that she was left in just her chemise. He swept her up and deposited her on to his large four-poster bed. He tugged his shirt over his head and lay with her.

Gwen felt light headed. Donnchadh seemed to know exactly what to do to her. She yearned for more but was scared to reach for it at the same time. She was aware when he sent her crown flying and it tickled her that he wanted her with such abandon that he flung it like that. When she ran her hands over his chest after he shed his jacket, she could feel the delicious heat of him. He was all smooth muscle and fire scorching her fingertips. When he was behind her unlacing her dress, she was briefly filled with trepidation. It pierced the fog of her mind that this was really happening. She was about to have sex with this strong, handsome, big man, her husband. She was about to lose her virginity to him and she was not quite sure how they would fit. However, he was being so gentle with her. When he traced her ear with his tongue, she was sure that she would burst into flame. She wanted more from him. She wanted to hold him, to feel him. Then he had bitten her neck and that was it, a pleasure shot through her that briefly cause her to lose control. She was vaguely aware that he had slipped her dress from her and again when he laid her in bed and joined her. "Oh Duncan! I cannot even begin to tell you what you are doing to me! I want you so badly." She reached a hand behind his neck and pulled him to her for a soul-searing kiss. He growled into her mouth and devoured her.

"Are ye sure ye want this dearest? If ye need, we can stop now, and wait until tomorrow. If we continue much longer, I fear it will be even more difficult tae stop. I want ye so much I ache with it, but I dinna want tae hurt ye or push ye tae far tae soon." He pulled back to look at her. One hand caressed the tops of her breasts where they rose from the neckline of her chemise.

"If I was not sure I would not have let it get this far," she reassured him. She shifted under his touch wanting more. "I want this. I want you. Now!" She moaned the last. She stopped his hand where it traced designs on her chest and guided it down her body so that he could raise the hem of her chemise and then back up underneath.

He clenched his teeth and his breath came out a hiss. "Ye are so wet lass!" She had no time to react because he began to stroke her. He played with her. Kissing her deeply and his tongue mimicking the press of his finger within her. She shifted anxiously beneath him. Her hands explored his chest and arms. Eventually her hands strayed down his body as he continued to pleasure her with his fingers. She moaned and her hips rose to meet the thrust of his fingers. Her hand fumbled to get beneath his kilt, and when she did, she wrapped a hand around his rock hard shaft. He jerked in surprise and growled.

He broke the kiss panting. She did not stop stroking him. "MMMM Lass! Ye dinna ken what ye are doing tae me!" He ground out and grabbed her wrist to still her hand. "If ye keep that up, this will no last long and I want tae make this pleasurable for ye" Once she let go of him, he got up and shucked his kilt.

She gasped at his naked form. She had seen naked men before, but none of them looked like him. He was all hard planes and chiseled angles. His face was stunning and his body was something any woman in her right mind would fantasize about. He stood at the edge of the bed for a moment allowing her to take stock of him. His eyes were filled with a heat that had her melting. She looked down his body and her eyes lingered on his impressive manhood. He put any other man she had seen to shame. While she was eager for him, she was a bit concerned about his size.

Donnchadh read the appreciation in her gaze as she drank him in. He was painfully hard and was not sure he could wait any longer. He wanted their first time to be pleasurable for her and he hoped that it would not be over too soon. He made his way across the bed to her and decided to speed things up a bit. She lay there watching him approach. He reached for her, grabbed the neck of her chemise, and rent the fabric all the way down to the hem. He groaned his appreciation and sank onto her body kissing one of her breasts and then the other. Her nipples were tight little buds. Everywhere he touched, he set her on fire. She writhed beneath him and he gently pushed her thighs apart and settled between them. "There is no going back now Gwen ye are my wife in every sense of the word." He whispered as he thrust into her. She gave an abbreviated whimper, sucked in a pained breath and her nails dug into his shoulders. He felt her tension and it took him a moment to realize what was going on. Christ, he berated himself; he had torn through her maidenhead like a rutting beast. He held himself still within her and kissed her neck as he tried to comfort her. "I am so sorry my love! The pain should pass soon, I promise ye. I should have taken more care tae make sure ye were ready for me. It will never be like this again. It only hurts the first time." He felt her fingers loosen their death grip on his shoulders so he flexed his hips experimentally.

She inhaled a sharp breath. "Oh God! Duncan! That feels good!" He needed no further encouragement. He kissed her and began to thrust slowly. Her hands roamed his back and her legs wrapped around his waist. She was so tight and hot around him. The pleasure was almost unbearable. Her body rose to his thrusts and her moans became louder. "Yes! Don't stop!" She cried out as he drove into her harder and faster.

She loved how he felt inside her now. At first, it had hurt so much but now, that pain was forgotten as if it had never been. She just wanted more of him. He filled her. She did not know how he would fit all of his girth within her, but not only did he succeed, it was one of the most pleasurable things she had ever felt.

"Gwen! I canno last much longer. Ye are driving me mad! Ye feel so good!" he rasped into her ear as he thrust harder. She felt the pressure building within her, her body began clenching around him. "Oh Duncan! Oh God Duncan!" She writhed in his arms and it pushed him over the edge. He gave a few more quick hard thrusts and roared his release. He partially collapsed on to her. She chuckled softly and stroked his hair and back as they both regained their breath and recovered.

Chapter Nine

Sunday morning dawned cool and clear. Gwen and Donnchadh had woken early, made love again, and watched the sunrise. 'Well my lady wife. Are ye ready tae make it official before the clan this morn?" he kissed the top of her head while she nestled in his arms. She giggled then and smiled against his chest as if she were shy.

"Aye m'lord husband. I am. Unfortunately, you know that means we have to get out of bed right?

"Aye. I am aware, and as much as I would love tae stay here, the thought of marrying ye all over is the only thing that could possibly coerce me tae vacate this bed and chamber for any amount of time. And once we have made it official afore the clan, ye will be all mine again and we shall no leave this room any time in the near future, because I dinna want tae share ye until I have tae."

They startled a moment later when there was a fierce pounding on the door. "M'Laird! Ye need tae rise and ready yerself! Ye over slept and I am here tae help ye!" Molly called from the hallway. Donnchadh slid out of bed. He pulled the fur coverlet up over her chest, wrapped a length of sheet around his waist, and went to open the door. Molly slid into the room as he opened it and very quickly shut it behind her so that no one would know Gwen had spent the night with him before they were married before the clan. "How fairs my favorite nephew and his lovely wife?" She went to the side of the bed to check on Gwen who was blushing furiously.

"Grand, if a bit tired." Donnchadh spoke for them and winked at Molly. "As I am sure ye ken the lass can cook and we....celebrated well in tae the night after our late dinner."

"I am sure ye fair wore the lass out. Now be a good lad, go tae your lady's room and get dressed while I see to her here."

"Mmm MY lady. I like that! I will see ye at the kirk my lady."

Before she could respond, he was out the door with a bundle of clothes and tartan. They would both be wearing the clothes they wore last night for their wedding today. If possible, Gwen was even more nervous than she had been the night before. Molly pulled a new chemise from the wardrobe and assisted her in donning it and then gown. This time she also brought out a small jewelry box and withdrew a delicate silver necklace of intertwined trefoils with a sapphire set nestled amongst three of them. She gasped at its beauty. "The ring Donnchadh gave ye was part of a set that his da had commissioned for his mam. Donnchadh dinna ken, but I kept it hidden just for this day. Iona would have adored ye. She would have been so proud of her wee lad. She would be bawling ere she were here. Tis all I can do no to cry meself. Come now lass, lets get ye tae the kirk. Yer man is waiting"

"Thank you Molly. That means a lot! I know we have only known each other a short time, but I hope I can make him happy."

They exited the castle and stopped in the garden. Molly had another wreath made for Gwen. This one of heather and white roses and some blue forget-me-nots. "Oh Molly, it is stunning!" Molly placed it on her head and they continued to the kirk. Once they were there, it was determined that Gwen would walk the aisle on her own, as she had no one to give her away. With help, Molly pulled the doors open and Gwen made her way down the aisle to Donnchadh. He stood at the alter beaming at her. She smiled nervously back. All attention was on her as she proceeded toward him. Finally, everyone was seated. The priest gave a brief sermon on faithfulness and the sanctity of marriage. He called for the attention of the congregation and began the ceremony. When he asked if there were any who thought they should not marry, she felt Donnchadh's arm tense under her hand.

"Aye! I have a reason!" It was Archie with his mother behind him. "He is a bastard thus unfit tae lead and we dinna even ken who her family is! Even if he were no a bastard, he still needs tae marry to make alliances with other clans."

Donnchach pushed Gwen partly behind him. "Is that so brother? Is there anyone else who feels this way?" he all but roared. A few men including Brogan stood up and nodded. Donnchadh saw red. This was his wedding day, this should not be happening. He was ready to draw his sword in defense of his rights and his wife. Before he could react, Cameron stood next to him.

"His da recognized him and even signed deeds and will stating that he is the laird of the MacLeods. We all respected his da and afore now, and best I ken, we have all respected Donnchadh. He has been a good and fair leader since his da passed. Can any of ye gathered here name a time where he has no given all he has for us? Even when he lost Dair, he continued to do his best as Laird, and then Cait, who among ye could have dealt with that loss so soon after Dair and seen to the running of the clan. He gave himself up for us. He kept going for us, his clansmen. He no longer laughed as he used tae, or smiled. However, he remained steadfast as our laird. Now tis true we may no ken her family. Nevertheless, she is a MacLeod and she has brought him back tae us as he was before. We have all taunted him this past week keeping them apart and he took it in good humor. We have our old Donnchadh back and this lovely lass is the reason. So instead of giving them grief, ye should be thanking her, as I do." He turned and dropped to his knee in front of Gwen and put his fist over his heart. "My Lady MacLeod, there are no words that I can say tae make ye understand the magnitude of my appreciation. A year ago a hole was ripped in our clan. And ye have begun tae stitch it back together. Ye have given us back the part of Donnchadh we have all missed. Ye are an amazing woman and I can no imagine a better wife for the Laird of the MacLeods. As long as, I live Lady Mairead MacLeod, ye have my fealty and my protection."

Gwen squeezed Donnchadh's hand as Cameron spoke, unsure of what to do. He just smiled softly down at her and nodded. She let go of his hand and then addressed Cameron. She offered him her hand to help him up. "I accept yer fealty and protection and I hope that I can do ye proud as wife tae yer laird." She raised up on her tiptoes and kissed his cheek. Her kiss had surprised him and he looked to Donnchadh, expecting some sort of jealousy. He saw nothing but pride in his face and then understood that this was simply how she was, not flirting, simply charming and affectionate with those she was close to and it warmed his heart. She was indeed perfect for Donnchadh! He took her hand and kissed it and then stepped down from the alter and turned again to the congregation a fist raised skyward. The majority of the clan cheered. "Now, our lady has two champions. If ye have a problem wi her, ye will have tae go through me and our Laird."

"That is no the point at all!" Archie still stood in the center of the aisle and rolled his eyes. A few of the men that supported him had sat down, but it was too late. Donnchadh had already made a mental note of the dissenters. "He is unfit as Laird and she is even more unfit to be lady of this clan."

"Is that a challenge brother dear? I would think carefully about yer next words."

"Aye! Tis a challenge. Here and now! I deserve tae be laird. Ye have usurped my place long enough!"

"So be it!" Donnchadh drew his sword and turned to Gwen. He kissed her fiercely and then whispered, "Dinna fash. This will all be in the past in short order and we can begin our life together. Ye stay with Cameron and if aught gets out of hand he will take ye tae my chamber." She nodded mutely at him, her eyes wide. "Cameron, I am sure ye dinna expect yer vow tae be acted upon so soon, but I need ye tae protect my bride should anything happen."

"Aye m'laird. With my life!" He drew his sword and stood before Gwen, between her and the congregation. He rested the tip on the ground and leaned a bit on the hilt, looking as if he had not a care in the world, but the reality was that he was ready to pounce.

"Come brother. Draw yer weapon and let's see this done. Ye have been a thorn in my side for far tae long. Once I defeat ye, ye and yer mother are tae leave MacLeod lands. I will not have ye inciting trouble amongst my people. I will allow ye tae take some money tae see ye tae Edinburgh but beyond that, ye will be on yer own." His voice was emotionless.

"Ye can no do that!" Archie's voice cracked as he yelled.

"Oh aye. Aye I can. I am laird brother. My word is law." He swung his sword and caught Archie across the chest, slicing his shirt and leaving a thin red line of blood to bloom across the white fabric. Archie yelled with rage and charged Donnchadh, his sword held before him like a lance. Donnchadh simply stepped to the side and then smacked Archie on the butt as he stumbled past. Archie let out an indignant cry and spun around swinging wildly.

"Come now lad. Concede defeat. I have no desire tae hurt or humiliate ye. I just want tae have my wedding in peace."

"Ye will never have peace as long as I live!" Another jab and then a slash, both of which Donnchadh easily avoided. The next time Donnchadh swung his sword, he caught Archie on his right forearm leaving a deep gash. "You bastard!" His voice rose a bit higher, sounding almost like a girlish falsetto. He charged again, this time he caught the sleeve of Donnchadh's shirt and sliced it.

"Ye wee rat! This is my best shirt and on my wedding day I am supposed tae look my best for my bride." He advanced on Archie with deadly intent. Archie swung his sword wildly and

Donnchadh knocked it easily aside. He made another swing, at which point Donnchadh decided he had enough and disarmed him. The sword skittered over the stone floor. Gwen watched all of it with a mixture of horror and awe. Donnchadh pinned Archie to the back wall of the Kirk with his sword pressed against his neck, ready to pierce flesh. Archie's mother cried out and ran forward. She grabbed Donnchadh's arm and tried to jerk the sword away from Archie's neck. He did not budge. She cried and begged for mercy for her son.

"Ye would have me show mercy woman?" his gaze never wavered from Archie's pale terrified face.

"Please! I loved ye as my son and raised ye as such. Dinna break your mother's heart!"

The laugh that escaped Donnchadh then was bitter. It made Gwen long to go to him. "Ye loved me not woman, and all ken it. The only love and kindness I experienced aside from times when it was just me and my da, was from Molly! She is ten times the woman ye are and has a heart far bigger. So nay, I will no show ye mercy as any mother, let alone mine. My mother lies near this very spot and her sister Molly now holds a place of honor in my house hold. Ye are unworthy of the title of lady. However, I will show ye mercy as a human being. I am no so cruel as tae kill any who disagree with me. So now is your chance, and mind ye it will be short. One of my men will take ye tae the keep, and ye may pack some clothes and personal belongings and naught else, ye will also be given some coin. Then ye are tae leave Dunvegan forever. I banish ye, and if ye ever set foot on my land again the consequences will be severe." He lowered his sword as Finola went to Archie and pulled him out of the kirk despite his arguing. Two clansmen went with them to ensure their compliance.

Donnchadh turned back to the altar. "Will ye still marry me lass? Even as sweaty and ill-kempt as I am?" he motioned to his torn sleeve. Cameron sheathed his sword and offered Gwen his hand as she descended the few steps from the altar. Once at the bottom she ran to Donnchadh. He caught her, and buried his face in her hair for a moment.

"Aye Donnchadh! I will take ye any way I can get ye!" She raised up on her toes and gave him a quick kiss. His clan cheered among them.

"Ahem! May we continue? While the Lord is ever present, we people have needs like food and drink." The priest interrupted good-naturedly. The wedding continued without further issues. Once the vows had been said, they headed to the great hall for a mid-day meal and celebration.

Gwen could not stop smiling, and neither could Donnchadh. He was happier than he had been in years and his lady wife was the reason. He had Cameron check to make sure that his half-brother and stepmother were quit of the castle. He wanted no further troubles on his wedding day. As they sat enjoying their meal, Donnchadh picked up one of Gwen's hands and kissed it. "I am sorry for how our wedding turned out my dear." He whispered.

"Ye have nothing tae be sorry for sweetheart. Did ye plan on yer brother and Finola making a scene? Did ye plan to have tae fight yer brother and draw blood? If so, ye need tae tell my fortune and tell me just how happy my husband and I will be together."

"Och I need no be a soothsayer tae tell ye that. We will be blissfully happy, I will see to it." He leaned forward and kissed her. The people who saw clapped and yelled in their favor.

"M'laird, methinks my little Kenna will have a friend here at the castle afore too long from the looks of ye two!" Lottie proclaimed with a smile. There was much laughter about the statement. Donnchadh grinned and Gwen blushed. She resolved to tell him that night that she still would not be able to get pregnant for about another year due to an implant. She hoped he would understand.

When pipers entered and began to play lively tunes, the assembled party moved tables and benches so that they would have room to dance. There was an amazing feeling of joy that filled the hall and encompassed the clan. Donnchadh looked at Gwen somberly for a moment. "Thank ye love. Ye have given my clan a side of their laird that they missed and ye have given their laird a fresh start. I cannot recall being so happy since the last time Alasdair and I hunted together and were caught in a snowstorm. We holed up in a shack used when herding sheep in distant fields and proceeded tae drink ourselves stupid..well more stupid. DInna sleep much but drank and talked much of the night and made our way back half-starved and drunk the next day. Och Molly was sore at us for that one. Anyhow, I am glad ye came in tae my life. Nae matter how it happened. Now will ye dance with me m'lady wife?" He stood and bowed offering her his hand.

"Aye m'laird husband. That sounds grand!" She smiled and took his hand and they made their way around the table to join the others dancing in the reels that the pipes were playing. Gwen danced until her feet were sore. It seemed that all of the clansmen wanted to dance with the laird's new wife. Finally, Cameron cut into a dance and spun her about the floor.

"Ye two look fine together. I am glad ye found each other. If ye need aught, ye call on me," he told her as they danced. Once the song came to an end, he escorted her back to the chair at Donnchadh's side. "It seems that our lovely lady is fair worn out from all the dancing. Perhaps ye two should rest a bit before dinner. Ye ken? Get the lass off her feet." He whispered the last rather loudly and the clansmen all whooped with laughter.

"Aye, laugh all ye like lads. I am the one that gets her tae himself!" Donnchadh retorted and scooped Gwen up into his arms to make his way from the hall. Their exit was marked with ribald comments as to what they could do until dinner. Gwen buried her face in his neck and her shoulders shook with laughter. He all but ran up the stairs to his chamber and kicked the door shut behind them. He sat her down on the bed then sat next to her. He noticed that she looked a bit forlorn. "Is aught amiss?

She started at her hands and shrugged. "Depends on what you mean by amiss. There is something I need to tell you but I am worried about how you may react."

"Dinna fash. I could no be upset with ye if I tried right now. I am far tae happy. And if it is aught serious, I will be respectful about it. Tell me and we can handle it together."

"Well you know I am from somewhere else," she swallowed hard and met his gaze. "And where I am from things are different. So I just need you to listen to me for a minute and not interrupt at all." She waited for him to nod and then stood and began pacing. "I know that this could change how you feel about me, I could lose you, but I don't want to keep anything from you. A husband and wife should not keep secrets like these from each other."

Donnchadh's heart was pounding and his brow furrowed. His anxiety was getting the better of him. "Och lass! Just tell me! The suspense may literally kill me."

Her head jerked in his direction and her eyes were wide and full of unshed tears. He immediately regretted his hasty words. He motioned for her to continue. "You see Duncan, I am not just from another place, but another time. I was born in the year 1993. I am 28 years old and I served in the military. Lottie mentioned us having a child. I can't have a child for about another year because of....because of a treatment I received. I know this all seems insane, but I have proof in my chamber." Donnchadh was staring at her. He was unsure what he expected her to tell him, but it surely was not this. He closed his eyes and pinched the bridge of his nose. He had told Molly that he would follow his instincts about Gwen. Now he was not sure.

When he spoke, he sounded almost detached. "Hmmm ye have a lot to explain. I asked ye afore, when ye told me yer real name if there was aught else. Ye said nay. Ye lied tae me."

She backed up from him a step and her shoulders slumped. "I am so sorry Duncan. I was scared what would happen if you found out. I was trying to protect myself."

His eyes narrowed on her, "Dinna call me that. Ye have lied tae me and led me on. I dinna even ken the slightest bit about who ye are. I thought I kenned at least a little. But ye make a fool out of me! Did ye withhold it from me until we were married and consummated so that I might be forced tae protect ye should ye be branded a witch?"

She shrank back further still and bumped into the wall. Tears rolled down her face. "No Dunc....Donnchadh. I would never do that. I didn't expect to be here long enough for it to matter, and now it does. I am sorry I kept it from you! I am not a witch, I swear to you!"

"Dinna swear to me. Tis only words that apparently mean naught tae ye. Ye said ye canno have children?"

"Not right now. In another..."

He cut her off "Good. So that means I need not worry about issue from our coupling last night and this morning. I will petition the church for an annulment on grounds of instability of the mind on yer account."

Her legs gave out then and she slid down the wall. "Donnchadh no! Please!"

"Och ye beg my protection, or my mercy?"

"Neither! I beg your forgiveness and understanding! I am not mad and I am not a witch. I was merely caught up in something that landed me here. At first I wanted nothing more than to go home, but now, I couldn't imagine my life without you." She held her hands over her heart as she pleaded with him. Her voice was thick with tears. "Please Donnchadh...please. I have proof in my wardrobe. And I promise you that this makes no difference in what you know of me. I am still the same person that you care about and that cares about you."

"Ye are the same person that lied tae me. Aye, go tae yer chamber." A look of hope flooded her eyes at that, and it hurt him even more. "Wait for me there. I will be there once I have gathered my thoughts and decided what I am going tae do. I will follow ye and lock ye in." She gasped as if he had struck her, but he did not look at her. "I canno have ye running off or disappearing on me."

Gwen said nothing more. She slowly got up using the wall to support herself. She ached from kneeling on the floor. Donnchadh made no move to assist her. She had known it was a risk to tell him about the reality of herself. She had gambled on the growing affection she saw from him and felt between them. The trouble with gambling was that there was always a chance that one would lose. In casinos the house always won. The same thing had happened just now. The house won. Her mind raced trying to process everything and figure out what she should do next. All she really wanted to do was curl up on her bed, close her eyes, and pray that when she opened them, this would all be a bad dream, and Donnchadh would still care for her. She slowly made her way to her room. Once she was inside she went to her wardrobe and stared at it. She heard the door shut and the lock click followed by the sound of Donnchadh's boots on the stones as he returned to his chamber. She felt numb. She opened the wardrobe and withdrew her pouch. She pulled out her phone, her ID, her car keys, her money, and a few other odds and ends. She set them all on the trunk at the foot of her bed and went to sit in one of the chairs before the empty fireplace. The sun was still out and warming the stones so there was not a chill. Hopefully Donnchadh would come around or at least check on her before it got too late because the nights were still cold. She closed her eyes in an attempt to calm her mind, and dozed off, exhaustion finally catching up with her.

Donnchadh sat on his bed. His heart ached. He had married and fallen in love with a lunatic. She had seemed so perfect for him but then that illusion had shattered. She had to be mad. There was no way anything she said could be real. She had hidden her identity from him and then lied. Perhaps this was not truly her fault. Perhaps some mental instability compelled her to act like this, to lie and concoct such stories. He was unsure how long he sat there on his bed but eventually he heard a gentle tap on his door. He opened it to see a tray laden with food set on the floor. So it was dinner time. He gave a bitter laugh and picked up the tray. They thought that the lovers were too busy to make it down to dinner. Little did they know. He was grateful though since it meant that he did not have to face anyone at the moment. He was not fit company. He ate a bit of the chicken and some carrots and bread. He could not stomach any more than a few bites. He sat back against his pillows and tried to untangle the mess of his thoughts. What was he to do with her?

He opened his eyes to a cool room and day light. He looked out the window and saw that the sky was filled with gray clouds. They perfectly matched his mood. It struck him then that it was morning. He had fallen asleep without going to see what Gwen supposedly wanted to show him. He sighed and opened his door to find a tray of breakfast in the hall waiting for him. He took it in and sat it on the table between the chairs in front of the dying fire. There was enough for two. Heather decorated the tray and there was even a plate of the shortbread Gwen had made. It made his heart clench in his chest. He sat down in one of the chairs. He kept trying to bring himself to go to her chamber but he couldn't do it. He heard nothing. Her chamber was beside his, had she been crying or upset he surely would have heard it. After building up the fire he finally decided that he could wait no longer. He unlocked the door and stepped inside. He was concerned for a moment when he noticed that her bed was untouched and the room was freezing but then he saw the top of her head as it rested against the wing of one of the chairs. He noticed the odd items on the trunk and approached to look at them. He tried to be quiet so as not to wake her if she slept. He had never seen anything like these. The card with her image caught his attention. It stated her name and the date of her birth and the year in which the card had been issued as well as some other information he was unsure of. She had said she was born in 1993, the card said the same and it had been issued in 2019. Could she be telling the truth? What would be the point of creating something like this for a swindle? He picked up the thin black box. When he brought it up to his face to examine it, it lit up and he almost dropped it. It displayed a close up image of her with a dog and a cat on either side of her face and asked for a PIN. He quickly sat it down. He examined the other items, becoming more and more confused. All of the items on the trunk were extremely well crafted and the little black box was astonishing. He leaned against the bedpost pondering what he was looking at. He decided to wake her and see what she had to say about her belongings. He went around the chair to find her curled into as tight as ball as possible. She hugged her knees to her chest and her head was bent forward. Even in sleep, she looked sad.

He longed to comfort her. He touched her hair and softly called her name. She did not respond. He knelt down to get a closer look and to try and wake her again. This time he touched her cheek. "Gwen, lass, time tae wake up." He realized that her skin was cold, almost alarmingly so. "Lass! Ye need tae wake up!" He ran his hands down her arms. She shifted her head a bit and a small sound escaped her lips. He grabbed her hands in an attempt to get her to respond and draw her up out of the chair, surely, he reasoned, she was just trying to get back at him for how he treated her last night. Perhaps she was trying to purposely worry him. His breath caught when he felt her hands. They were like ice. She still did not fully respond to him. Only another small sound. "Christ! What has happened lass? Why will ye no wake for me and why are ye so cold? Come on Gwen. Ye need tae wake up and show me these things of yers!" He was almost shouting now. He heard someone coming down the hallway. He got up and quickly shoved all of her belongings into the trunk they had sat on.

"What are ye two doing in here?" Molly asked. She had noticed the open door and peered in to see Donnchadh standing near the chair a look of concern on his face.

"We...we had a disagreement yesterday. I told...she stayed in here last night."

Molly knew he was not giving her the entire truth. "Well are ye both settled now? I have tae admit I find it surprising that she stayed in here as the bed is untouched and there is no fire and does no look to have been one at all since yesterday morn, tis freezing in here." She frowned at him. "Where is the lass?"

Realization struck him then. Last night he had locked her in and had not even lit a fire for her. He had done nothing to care for her. He would have offered his enemy basic comforts if they were a guest in his house and he had not even done that for his wife, mad or not. He scooped her up out of the chair then and took her back to his chamber. Molly watched with growing concern as she saw how pale and unresponsive Gwen was. Her hand hung limp as he carried her. Donnchadh laid her on the rug before the fire and stoked it some more and then rushed to pull the covers from his bed. He wrapped them around her and then pulled her partially into his lap. "Come on lass. Wake for me. I am sorry. Christ I am so sorry!" She did not move. Molly had followed them.

"Ye left her there without a fire all night? Are ye daft! Ye will be lucky if she dinna catch her death!" Molly raged at him. "I told ye tae follow yer instinct! I told ye tae take care of the lass and that she was important tae ye and the clan! And this is what ye do ye boidseir! How could ye?! Are ye truly that petty? Has Finola rubbed off on ye that well?"

He did not look up from Gwen but he flinched at her yells. She was not wrong. He recalled every word she had told him and each statement ripped out another little piece of his gut. He wished he could take her place. If only she would wake up, or warm up. Her breathing was so shallow that it scared him. He fought back tears. "How can ye ken that Auntie? How can ye be sure?"

"I read both of yer tea leaves ye great arse! And they have no told me wrong yet. I thought that the lass would have enough time with ye, that when ye fought, ye would be able tae get it through yer thick noggin that she cared and was the one for ye. Clearly both the leaves and I underestimated just how hard headed ye are! Ye had best pray ye dinna lose her lad. She was meant tae be the great love of yer life. There will never be another. The leaves told me that if ye lose her ye will be forever alone and yer clan the worse for her loss." She sat beside Gwen chafing her hands in an attempt to warm them. "We need tae get her in a hot bath tae bring up her temperature. Her lips are nigh blue. Pull her up full against ye. Take off yer sark and hold her close tae yer bare skin while I get a bath brought up."

Donnchadh did as he was bid. He thought that she might be a bit warmer than she was when he found her, but it was still a shock when he pulled her to his bare chest. He sucked in a breath, wrapped them both in a large blanket, and sat there while Molly oversaw the preparations for the bath. The lads carrying the water in glanced their way on occasion but he did not shift his attention from Gwen. "Come my sweet love. I need ye tae wake up and chastise me for my stupidity. I need tae hear that sweet voice call me yer Duncan again." Tears began to roll down his cheeks as they poured the last of the warm water into the tub.

"Come lad. Let's get her out of those clothes and in tae the bath." Molly began to remove blankets and helped him beto undress her limp form. Each limb that was moved and flopped back unresponsive was like a dagger in his gut. He had done this. She was like this because of him and it was eating at him. Finally, when they had her naked he began to gently place her in the warm water. When he had her most of the way in, her eyes shot open and she screamed as if in pain and was clawing at him like a cat trying to get out of the tub, leaving red welts down his shoulders and arms. She even drew a bit of blood.

"We need tae warm ye up lass. Just a minute more and we can take ye out of the tub." He tried to calm her as he restrained her wrists. Her eyes were huge and her breathing fast and heavy between moans of pain. She fought him a moment more and then passed out.

"Gwen?! Lass? Come on! Wake up again for me! What's wrong?" He looked at Molly in terror.

"Get her out of the water! Let's get her dry and in bed! I am not sure what is wrong!"

Gwen's head lolled to the side as he dried her. It was as if she was dead and the very thought scared Donnchadh more than anything did. He realized that he could not lose her. He crawled into bed with her and pulled her body against his. She seemed to be warming up. He just hoped she would wake again soon.

Sleep had been a relief to Gwen yesterday and she barely registered the temperature change. The cold had enveloped her and wrapped her in a pleasant numbness last night. She had woken to excruciating pain. Donnchadh had put her in what felt like lava. It was a pain like nothing she felt before and he was not allowing her to escape it. He held her there and let her suffer until she passed out.

She awoke a little while later feeling warm if a bit achy. She began to panic when she couldn't move. She had no idea where she was, only that she was restrained. She fought to free herself.

"Shhh. Shhh. Gwen, tis me Donnchadh! Ye are all right. I was just trying tae get ye warm." He let go of her and tried to calm her.

She scooted back across the bed wide eyed and terrified until she bumped into Molly on the other side. "What...what happened?" her voice came out in a rough croak.

"Get some water for the lass." Molly directed Donnchadh. He was glad to have something to do because seeing the look on Gwen's face was heartbreaking knowing he was the cause of her fear. "How much of yesterday do ye remember Lass?"

She took the offered water and sipped. "There was the fight and the wedding and lots of dancing....and then....." She was quiet for a moment and then met Donnchadh's gaze. Her eyes were filled with sorrow. "Then I told Donnchadh some things he didn't want to hear. I went to my chamber and .....and he locked the door. That is all I remember." She no longer looked at him. She stared at the wall.

"What in the seven hells were ye thinking lad? I ought tae box yer ears!" Molly railed at him when Gwen said nothing more. Then she spoke softly to Gwen. "Ay dearie, t'was just so. Ye were in yer chamber without a fire all night and caught a terrible chill. Donnchadh found ye in a chair in yer room freezing and unresponsive. We had tae try and warm ye up as quickly as possible."

Gwen blinked then but did not focus on either one of them. "Hypothermia. I caught hypothermia. Fuck. No wonder I feel like hell." She pulled her knees up and leaned her head against them.

"Are ye feeling warmer lass? Is there aught ye need? What can I do tae help ye?' Donnchadh was almost frantic. She looked up at him then. Her eyes looked as cold as she had been when he found her. He sat back from her a bit.

"No. There is nothing." She responded flatly. "Actually yes, there is something you can do. Help me back to my room. I clearly pushed you too far yesterday. I will sign any annulment papers you want on any grounds you want to claim." She began to get up off the bed.

"Nay lass I will no do that!"

"Fine. Just send someone up to light a fire for me in my room then." She stood and took a step. She would have fallen if not for Molly catching her arm.

"Perhaps ye should stay where ye are o' the now dearie." Molly said gently.

"No. Thank you though Molly. I appreciate your help. If you could just help me to my room and then send for someone to light a fire and bring me up some tea and warm broth I will be fine." Donnchadh was at her side and reached for her arm to help her. "Don't touch me!" She growled and withdrew from him. He let his hand fall and stood watching helplessly as his aunt guided his wife away, perhaps for good.

Once they made it to her room, Gwen sank down into her bed and burrowed under the covers while Molly made sure she had everything within reach and told her she would have a maid right up for the fire and have her bring the tea and broth as well. Gwen nodded mutely. Once Molly was out of the room, she could not hold it any more. A sob clawed its way out of her throat. She cried into the pillow. She turned her back to the door and buried her face in her pillow when the maid entered and lit the fire. She left the tray on the table between the two chairs. Gwen did not acknowledge her at all even when she left. Tears continued to spill down her face as sobs wracked her body. She had thought she might actually have had a chance at happiness with him. She thought she was falling in love with him....who was she kidding, she had fallen head over heels in love with him. But she had screwed the pooch. Her truth was too much for him.

Donnchadh could hear her sobs. He wanted desperately to go to her but Molly had advised against it. Telling him to give her time. He sat before his fire and listened until her cries softened and then continued to listen in the hope that he would hear her door open and her footsteps as she came to his room. That did not happen.

Once she felt like she didn't have any more tears she got up and sipped at the tea and attempted to eat some broth. She couldn't stomach much. She sat before the fire simply soaking up its warmth. She did not move except to use the chamber pot. She could hear people moving around the castle preparing for what she assumed must be the evening meal judging by the elongating shadows she glimpsed out her window. Still she did not move. Another maid came in and brought more tea and broth and stoked the fire and left. She sipped the tea, ate a few bites of bread with some broth, and then crawled into bed.

Donnchadh sat alone in the great hall. Dinner had long since been cleared and his clansmen now let him be. Cameron had approached him at one point and asked how his lady wife was and told him that they were worried since they hadn't seen her since the midday meal the day previous. Donnchadh grunted that she was just fine and proceeded to ignore everything else. When the fire in the hearth finally died down he trudged back to his chamber. Despite the roaring fire waiting for him. It was cold and empty. The tub had been cleared away and Gwen's clothes had been cleaned up as if she had never been there.

The sounds of the castle woke Donnchadh the next morning. Depressed and alone he decided that he needed to take control of the situation. He went down to the kitchen, prepared some breakfast and took the tray to Gwen's room so that he might dine with her. He knocked and got no response. He gently opened the door. He did not see her at first. He saw the rumpled bed and then looked to the chairs. She was sitting just as she had been when he found her. His heart stopped for a moment. He took another step into the room when she finally responded.

"Ye can leave the tray on the trunk there. The other is on the trunk by the wardrobe; if ye could take that down with ye I would appreciate it." She had not realized it was him. He sat down the breakfast tray and looked at the one from last night. It was barely touched. His gut clenched. That was not good for her. She needed to eat.

"Might I join ye lass?" he asked as he made his way to the other chair.

"This is your castle and you are laird. Do as you wish. Did you get the annulment you wanted?" She did not look at him, instead staring into the fire.

"I do no desire annulment lass. I spoke in haste the other day. I want ye for my wife as much now as I did the eve ye and I wed." She turned to look at him then with red-rimmed eyes.

"Why? What changed? I am still the one that lied to you, the one that you don't know."

"I told ye I spoke in haste. I was hurt that ye kept it from me for so long. I still care for ye and I can no tell ye how sorry I am for my actions and for how ye had tae suffer because of them! Show me yer belongings lass. Explain them tae me. I caught a glimpse the other day and I admit I am intrigued." He went to her trunk and dug out the items he had shoved in there the other day. "Start with this one. It confused me the most." He handed her the iPhone.

She sniffled it and took it from him. Thankfully, she had turned it off when she was at the festival and only turned it on the other day. It had been in power saver mode so she still had nearly a full battery. She lifted the screen to her face and it unlocked. Donnchadh watched in awe. "How did ye do that? Tis like magic!"

She laughed softly. "I guess it kind of is. It is called technology. It has very small cameras…..um" she thought for a bit of how to describe it and decided that some of the anachronistic responses that the cast gave at faire might get close enough for him to understand. "It is kind of like a miniature portrait painter. There is one on each side that captures images. Like the image on my background. That was taken with the one on the back. That is me with my dog Isolde and my cat Tristan. I still believe they were soul mates." She smiled at the image. "I still miss them. Probably always will."

"Did ye leave them behind then?"

"No, they left me behind. I lost Isolde (she motioned to the corgi) to lymphoma, a sickness that leads to the growth of lumps in the chest and causes the one that has it to be very ill, and it is not often curable if you catch it in late stages as I did." She clicked a little block and then began thumbing through various images of her dog and cat. Some she took with them, in others the two animals were curled up together. The one that caught Donnchadh's attention was of Tristan grooming Isolde, the dog looked blissfully happy. "I still think that they were soul mates. I never saw another cat and dog like them. I had her since she was a puppy and Tris was a rescue. He was already 9 years old when we got him. You would never have known that they were not raised together. He loved her. He would groom her every night before bed. When she passed Tristan grieved terribly for her. He got very ill as well. I had him for just over a year and a half after I lost Isolde. He had lymphoma just like she did. I like to think that they are together forever now and will be waiting for me on the other side of the rainbow bridge when I die on day." She shook her head and sniffed.

"I am so sorry ye lost them like that. It looks like ye loved them well." He looked over at her and she gave him a watery smile. "So is that all this wee box does?"

"No. It is also how people communicate over long distances. All sorts of things. In fact, can I ask you a favor? Can I take a picture of us?"

"Picture? That is what the tiny image is called?" She nodded in response. "Then aye. Will I feel anything?"

"Thank you! And no, you won't feel anything. You just need to sit still for a moment and smile. Let me sit on your lap for a moment." He opened his arms so that she could settle comfortably. She pressed something and then held the box at arm's length. He could see his reflection even clearer than the loch or the most polished mirror. It was astonishing! "Smile!" she told him and then pressed a circle on the face of the box. "One more!" She was laughing this time. Again, he could see their reflections. She told him to smile again and this time she turned and kissed his cheek. She captured that moment, when his smile became surprise. She stayed there on his lap and showed him the images.

"T 'is so clear! I have never seen the like! I do find that I prefer the second one." He winked at her. "Does this mean ye have forgiven me lass? That we are alright again, and ye will stay my lady wife?" She sobered a moment while they sat there looking at each other.

"Do you honestly believe me now?"

"I canna deny what ye are showing me. Aye, I believe ye."

"Swear to me you won't ever pull a stunt like the other night that I am still recovering from, and we can work on this forgiveness thing. If anything like that ever happens again I will leave so fast your head will spin."

"I swear tae ye!"

"I will remain your wife then Donnchadh."

"No like that."

She raised a questioning eyebrow. He decided to explain what he meant. "Since I found ye unmoving the other morn I have wanted nothing so much as tae see ye smile at me and call me by yer pet name for me. I long tae be yer Duncan again. I can no tell ye how sorry I am that I was such a colossal arse!"

"It is forgiven. I like it when you are my Duncan". She kissed him then. He wrapped his arms around her and growled deep in his chest. Their tongues mated and they were both breathless when he pulled back.

Chapter Ten

G wen and Donnchadh spent the rest of the day in her chamber. She showed him her ID, lipstick, and car keys. He wanted to hear more about where she was from. She also wanted to hear more about his life. By the time evening fell the realized they had missed the noonday meal. Their stomachs were growling as the made their way to the hall. Once they reached the table Donnchadh stood and called for everyone's attention. "I should apologize tae ye all. My mood has been foul of late because I dinna listen tae my lady wife and we had a disagreement. My behavior was unacceptable and the like will ne'er happen again. So I beg yer forgiveness as well as that of my Mairead." He turned to her and stroked her cheek. "I am sorry my love."

Gwen stood and wrapped her arms around his neck in a tight embrace. "Ye are forgiven m'laird"

Donnchadh raised his mug, "Tae Lady Mairead MacLeod! May I prove worthy of ye!" Everyone in the hall raised their vessels and drank deeply. Dinner passed without further incident. Before they left the hall, Cameron approached them.

"My Lady, if our laird is ever so thick headed again, ye come tae me. I will nae be as thick headed and would happily wed ye in his place!" He gave an exaggerated bow. Donnchadh cuffed him upside his head and laughed.

"As if she would choose ye, when she has such a devoted husband who has learned his lesson? Ye would be a poor substitute."

"A man can but try m'laird! And when a lady is as lovely as yer wife, hmm a man might try doubly hard." He winked at her.

Months passed and summer wore on. Gwen and Donnchadh reached an even keel and were rarely far apart. She had taken to riding the land with him and it had become a common sight for the clan, to see them racing about the fields on horseback. So far, he had not been able to beat her, but he could draw even with her. She provided a voice of reason amongst heated disagreements. It became clear to all that Donnchadh doted on her. He watched her whenever he could and they would often disappear together. Summer Solstice was fast approaching and the clan was making preparations for the bonfires and celebrations. They had relative peace. Donnchadh and Gwen had not fought, and the MacDonalds had been oddly quiet for this time of year.

One rainy morning Donnchadh was notified that riders were approaching. By the time he was able to pull himself away from Gwen, the visitors had been escorted to the great hall. He was in a fine mood and Gwen had promised to join him after she dressed. He loved the moments that they could grab and sneak away from the clan to love each other. His mood immediately blackened when he saw who was awaiting him. It was his step mother and brother with another woman. He took a deep breath and prepared himself for a verbal battle. "I told ye that I would no tolerate ye back on my land. I told ye that there would be consequences should ye return. Yet here I see ye. I have had a belly full of yer trouble! Tell me what ye want afore I take my temper out on ye!"

His stepmother stepped forward. "Tis funny ye should say that ye have had a belly full Donnchadh, when it is ye who gave a belly full."

Donnchadh was supremely confused by what she was saying. In that moment, Gwen walked up beside him and took his hand. She had not been too far behind him when he left their chamber. She did not like what she saw and had a terrible feeling. She squeezed his hand and he looked down at her, his eyes softening. He raised her hand to his lips and kissed the back of it.

Finola snarled. "Och t' is so disgusting that ye could act thus in front of Brigit!"

"Speak plain woman! I dinna ken what ye mean!"

"Oh ye want plain do ye? Is this plain enough?" She gestured toward the woman he assumed was Briget and she removed her cloak to reveal a swollen belly. "She is carrying yer bairn!"

Donnchadh was in shock. This could not be possible. He had only been with Gwen since well before they married. He glanced quickly at Gwen and squeezed her hand hard. He didn't know how she would take this, but he couldn't lose her. "That is impossible! I have been wi' no other woman aside from my wife!"

"Ah but there was one evening, brother."

"Perhaps we should take this to the library Donnchadh." Gwen interrupted. "Surely we dinna want the entire clan involved." He nodded mutely at her wisdom and began to lead her there when Brigit spoke as she claimed his other hand.

"Would ye assist me upstairs m'laird? I find I canno balance as well anymore now that I am carrying yer bairn." She placed a protective hand on her stomach. He looked at her for a moment and then at the people gathered. He wanted to shake her off but he was in a difficult situation. He would be blamed if she were to fall or get hurt. He longed for nothing so much as to ignore her, take Gwen in his arms, and leave the rest of them behind. But as laird he could not.

"Very well." He relented and let her take his other arm. As they approached the stairs, she stopped them.

"The stairs are no wide enough for the three of us Donnchadh. And I am worried I could stumble"

He ground his teeth and looked to Gwen. "She is right about the stairs love. They are no wide enough for the three of us comfortably. And if she is indeed carrying my bairn, I do bear some responsibility."

Gwen fought to maintain her composure, gave him a weak smile, and nodded as she released his arm. Brigit yanked him forward then and Archie and Finola breezed past her on their way up the stairs. They both gave her a rather smug look that she found very odd considering the situation. She was left to follow. She caught up with them at the library. Brigit was already seated, as was Finola while Archie and Donnchadh stood. A look of relief passed over Donnchadh's face when she entered and he held his hands out to her.

"So ye are going tae rub her in my face are ye?" Briget spat at him.

He scowled at her "I have no need to stoop to anything like that. She is the woman I love! She is my wife. I merely try tae treat her as a loving husband would." Gwen gasped quietly at his statement drawing his attention. He eyes softened when he looked at her. "Aye dearest. I love ye. I wish the first time I told ye would have been more romantic." He gave a sad laugh. She stepped to him then, wrapped her arms around his waist, and squeezed. He embraced her as well and was unwilling to let go. He could hear sounds of indignation from Finola, Archie, and Brigit. He could not bring himself to care though. When Gwen relaxed her hold on him, he resituated her so that she was close to his side and he had a protective arm over her shoulder.

"Now, I need tae ken the meaning of this. Because honestly I dinna believe this woman could possibly be pregnant wi' my offspring!" He addressed Finola.

"Well ye see Donnchadh dear boy, she is indeed. The week before ye declared ye were tae wed her," she pointed at Gwen. "Apparently ye had yer way wi' my poor Brigit. Surely, ye remember that dinner. Maud made her opinion on that woman known and then the both of them left the table. Ye and I talked for a while and by that point ye were a bit in yer cups so I bid ye stay down stairs so ye dinna hurt yerself. Brigit went tae check on ye and found ye sitting by the fire in the great hall. She told me later that ye had been quite hot for her. She said that ye had sex with her right there in that chair. There were even witnesses.

Donnchadh felt Gwen go stiff beside him. She looked up at him, her face full of worry. She whispered to him then. "Ye thought it was me…". He jerked his attention to Brigit then. His anger flared. She could in fact be pregnant with his child then, but he recalled that his aunt had told him he was drugged that night. His anger mounted further.

"I see ye recall. And here I hoped ye would look back at it wi' the fondness I do." Brigit stroked her stomach. Donnchadh opened his mouth to speak but Gwen beat him to it.

"How dare ye! I was with him that night and he was violently ill! Ye drugged him!" She snarled at them.

"Och lass, no need tae be sore at Brigit. She did not mean for this to happen. She merely cared for my brother and this is what came of it. They have kenned each other for years and who could not return the affections of such a beautiful lady." Archie fawned over Brigit who smiled shyly up at him.

Gwen rounded on Archie then, "Ye arse! The lot of ye make me sick! I held Donnchadh while he repeatedly spilled the contents of his stomach from whatever ye gave him. Dinna even play at kindness or caring. I remember what happened at our wedding. There could be no mistaking that ye hated my husband. So tell me what does this gain ye, ye little prick?"

He feigned shock, rather poorly in Gwen's opinion. "Lass I am hurt that ye would think I would use a woman's delicate situation for my own gain. This gains me naught. However, it may gain something for the clan. It turns out that we discovered that our sweet Brigit is of MacDonald lineage. She could be the key tae peace between our clans." His sickly sweet tone pushed Gwen over the edge and she punched him, breaking his nose. He did not hesitate to retaliate in kind and backhanded her before

Donnchadh could intervene. She stumbled back wiped blood from her lip and readied herself to fight him when she heard Donnchadh roar as he tackled Archie to the ground and began to pummel him. Gwen stared in astonishment for a moment while Finola and Brigit tried to pull Donnchadh off Archie. Archie was no longer swinging his arms in an attempt to strike Donnchadh; he was reduced to trying to protect his face as blows rained down.

Gwen squeezed her eyes shut for a second and then yelled. "Enough!" She continued more calmly. "Donnchadh my love, let him go and let's go tae our chamber. We can have Cameron escort them tae chambers where they can rest and lock them in while we figure out what is going on and how we can handle this." She placed a gentle hand on his back drawing his attention. He allowed her to help him up. Once he was on his feet he noticed that she had only offered him her left hand which was unusual since she was right handed. He ran his hand down her right arm until he had a hold of her hand and when he did, she winced a bit. He looked down and saw that her knuckles were bloody. It shook him and he said nothing further as he pulled her from the room. She gave terse directions to Cameron as they passed him and he nodded his understanding.

Once they were in their chamber, he swung her around in front of him to assess the damage to her hand. "Come lass." He tugged her to the basin of water and rinsed her hand. It looked as if most of the blood had belonged to Archie, but her knuckles were red and they did bleed a bit where part of her fist connected with his cheek. He opened his trunk and pulled out some bandages. Once he was satisfied that her wound was sufficiently clean, he wrapped her hand with the strips of linen.

"Are you ready to talk about it now sweetheart?" she cupped his cheek with her left hand. He turned his sorrowful blue eyes to her and searched her face.

"I can no lose ye! We have dealt wi' so much and I thought our troubles were over. It has been so wonderful lately. My clan has been at peace and I have ye wi' me. I dinna want it to change. If this is true, if she is pregnant wi my bairn and she is a MacDonald, there are those that would support her. And they would use your….." He shook his head and stopped. He looked at the fire, and then out the window. He did not want to meet her eyes. It was too painful to think what they might bring up and how it might hurt her.

"They would use my what, my love?" She was being so gentle with him that it almost hurt him physically. She did not deserve this. She had dealt with enough being ripped from her home, traveling through time, being forced to marry him. He wondered if this would be what finally drove her from him. If it was, he could not blame her.

He swallowed hard and met her gaze. His eyes filled with unshed tears. "They will use your barren womb as an excuse tae demand that I divorce ye and wed Brigit." He leaned his head back in an attempt to stop the tears. "Things have no been easy for us and ye have been hurt by me because of our marriage. I can no begin tae tell ye how sorry I am for all of it lass. When I said I love ye in there, I meant it with every part of me. I was long overdue in telling ye. Losing ye will…will break me but I love ye and I want ye tae be happy and if being free of me will allow ye peace…" He could not continue. He backed up until his back connected with the wall and he slid down it. He rested his arms on his upraised knees and tried to maintain his composure as his heart began to crack.

She knelt before him and looked at him in concern. "Duncan, what do you mean they will use my barren womb? I am not barren."

He looked up at her then in surprise. "Lass ye are no wi child. I have no gotten ye wi' child since we wed, no for lack of trying. Brigit serves tae prove my virility. It has been months and nothing."

"You clearly didn't understand what I told you before. Stereotypical man only hears what he wants to. I am not barren. At least my inability to bear a child just yet has nothing to do with me being unable to ever have a child."

"Speak plain Gwen. I am getting a monstrous headache from all of this. What ye are saying makes little sense tae me. I heard exactly what ye told me. Ye could not have children because of some sort of treatment. Whatever that means"

"Oh my sweet husband." She stroked his cheek and then turned his head first one way and then the other. He raised his eyebrows questioningly at her. "What? I was just checking to make sure that there was no cotton in your ears so that I can be sure that you actually hear and understand me. Yes, what you said is partially true. However, you are leaving out part of it. I said at the time that I would not be able to have a child for about a year. I did not say I would never have a child. Granted, having a family was not a priority for me before, and I never went to a fertility clinic, but no physician ever told me there was anything wrong with my reproductive system. Once the implant has aged to a certain point, it no longer works and I can get pregnant. Which if memory serves, it should be reaching end of life sometime early next year. So only 7 or 8 months away at most."

"What is an implant? I dinna understand all of that. Why would ye have something in ye tae keep ye from getting pregnant?"

"There are several reasons women have it done. It can help regulate periods and hormones as well as protect against unwanted pregnancy. I was in the military and, things happened. Especially on deployment. People can get carried away in so many ways, and then a woman ends up with a pregnancy she doesn't want. I was protecting myself. The thing is, the implants are only good for so long. So women have to go get them replaced if they still don't want to get pregnant or take pills or something like that."

"I still don't understand what ye mean by implant."

She grabbed his hand and ran his fingers over a spot on her arm. "You feel that little rod there?" he nodded. "That is the implant that keeps me from getting pregnant. A military physician placed it there when I requested it." She bit the inside of her cheek and thought for a minute. She noticed his sgian dubh and it gave her an idea. She knew she had to be quick. She grabbed the dagger from his boot, unsheathed it, and dashed to the basin. She stood back to him and took a deep breath. She shook her hands to stop them from shaking too badly. She felt for the implant and then sliced the spot on the underside of her arm. She fought to contain a cry of pain when the knife pierced her skin. She knew she only had moments before Donnchadh reached her. She could hear him getting up and calling her name. She ignored him and dug into her arm to remove the rod. Her head began to swim and pain flooded her senses. Dear

God she thought, the man had better be worth it. She felt his hand on her waist just as she was able to remove the offending device. It plinked into the bloody water of the basin.

Donnchadh was unaware of what she was doing. She had explained the implant to him and he was relieved. There was still a chance that they might have a child together. It was beyond strange to feel the little thing beneath her skin. When she grabbed his dagger and made her way to the basin he could not understand what she was doing. Then he saw her move to press the knife to her arm. He could not get up fast enough. It was as if time had slowed just for him, but it sped up for her. Once he was on his feet he could see blood dripping into the water staining it pink. "Gwen! Lass Stop! GWEN Damn it woman! Answer me!" By the time he reached her, she fell into his arms. Blood flowed from a self-inflicted cut on her arm and her hand was covered in blood. "Christ woman! What have ye done?" He laid her down on the floor and grabbed the bandages he had used on her hand earlier. He spoke softly to her as he bandaged her arm. "I have never known a woman so prone tae trouble and harm as yerself." By the time he was finished her eyelids fluttered open. "What were ye doing lass? Ye nigh scairt me tae death!"

She blinked up at him and then sat up. He moved to help her and he let him assist her to stand. She went back to the basin, rinsed her hand, and pulled something out of the water. "Are ye daft woman? What is wrong wi' ye? Ye take my dagger and draw yer own blood! Tis insane! Do ye wish tae die?"

"Hush and give me your hand." She leveled him with a serious gaze. He held his hand out to her. She dropped a small thin rod onto his palm. He studied it, turned it over and examined it.

"What is the meaning of this?"

"That my love, is my implant. That was what was keeping me from getting pregnant."

"Did I hear ye correctly? It WAS keeping ye from getting wi' child? As in the past, was?"

She smiled at him then. "Finally he removed the cotton from his ears! Yes sweetheart. That was it. Now that it is removed, after a while, I will be able to get pregnant. So if your clan does not try to depose me in favor of Brigit, we might have a little bairn of our own before too long."

His eyes were wide. He scooped her up and held her close. "I never want tae let ye go. God but I want a family wi' ye more than anything! Dinna ever do anything like that again woman!"

She wrapped her arms around his neck gingerly so as not to put pressure on her cut. "I love you my Duncan." She whispered softly into his ear. He pulled back to look at her for a moment and then kissed her for all he was worth. He took a few steps and pushed her against the wall. He ran a hand down her body tracing the side of her breast, her ribs, her hips, and then down her leg. She needed no further prompting. She wrapped her leg about his hip and moaned as he nibbled the spot that made her weak in the knees.

He reached down with his other hand then pulled her other leg up so that her legs wrapped around his waist. He held her against him with one hand while they kissed and fumbled to move her skirt and his kilt out of the way. She loved the feel of his mouth on hers and pulled at the collar of his shirt so that she could feel his bare chest beneath her finger tips. When he had her skirt out of the way he ran a finger over the wet center of her. She pulled her mouth from his and leaned her head against the wall trying to contain a cry of pleasure. "Och ye are so ready for me. I love the feel of ye!" He whispered as he kissed her neck. She clutched at his shoulders

"I need you Duncan, please!" She tightened her legs about his waist. She pushed him over the edge with that. He shoved his sporran and kilt out of the way and thrust into her. She cried out at the sudden fullness. "Oh my God yes!"

He drove into her again and again. She clenched around him and he cried out. She made him feel wild. "Ye are so tight Gwen! I love the feel of being inside ye!" He pushed into her harder and with more speed. She moved with him. Each time he thrust into her it drew her closer to the edge. He was close and the pleasure almost bordered on pain. She was crying out and calling his name as her pleasure rolled over her and it pushed him over the edge. He called her name as he came into her. "I love ye my bonnie wife!" He panted as the held each other, neither wanting to move, basking the in the afterglow of their lovemaking.

"I love you, my husband." She leaned her head against his shoulder while she fought to catch her breath.

Chapter Eleven

A knock came at the door and Donnchadh helped Gwen to straighten her clothes before answering. When he opened the door, Cameron was waiting. "We heard an awful racket so I decided tae come check on ye…" he blanched when he saw the bloody basin and the blood on the floor. "Och is everything alright? I merely came tae rib ye, but it looks like a massacre in here!"

Gwen walked over, put an arm around Donnchadh's waist, leaned against him, and winked at Cameron. "Tis all fine Cameron. Just had tae spill a little blood tae get my point across and get my husband back in line after the debacle in the library."

"Ye are sure Mairead? I am here tae help if ye need."

"I am more than sure Cameron. Had ye arrived a few minutes earlier ye would have had tae wait longer for Donnchadh tae open the door and ye would have had more tae tease us about." Cameron had the grace to blush at her saucy response.

"Thank ye Cameron. Are our ……guests settled in appropriate rooms?" Donnchadh addressed him.

"Aye m'laird. They have all been dealt wi'. Archie and his mother are sharing a chamber and ye will no be happy about the next part. Brigit conned one of the maids in tae giving her the room Gwen used tae occupy. Had I kenned I would have stopped it and put her elsewhere but I think that it is best tae leave her there for now so that we do no cause a ruckus. I do no think that it would be wise tae draw more attention tae them afore ye decide what tae do. I can no say as I want them here longer than necessary. Things have been so peaceful of late and I would hope we could keep it that way. I hope I am no overstepping my bounds."

"Nay lad." Donnchadh placed a hand on his shoulder. "I am glad ye are involved and I am doubly glad that ye are so protective of my wife. I would make a deal wi' ye. I would have ye be my second. Your first priority though would be Mairead's safety. She is a strong woman but even then, there are some things she will need protecting from on occasion."

"I noticed that strength when she laid into Archie and withstood him. Twas impressive, she handled it better than a lot of lads I ken." He winked conspiratorially and then sobered. "I can no thank ye enough for the honor ye do me and the trust ye place in me. I will gladly serve as your second and protect our lovely lady."

"Wonderful! Yer first duty is tae make sure that those doors are nae opened and no one talks with them. I need tae take Mairead out of the castle tae get some air. We need tae clear our heads." He walked out of the room keeping his arm around Gwen and Cameron followed. They went to the stables and Donnchadh directed a groom to saddle Loach. "I am taking ye on an adventure that I think ye will enjoy my love. Tis something

I have wanted tae do wi' ye for some time and now seems like a good time."

"What are ye about Donnchadh? Don't we need Realta saddled too if we are tae go riding?"

"No if I do no want to let ye out of my arms. I mean tae have ye ride on my lap. I find I can no let go of ye just now." He squeezed her shoulder.

"Be careful out there m'laird" Cameron saluted and made his way back to the castle.

Once Loach was saddled, Donnchadh mounted and reached down for Gwen. She eagerly made her way up and cuddled into him. "Once we are out of the gate hold on tight. We are going tae fly. I have wanted tae do this since ye told me about yer ride on the beach." He guided them out of the castle yard and then went around the castle itself. He approached the loch and it was low tide. "Ready lass?" He asked her and she nodded her consent grinning while she wrapped her arms tight about him. He kicked Loach into a gallop across the flats. The sun tried to peek through the clouds while they flew over the flats. He could hear her laughing and looked down to see her smiling where she was nestled against him. As she got used to Loach's gait, she loosened her grip and leaned forward joyfully soaking in the scenery. He was so proud of his land and doubly proud of his woman. He wished that this moment could go on without ugly reality intruding. Loach seemed to enjoy the run as well, kicking up sand and splashing water. Eventually they slowed; he reined Loach in and pointed across to a rocky area at the edge of the loch not far away for Gwen to see. Loach snorted in indignation at not being allowed to run headlong and startled the seal basking on a large rock. Gwen gasped and covered her mouth with her hands.

She was so excited. She had never seen a seal in the wild. It was beautiful. It almost blended in with the rock and she would have had to work to make it out had Loach not startled it. It looked up at them and then decided that they were not a threat and laid back down to soak up what rays of the sun it could. She turned to look and Donnchadh grinning like a loon. She was sure that he would think her reaction childish but she couldn't help it. "Are there a lot of seals here? I have never seen one outside of an aquarium and then never one like this!"

He smiled back at her just as happily. He didn't always understand every word she said but he loved that she took such joy in his home. "Aye we see them on occasion. We have tae be careful when we ride the shore line sometimes."

"Oh this is wonderful! So beautiful! I can't believe I get to live here in this amazing place with my amazing man." She kissed his cheek. "I do think we still need to talk a bit more about what is going on."

"Aye. I do no like this situation for so many reasons. I can no stand Archie or his mother and I have no patience for Brigit. She has always been practically attached to Finola. I cannot bear the thought that she may be carrying my bairn. It enrages me that she is trying to insert herself in yer place. Even were I no married tae ye, I would NEVER even consider wedding her. I just pray that I will no lose ye over this." He leaned his forehead against hers. He let Loach wander as he would while they spoke.

She closed her eyes for a moment and inhaled his scent. "I told you earlier that I love you, and I meant it. That will not change for so many reasons. First, this technically happened before we were married. Second, you were drugged. I know what that is like and I would never blame you for that. I was drugged like that once and lucky enough to escape without too much damage."

"Ye humble me love. I must be the luckiest man in the world. Ye came tae me from another place and time. The reality of it is that quite possibly ye should not even be here. But I am not looking that gift horse in the mouth. Fate gave me my true love and I could not be more grateful. I want tae spend the rest of our lives making each other happy. I want to make ye so happy that these trials that we are facing seem like nothing when we look back on them when we are old."

"I agree one hundred percent. I just hope that we can smooth this baby thing over somewhat. I will not let her take over and I certainly will not sacrifice my husband to her. I know your clan might benefit from an alliance with the MacDonalds, but there has to be a better way. And if the MacDonalds are such enemies, how did they just find out that Brigit is one of them? There is not a whole lot that makes sense here. There is a saying where I come from, that everything you need to know, you learn in kindergarten. Kindergarten is for very young children before they attend school so that they can learn how to behave and interact with other children and things like that. Well, it looks like I didn't learn some of the big lessons. I didn't learn to share and apparently I don't play well with others all of the time. I want that woman gone and out of our lives. If she does have your child," She took a deep breath, "I will raise it as yours and mine, not as Finola did for you but as a real mother. No child should suffer what you did. I cannot stand

Brigit, but I would not punish a child for its mother's sins. I would not want her around at all though. I don't think I could deal with seeing her regularly, because I honestly doubt she would let it go. She would still want to be the center of attention.   And like it or not Donnchadh Maxwell Callum MacLeod, you belong to me. You are MY Duncan and no one else's."

"I would not have it any other mo chroi. Just as ye belong tae me. I understand that ye want her gone. Honestly, I am trying tae figure out a way tae get the three of them gone sooner rather than later. They are all snakes. It means a great deal that ye would be willing tae take on the bairn. And while I would welcome a child, I did no want it to happen in this way. I want a bonnie little lass wi' her mother's curls and spirit who will race her da about the isle on horseback or a braw wee lad who will grow up big and strong wi' his mother's spirit, and perhaps her mean right hook as well!" She laughed with him then.

"I would adore a little boy with his father's eyes and smile! Of course I would likely never get anything done because the two of them would have me so wrapped around their fingers." She sighed and laid her head on his shoulder. "Oh Duncan. I want that so much it hurts. I would love to have both a boy and a girl with you. Our own little family and they would have their great auntie Molly baking them shortbread all the time and she would spoil them rotten."

He placed his hand on her stomach and looked at her. "Aye I want that as well mo chroi. Just think, it is possible that this time next year we could already be a mam and da to a wee bairn of our own making." She held his hand there and kissed him.

"I can't wait!"

"Neither can I. I find that I am hungry for ye again!" He tightened the reins and urged Loach into a gallop back to the castle. Gwen's surprised laughter rang across the loch.

When they returned to the castle, Cameron was waiting for them. "The fat one has been raising a fuss since she realized she dinna have free range of the keep. Been pounding on the door, screaming, and throwing things. I was just about tae ride out tae get ye."

"What about Archie and his mother?" Donnchadh asked.

"Nary a peep from them. I think they expected the limitation of their movements."

"Hmmm well that is something at least. See Mairead tae our chamber and I will see tae the fat one as ye called her."

"I think ye should take Cameron wi' ye. I do no think it wise tae be alone wi' her. In light of the current situation, I think ye need tae be careful. I can get tae our chamber fine on my own and wait on ye there after I check on the kitchen and see if Molly needs aught."

"Mo chroi I dinna want tae involve more people than necessary. I am no exactly proud of how this problem came tae be."

"Sweetheart I trust Cameron more than anyone except ye or Molly. I have no doubt we can trust his discretion. And if ye think on it, he would be fulfilling one of the duties ye specified for him." Both men looked at her in confusion. "He would be protecting me."

Donnchadh arched an eyebrow, "And just how do ye figure that?"

"Easy. The most reliable predictor of future behavior is past behavior. Having seen what I did and knowing what I know of her, I am reasonably certain that she will throw herself at ye without hesitation. She has shown that she is comfortable wi' subterfuge and should no be trusted. She seems more than willing tae do whatever she needs tae in order to displace me. If ye approach her alone I have nae doubt that she will proclaim that ye again had yer way wi' her because ye still cared for her as Archie insinuated. So tae that end. Cameron would be protecting me from her machinations at that point. So he would be following yer directions to the letter."

"Yer wife is a smart one Donnchadh! I can no say I disagree wi' her logic. I think ye have met yer match lad!"

Donnchadh put his head in his hand. "Seems I have. Very well. Come along Cameron. It looks as if ye will be protecting my lady's honor." He kissed her and Cameron sketched a ridiculously elaborate bow that left her giggling. As they walked away Donnchadh called back to her. "I will expect tae find ye in our chamber when I am done!"

"Of course m'laird." She raised her voice so she could be heard as they approached the stairs. She had to tease him though. She cocked her head to the side checking out his legs and ass as he mounted the stairs. "I hate tae see ye go! But I love tae watch ye leave!" Donnchadh stopped abruptly spun on his heel to catch her checking him out. He was so abrupt that Cameron bumped into him. He stared at her in absolute shock. She whistled and wolf called at him and then blew him a kiss and flounced off to the kitchen. She could hear Cameron roaring with laugher and Donnchadh yelling at him to shut up and then laughing himself. She was determined that this day would end just as pleasantly as it had started despite the interruption.

Chapter Twelve

Once she had spoken with Molly about the remaining meals for the day, she made her way upstairs. She had asked that lunch be a casual affair and that a tray be prepared for Donnchadh and her. Molly quickly agreed and hugged Gwen fiercely. "Do no let them get tae ye lass. This will all be sorted out. I ken it. Now take some shortbread wi' ye and go wait for my nephew." She got the feeling that Molly loved her new place in the castle. The servants treated her with respect and she was able to see to everything just the way she liked. As she headed upstairs, she decided to take a detour and make sure that Archie and his mother were still safely contained. She quietly approached their door and could hear them talking within. She pressed her ear to the door.

"Tis going as planned Archie. It is just a matter of time. Brogan will support the claim. If Donnchadh does what he thinks is the oh so honorable thing in order tae keep peace, marries our Brigit and gets rid of Mairead, there are one of two outcomes. Either she will kill him in his sleep after a time and ye will lead the clan or, one of our blood will lead the clan when Donnchadh dies and he will be none the wiser. Tonight ye will pick the lock and we will confirm our plan wi' Brigit and Brogan."

Gwen blanched and ran to her chamber. She just made it inside and slammed the door when she spilled the contents of her stomach into the chamber pot. They were plotting Donnchadh's death. She had to think quick.

When Donnchadh entered the chamber Brigit approached him and wrapped her arms around his neck. She did not seem to notice Cameron. It looked as if Gwen had been right. "Come back tae renew our acquaintance, m'laird? Did ye miss me? She pressed her breasts against his chest. Cameron cleared his throat as Donnchadh peeled her from him.

"What is the meaning of this then?" She put her hands on her hips. "Why do ye bring that lout wi' ye? Surely ye and I need some time alone tae get reacquainted. I can forgive ye yer time with her since ye dinna ken about me and the bairn."

"Cameron is my second now. And I would never welcome the chance tae get familiar with ye. I merely came tae ask that ye cease in yer destruction of my home. If ye dinna stop I will have ye locked in the dungeon where ye can no harm anything. And cease yer caterwauling as well. Ye are giving every one headaches!"

"Is this yer way of denying our bairn? Will ye deny it and leave us tae rot? Ye are too cruel tae lead a clan!"

Cameron and Donnchadh looked at each other and rolled their eyes and then turned their attention to Brigit again. "Listen close woman. I did no say any of that. If, and only if the child is mine, I will acknowledge it and my wife and I will raise the child as our own. It will never ken that it was birthed by a harpy. Ye will be exiled and should ye return ye will be put in the dungeon until such a time as I have decided that you have suffered enough, and then I will see ye hanged." His voice was deadly quiet. Her eyes were large with fear and she backed up from him. He advanced on her and continued, "So I would advise ye tae shut yer gob, mind yer manners and watch what ye say. Ye are at my mercy now and I am tired of the games."

"Ye can no do that!"

"Oh? Can I no? That is news tae me! Last I kenned I was the laird here and my word was law. Have ye been listening tae my brother then? He had the same problem believing that I am laird of my own clan." Her eyes widened and she looked away at that. She would not meet his gaze again. Donnchadh thought that an odd response.

"Come Cameron. I find that I have no more tolerance for this madness. If anyone hears aught from this chamber, throw her in the dungeon. I don't care when and I don't care how. My only concern is that the bairn no be harmed."

"I shall see tae it Donnchadh." With that they both quit the chamber. Donnchadh gave further instruction that he was to accompany any one that went in to tend the fire or bring her food. She was not to talk to anyone, nor were they to talk to her. When he entered his chamber he was just able to catch Gwen as she flung herself at him, and wrapped herself around him. She seemed deeply upset. He held her and sat on the bed with her. "What is the matter mo chroi? Who do I need tae kill?" He brushed her hair from her face.

"That is not quite the issue." She sniffed "I overheard something that truly scared me." There was a knock on the door and she bade them enter. It was a servant wth a tray of capon, cheese and some bread along with his ale and her mead. The servant placed it on the small table. She asked him to take care of the chamber pot as well. She continued once they left. "I finished in the kitchen and came back here and decided to detour and check to make sure that Finola and Archie were still confined and not throwing a fit. When I reached the chamber door I heard them talking. It sounds like they were planning to use Brigit to get to you. Brogan is supposed to support Archie and eventually Brigit was supposed to kill you in your sleep so that the child or Archie would inherit. Finola made it sound like they were sure the child wasn't yours and was happy telling Archie that at least one of their bloodline would rule the clan even if Archie couldn't directly." Donnchadh stared at her, unspeaking as he processed what she was saying. Then he remembered Brigit's reaction when he mentioned her spending time with his brother. It all made sense. "Please say something Duncan! I am worried! They said that they were going to pick the lock tonight and cement plans with Brogan and Brigit"

Donnchadh kissed her forehead and pulled her to his chest. "All will be fine my love! I promise ye! What ye just told me answered some big questions we all had and I ken exactly what is going on now. Tonight will not be restful but it will provide a resolution. I will be waiting for them when they pick the lock and I will already have Brogan in the dungeon. It would make it easier tae convince the clan if Brogan were tae confess his involvement."

"You already have the means to see that he does Duncan. Just tell him that they confessed everything and even blamed him for masterminding the part about Brigit killing you. I would bet he would tell you all the details. Just treat him like you couldn't believe he could do something like that."

"Och ye are a scary one Gwen. Remind me tae never get ye upset at me again. Ye can hit like a lad and have a devious mind. I like it though." He kissed her and then leaned his head back and closed his eyes.

"Yeah well, between the military, crime shows and a show called Cops that I watched growing up, my ideas and sometimes my actions may be a little out there in comparison to most here." She said sheepishly. "Are you hungry at all?"

He still had his eyes closed while he listened to her. He chuckled and nodded bringing his chin down so that he could look at her. She shifted briefly on his lap and reached for the tray. She offered him a piece of capon from her finger tips. He smiled and took it, kissing the tips of her fingers as he did so. "Mmmm best way I have ever eaten roasted capon. I think it even tastes better this way!" She giggled at him and offered him another piece. For a time, they sat talking quietly and feeding each other. Eventually they drifted off cuddled up together in the chair drained by the events and emotions of the day.

The evening meal had been subdued and somewhat solemn. It did not go without notice however, that Cameron now sat to Donnchadh's left and Gwen to his right. Molly sat on the other side of Gwen and the four of them spent most of the meal deep in conversation. "So it looks as if my nosy wife may have saved us some trouble." Donnchadh winked at her as he spoke softly. He did not want anyone else to hear. "Cameron, after the meal, ye and I will corner Brogan and address the earlier situation with him. Mairead overheard plans that Archie and his mother made tae sneak out this night and confirm a plot tae do away wi' me wi' Brogan and Brigit. We are going to detain Brogan and question him."

Chapter Thirteen

ameron and Donnchadh cornered Brogan as he was finishing his meal. They escorted him outside and sat him down on a rock by the Loch. They did not want anyone to know what they were about. And if they had turned Brogan against him, who knew who else they could have on their side. "We need tae talk Brogan. I ken that we have been at odds on occasion, but we have always gotten along. I enjoy yer company. I have a problem though. As ye ken Finola and Arche have returned wi' Brigit claiming her bairn is mine."

"Aye. I have heard as such and have seen no reason to doubt them. Ye have no been yerself of late and ye slipped wi' the lass. So make things right and dispose of Mairead and take the mother of yer child tae wife." He sat with arms crossed and shrugged like he hadn't a care in the world.

Donnchadh looked out over the loch. The moon shown on the water and gave him some peace when he desperately needed it. He ran his hands through his hair and thought about his next move. Cameron stood behind Brogan and nodded reassuringly when Donnchadh looked at him. "All right lad. Here is what is going tae happen. Ye are going tae tell the truth of the situation and renounce any connection tae those two and set about regaining my trust, or ye can continue this madness and ye shall be exiled once all is uncovered. Ye will never see your family or clan again." Donnchadh's voice was low and menacing.

Another shrug. "The truth is out m'laird. The bairn is yours and the woman is of MacDonald stock. Ye have the means tae end a long feud in yer hands."

Cameron laughed bitterly then. "I kenned ye were hard headed man, but this just beats all. Listen well and dinna bedevil our laird any more. We ken all! Everylast detail right down tae yer involvement. They spilled everything when they realized they were in trouble and wanted to make it out safe." Brogan's eyes went wide. "Aye, I see ye comprehend now."

"They said that ye are the one that masterminded my downfall and death and that ye were set tae support Archie's claim. I can no tell ye the pain that caused. I dinna think ye would do such a thing. I told them that they had tae be lying, ye have been my friend for years and you could no possibly betray me like that. But they insisted and they even admitted that the child was no mine."

At that Brogan slipped off of the rock onto his knees. "Och M'laird I dinna plan yer death! I could never. Whatever grievances we might have, my respect for ye trumps them. I had very little tae do wi it in reality! Aye, I was tae support Archie's claim. That was it! I swear tae ye!"

"Hmm if that is the case then who is the real father of the bairn? They did not want tae share that one wi' me."

"Archie is the father m'laird. They shared a bed the very night of that dinner and most since."

Donnchadh met Cameron's gaze. He was relieved that his suspicions were true. Gwen would be relieved as well! She would be the only woman to bear his children. "And just how was it determined that Brigit was a MacDonald? Or is that even true?"

"Tis partly true. Well at least as far as I ken. When they left the castle, they ended up on MacDonald Land. Archie did some fast-talking and they were not killed. When they were taken before the Laird and one of his clansmen thought he recognized the Brigit. Turns out, she was his niece. She and her mother had disappeared long ago. So Lady Finola and the Laird agreed that if ye would marry the lass, they would consider peace. Personally, I thought the idea of peace was grand. Therefore, I went along. I swear tae ye, I kenned naught about a plot for yer death. Please have mercy m'laird!" he clutched at Donnchadh's kilt.

"Ye have given me much tae think on. I am giving ye some trust and if ye break it, there will be hell tae pay! Go find yer bed outside the castle this night and come find me mid morn tomorrow and speak of this tae no one. If Finola, Archie, or Brigit reach out tae ye, I expect ye tae report it tae me immediately! Understood?"

"Aye m'laird! I understand and I shall see ye on the morrow!" he scrambled up from where he knelt and made his way back to the village.

"I am both relieved and worried. The fact that the bairn is no mine is a weight off my shoulders and I can no wait tae tell my wife, but the involvement of the MacDonalds makes me leery. The laird has not proved the most reliable man." Donnchadh ran his hand through his hair as he and

Cameron trudged back up to the castle. The moon was high in the sky and the denizens of the the castle would all be setting in for the night if they were not already settled. He figured that Gwen and Molly were in his chamber sharing a glass of mead and waiting for him, and that he had a short time before his brother tried to finalize his plan.

He and Cameron reached the door to the guest chamber just in time to hear the scratching of the lock and Finola hissing at Archie to be careful and hurry. Donnchadh arched an eyebrow at Cameron leaned against the wall crossing his arms over his chest. "Hmmm seems like the lad learned something useful after all. Answers some questions for sure, like how he came by items I swore I had locked away when we were younger." He whispered.

"Indeed, resourceful little shite that one!" Camreon mimicked Donnchadh's posture as the two of them waited for the lockpick to complete his task. Finally after what seemed like hours, but in reality must have only been a few minutes, the door slowly opened and Finola gave a muted cry of success, congratulating Archie on his handy work. She stepped into the darkened hallway and gasped as she backed up and bumped into Archie who was close behind her. The glow from the fire in their chamber shed just enough light that she could make out the anger written on Donnchadh's face.

"Going somewhere stepmother dear? Tis a bit late tae be traipsing about the castle. I had yer meal brought tae ye so it can no be hunger that drives ye from yer chamber," he tapped his chin as if deep in thought, "ye have a chamber pot and divider, so it can no be need of the privy, yer fire is lit so it can no be need of kindling. Can ye thank of any other reasons Cameron?"

"None come tae mind m'laird. None that are honest and forthright at least." He narrowed his eyes at them. "So what is so dire that ye needed tae pick the lock of yer chamber?"

Lady Finola opened her mouth and then closed it, she opened her mouth again yet nothing came out. She repeated this a few times. "Enough! I have no patience for this farce. It has been a painfully long day and my bed and my wife beckon me. So how about this. I will tell ye why ye are attempting tae sneak about my castle in the middle of the night" Finola opened her mouth to interrupt him, "Aye MY castle. Now haud yer wheesht and listen tae me." He pressed on. "Ye thought that ye could concoct this grand little scheme tae rid yerselves of me and place Archie as Laird. I ken the whole thing. Ye thought ye could conn me intae setting aside my lady wife in favor of Archie's mistress." Archie made an indignant sound but Donnchadh did not give him a chance to speak. "Aye, I ken that the bairn is no mine. And while I want peace wi the MacDonalds more than ye ken, I am no willing tae sacrifice my love for it and I certainly am no willing tae take on his bastard. So in short, I will no divorce Mairead, I will no marry Brigit, Archie will not take my place, and ye will no kill me. But ye will spend some time in the dungeon while I decide what tae do wi' ye both. And I also ken that Brogan was involved and I will deal wi' him as well. Brigit may stay where she is o'the now as I will not sentence a pregnant woman tae the dungeon. Perhaps after Beltan I will use her tae bargin wi' The MacDonald for peace. Cameron would ye see these two to the dungeon and put in separate accommodations. I have an aunt and a wife that are surely thinking the worst by now and I am bound tae have my hands full."

Cameron chuckled and nodded "Good luck wi' that lad! Another reason I dinna marry!" and then as if a switch had been flipped he scowled at the prisoners. "Ye heard yer laird, MOVE!" He grabbed their arms and made his way down the hall.

The walk to his chamber seemed longer than usual. When he approached the door, he could hear the women within taking. He softly opened the door to the sight of them sitting in the chairs by the fire having an animated conversation. It soothed his heart to see them both so happy and getting along as if they had known each other forever. Gwen looked up at that moment and saw him. She practically jumped out of her chair and threw herself at him. He caught her and squeezed her tight. "Are you ok sweetheart?" she asked softly. He loved when she called him that, really he loved any pet name she called him, but sweetheart and Duncan were his favorite. They made his heart beat faster.

"I am grand my love. Ye saved me and my clan." He set her down and greeted his Auntie.

"Well come sit down and give us the details lad!" she motioned to the chair Gwen had vacated.

He sank into it and pulled Gwen on his lap. It felt natural to him to have her there. "Ye saved us wi' what ye overheard Gwen. They did indeed plan tae kill me. It was as ye heard and worse. Brogan was in on it, but no involved wi the plot tae murder me, but the did engage wi' the MacDonalds. Brigit is one and they relayed that the laird indicated that he would consider peace if I wed her." Gwen drew in a sharp breath and looked away from him then. She knew how important his clan and peace were to him. He placed his index finger below her chin and turned her face back to him. "I will no let ye go Gwen. No matter what! Ye are my heart. It will be fine. This means that the old man is at least open tae negotiate peace and that is the important part. We talked about it before. Ye are mine, end of story. The vows I gave ye are forever. Dinna ye forget that love!"

She kissed him softly then, wrapped her arms around his neck and buried her face against his neck and fell apart a little bit. For a time they all sat there in silence and Donnchadh relished it. He held Gwen and stroked her back as she calmed. Molly looked at them with her head tilted. "Ye two are quite the pair. I did well."

Gwen shifted so that she could see Molly. She asked what she and Donnchadh were both thinking. "What do you mean you did well?"

The old woman laughed. "Guess I may as well tell ye since the lad kens that ye are indeed from the future." Both of them stared at her in shock. "I brought ye here for my nephew. I read the signs and saw ye. I kenned ye would bring him back tae us and be important tae the clan."

Donnchadh shook his head slowly. "So ye are the witch they claim. That is why ye were so concerned wi' our tea leaves. Ye wanted tae make sure ye got it right aye?"

She reached over and patted his knee. "I always kenned ye were a smart one laddie. Now I ken that I dinna get ye a wedding gift, but there is something I can do that I think will please ye lady wife tae no end." She fixed her gaze on Gwen's questioning face. "I can give ye a day back in yer time, where ye were just afore ye came here."

Gwen felt Donnchadh tense. She could not believe what she was hearing. She could go home! But she didn't really think of that as home any longer. "Nay!" Donnchadh answered for her, "Ye will no send her away." Gwen looked at him, struck by his upset.

Molly laughed as she winked. "Och lad I am not so cruel! I meant that I could let ye both have a day in her time together. As in, ye go tae sleep now, wake up in her time enjoy yer day, and then end up back home afore the Beltane fires are lit. I would no dream of separating ye two. I worked tae hard tae get the lass here and besides I want a grandniece or nephew from ye two before tae much longer." She winked.

Gwen could not believe what she was hearing. A chance to see her loved ones again and she would be able to introduce them to the love of her life. "Donnchadh I would love that! I would love tae see my friends once more and let them know I am safe. And to be honest I would kind of like to show off my sexy husband too! None of my friends landed any as handsome as you. I may be biased but..." she shrugged and giggled. "Please sweetheart?"

Donnchadh's head spun. He was ready for the day to end and to curl up in bed with his wife. He believed she was from the future, well he mostly believed, and he understood that his auntie was a witch. But him time traveling was too much. He looked at Gwen, saw the hope, and love shining in her eyes and he realized in that moment that he was completely hers and if there was something within his power to do that would please her, he would do it. He was hers body and soul and he could not have been happier about the fact. He took her face in his hands and gave her a quick kiss and then looked at his aunt. "Ye are sure this is safe?"

"Aye lad. I would no offer if it was no."

"What if aught should go wrong? What if we can't get back for some reason?"

"Ye will get back just fine. Tis only a day. I do have a contingency plan though. Should ye no get back that night, go back tae the hotel and wait. Help will come tae ye in the purple hour. But that is just in case of emergency lad."

"Alright then. So I assume we need tae go tae bed in our clothes then?"

"Ye do for sure lad as ye will have nothing waiting for ye there. Gwen, I will be putting ye back to the day afore ye came here. At the end of the day, instead of going tae dinner go tae the back of the faire as you did afore. Just before the festival day ends. Ye ken?"

"That is amazing! Of course! I know exactly where to go!" she hopped up from Donnchadh's lap and bounded over to hug Molly. She was like an excited child. "I can not thank you enough for this! It means more than the world to me! And to have my Duncan with me! It is amazing!" Molly smiled indulgently at her. She was pleased with the woman she had chosen for Donnchadh.

"Tae bed wi' ye now, I will see ye tomorrow eve. And I promise ye will no feel a thing, And I will inform Cameron the two of ye will not be around at all tomorrow, so he will see tae things for ye." She hugged them both and left the room.

"Well I guess it is bed time then mo chroi." He offered his hand to Gwen. "It will be odd being in bed wi' ye, both of us fully dressed wi'out the intention of undressing immediately thereafter." He winked at her and raised her hand to his lips.

Once they were settled on the bed Gwen lay down in his arms facing him using his chest as a pillow. "Are you nervous sweetheart?" he did not say anything but she felt him nod. "It will be alright I am sure. Tomorrow is going to be amazing! And honestly there will probably be some scary parts for you. But I will be there with you and I know how it all works." She stroked his chest with her fingertips.

"That is oddly reassuring yet concerning at the same time dearest." He chuckled as they drifted off to sleep.

Chapter Fourteen

Gwen stretched and her hands hit the headboard. She stopped and felt it for a moment, It was smooth, not Donnchadh's beautifully ornate headboard back home. She nearly jumped out of her skin when the alarm on her cell phone went off. Donnchadh sprung out of bed, his sgain dubh drawn ready to take on an attacker. Gwen crawled across the bed and quickly swiped across the phone screen to turn off the alarm.

"Are ye alright lass? What was that? Where are we?" It took him a moment to realize they were not under attack.

She grinned at him. "I am more than fine sweetheart! This is the hotel I was staying at in my time. My lodging. We made it, we are really here!" She sprang up from the bed and practically bounced across the room to her bag and began to withdraw the garb she had worn the first time he saw here. She was practically glowing with happiness. "I can't wait to see everyone and for you to meet them! Oh my gosh! SO much to share and show you!" She was changing out of the chemise she had been wearing and stepping into the bathroom. "I am going to get a quick shower. Care to join?"

"What is a shower?"

"It is like a warm indoor waterfall for bathing oh and the …privy is in here too. You use this" she motioned to the toilet and lifted the lid to show him. "So, shower?"

He looked past her at the bathing chamber. It seemed innocent enough. "Aye lass. I think I shall join ye. We are here for but a day, so I may as well take advantage of all the things I can." He winked and dropped his kilt. Gwen started the shower while he finished getting undressed. She stuck her hand in to test the water and decided it was warm enough. Donnchadh was still a bit hesitant as he watched her step in to the shower. It did look pleasant and the water streaming over her body was lovely. He stepped in to join her and the warmth of the water surprised him. She had not been joking when she said it was warm. "This is amazing lass! It feels wonderful."She moved to the other side of him so that he could stand in the cascasde of water while she soaped up her hair.

She grinned at him as he stood beneath the spray of water. He looked like he was truly enjoying it. She tapped him to get him to move so that she could rinse her hair. He smile and moved. He watched her every movement. "Would you like me to wash your hair Duncan?" She offered when she was done with hers. He did not have to be asked twice.

"Aye! I would like that very much!"

"Ok, get your hair good and wet and grab that wooden bench right there and have a seat." The hotel had some nice amenities. The rooms were large with large bathrooms and the showers were almost luxury. The showerheads were even the large round disks like rain heads. They had thought of everything. Once he sat down, she squeezed some of her marzipan-scented shampoo into her hand and began to massage his scalp until there was a rich lather. Donnchadh was moaning in pleasure as she finished. "Go ahead and stand up and rinse it all out." One he got all of the soap out he turned to her. His pleasure in her massage quite evident.

"That was amazing lass!" He pulled her to him and kissed her deeply. He pulled her under the spray of the water with him. She smiled against his mouth and ran a hand down his body until he reached his manhood and cupped it. He growled then and shifted, pressing her against the wall and lifting her legs around his waist. She gave a small squeak when he lifted her, and then wrapped her arms around his neck. He lowered her on to his length. It was her turn to moan in pleasure. She leaned her head back against the wall of the shower as he kissed her neck and pounded into her. Filling her as only he could. She cried out as he hit her g-spot. She clung to him digging her nails into his back and it drove him wild. He fucked her tight wet heat even harder causing her to gasp. She felt as if her body was a thing of sensation that had been fashioned just for him. He kissed her and swallowed her moans. She could feel her pleasure cresting as his hips drove his cock deeper into her and his rhythm becoming almost frantic as he approached his own release. She cried out as her body clenched around him as she came. He groaned as her body squeezed his cock and he came calling her name. Both of them stayed there for a bit trying to calm their breathing.

They rinsed off kissing here and there and then got out of the shower. Gwen checked the time and was relieved to see that there was still plenty of time to get dressed and make it to faire. Donnchadh was thoroughly amused by her excitement. She pulled on her chemise as he put on his saffron shirt. She stopped to watch him as he laid his belt and tartan on the floor and pleated it. Once it was pleated to his satisfaction he laid down and wrapped it around himself. He stood up and picked his kilt pin up off the nightstand and placed it near the bottom edge where the fabric overlapped. "Ok, that is so cool and kind of sexy. I always wondered how men got into real kilts."

He laughed and leaned into give her a quick peck as she settled her skirt high on her waist. "Now ye ken the secret." He winked. "Need any help mo chroi?"

"No. I got it. This is an old habit to me." She shrugged on a tapestry covered bodice while he lounged on the bed and watched as she began to lace it. He noticed that she laced it much tighter than she did most of her dresses at home. He laughed outright when she bent over to adjust her breasts so that she would be comfortable. She made a face at him when she stood up and continued lacing. She turned to the mirror to finish up the last bit and fluffed to make sure everything looked alright. Donnchadh got up behind her and slid his hands down her shoulders to tease the exposed tops of her chest and then venture down to pull her back against him in a tight hug. She giggled and leaned her head back against him and ran her hands up and down his arms.

"I dinna ken if I can let ye out of the room like this! Men will be leering at ye and I do no ken how I will handle that."

"It will be fine sweetheart. I can tuck them in a bit if that helps. Just know that this is tame compared to some of what you will see today. So don't go staring at too many women or I might get jealous."

"Nay ye are fine mo chroi. I but tease ye. I am amazed ye can get yer bodice so tight though."

"It is more comfortable that way with this one, and it looks good. I don't often like how I look, but in this I feel so comfortable!" She winked and stepped out of his arms and set about getting her belt, pouch, and most importantly her mug. She also flitted about the room loading up a basket with odds and ends that he was unsure of the uses.

"Ye are beautiful my love, how could ye no like how ye look?"

She smiled softly and a little sadly at his bewilderment and thought a moment of how to best explain it. "I will just say this, my childhood was not great and I grew up being made to believe that I would never be good enough in so many ways. Fourteen years of that ingrained into my head, and that is not easy to overcome. Some days I like myself, some days I don't. The one constant is that I always like myself at faire." She looked off to the side for a moment and then met his gaze again. "I don't like to talk about it often because it still messes with my head sometimes."

"Och Gwen! My sweet love, ye are beyond worthy of everything and more. In reality I am no worthy of ye. It was yer strength and intelligence that saved me and thus my clan just the other day. That is no small feat and I shall be forever grateful! Ye are the most beautiful woman I have ever been lucky enough tae meet and yer heart is so soft and sweet. I could no have asked for a more perfect wife."

"That means a lot to me sweetheart!" She set her basket down on the bed and went up on tiptoes to kiss his cheek. "But for sure I am not the most beautiful woman you have ever seen. There are women thinner and far prettier than I am. Hell you will see a ton of them today."

He shook his head and frowned at her. "Listen well wife, when I say ye are perfect, I mean it. And why would I want a thinner woman when I have ye. Tis no as if ye are some great bloated whale. Ye have gorgeous curves in the right places. Ye are soft in all the right places in all the best ways. I do no think ye are seeing what I see. For all yer mirrors here are crystal clear and give a perfect reflection, I do no think ye are truly seeing. Ye are stunning! Do no doubt yerself or me." He turned to the mirror then and pulled her in front of him. He leaned down and whispered in her ear, "Let me tell ye true my love. Let me tell ye what the mirror really shows ye. He ran his fingers down her cheek. "Ye have soft fair skin dusted with freckles like little faerie kisses. And they must have indeed kissed ye in blessing. Ye have a lush body that I love and that will carry our children. They will nurse at yer luscious full breasts ." His hands traveled over her breasts giving them a loving squeeze and then skimming her sides and then settling on her waist. "Ye have hips that sway when ye walk in a manner that drives me tae distraction! And yer eyes love, yer eyes swallow me whole. So dinna say ye are no good enough. I will help ye let go of that belief. Ye are the best of everything lass. Let today be the first day ye start listening tae yer husband about yer appearance instead of that little voice in head. We will work on it together and maybe one day ye will not longer have days where ye dinna like yerself."

Tears spilled from her eyes as she turned in his arms, wrapped his arms around his waist, and cried quietly into chest as he held her and gently rubbed her back. She sniffled and tilted her head to look at him. "Oh Duncan thank you. There are not words to describe how much that means to me! I am sorry for falling apart like this."

"Hush mo chroi, no apologies. Ye are my wife and I would move heaven and earth for ye if I could. Now do we have a festival tae attend?" He wiped her tears away with his thumbs and then kissed her.

"I have to be the luckiest woman alive to have you for a husband! Yes we have a festival to go to. Come on." She grabbed her basket and put her Macleod of Lewis plaid over the contents. Now she proudly wore her MacLeod of Harris arasidh with a heather broach. "Before we head out, I need you to trust me. I told you about some things before but others could not be described. We are going to stop for coffee on our way and I will be driving us in my horseless carriage. Just think of it as having small horses under the hood. I will never do anything to put you in danger, but we will be going very fast, faster even than Realta." He nodded steeling himself for whatever was outside the door. He was both eager and, if he was honest with himself, a bit scared.

Chapter Fifteen

Nothing could have prepared him for the riot of color and sound that greeted him. Gwen took his hand and gently tugged him in the direction of the stairs that led down to the ground level. It was almost overwhelming. He could not stop looking around as she talked. He did not catch all of what she said as he gawked at what he assumed were the horseless carriages she had described. They were amazing. "Come on sweetheart. Let's go. Starbucks is calling my name!" she opened the passenger door of what looked like a blue box on wheels. Hesitantly he sat in the seat and waited for her to shut the door. She went around the car and got in on the other side and sat behind the wheel. She put a key in the base of the wheel and the engine roared to life. Donnchadh was a bit startled as she looked behind them and backed out of the parking spot.

"This is….something!" Donnchadh shook his head and looked around. He noticed a small handle above the door and grabbed it out of instinct.

Gwen chuckled. "Yeah, I imagine it is overwhelming. I promise that you are safe! I would never put you in a dangerous situation. I am really amazed at how calmly you are handling this."

"Well I accepted that ye were from the future, and Molly is a witch. This is just a product of that apparently so while I marvel at these things, there is no cause for me tae get overly upset. I am simply of the mindset tae enjoy what amounts tae a magic show for me."

"That is one way to look at it." He amazed her. He took this in stride and seemed so calm about it. She pulled into Starbucks and ordered 2 grande peppermint mochas and got an extra shot of espresso in hers. "Okay, this is much stronger than what you are used to so sip it slowly." She offered him one of the cups. As they pulled away from the takeout window she took a sip of her drink and moaned. "OH sweet lord! I have missed this!"

Donnchadh enjoyed watching her pleasure. She was truly an amusing woman in every sense of the word. He cautiously took a sip of his drink, it was indeed strong, and heavily tinged with mint. He did not find it unpleasant though. Gwen continued to sip hers as she drove. She turned on some bagpipe music and told him about things to expect at the festival. She carried on in a very upbeat and animated manner, which he could only assume was to be attributed to the beverage she drank. She had explained that hers was a bit stronger than his was. She was happy though and in that moment, that was all that mattered to him. They drove down a rough road that was lined with pine trees and had no civilization in sight and then turned off onto a dirt path that led to a large field where people left their horseless carriages. When she parked, he told her to wait as he got out and went around the car to open the door for her. "Why thank ye m'laird!" She grinned as she accepted his hand in assistance getting out of the car. "So would you mind if I told one friend what your name means? I don't want to tell everyone mind you, because you are my Duncan, but Chastity and I have known each other forever and she will freak when I tell her."

"As long as I am still yer Duncan that is fine." He kissed her and then watched her set about getting ready for the day. She pulled out her black leather hat and made sure she had her money and some little cards in her pouch. She left the basket in the car though. He asked her what it was for if she was not bringing it. "Oh, we will need to come back and grab it before we go home. It has a few things I want to bring with me."

He smiled at her and offered her his arm and they proceeded to the front gate of the festival. Donnchadh looked around while she purchased tickets. He was enthralled by this place and its people. The modes of dress were so different. Some women wore short pants that left most of their legs bare, some dressed in a similar fashion to Gwen, and others dressed in tight bodices and lots of leather and animal fur. One redhead in particular paid him quite a bit of attention even while she was talking with a group of people. He turned when Gwen put a hand on his arm and gave him a ticket.

They walked over to the back of the group of people that was gathering around the gate. Gwen could not contain her happiness. She was practically bouncing. She wrapped both of her arms around Donnchadh's right arm and flashed a huge smile at him. He leaned down and kissed her. "I love seeing ye this happy. I just worry that ye will miss all of this so much that ye will be sad when we return home."

"Want to know a secret??" she got up on her tiptoes to be closer to his ear, her breasts pressed against him distracting him briefly. "The reason I am so happy is that you are here with me, well that and perhaps the vast amount of caffeine I consumed on the way here. But that is beside the point. You are my happy place Duncan! Bringing you here is a real treat, but going home with you will be complete satisfaction for me. Today will end, our life together is just starting and as long as I am with you, I am blissfully happy!" He pulled his arm from her grasp and put it around her, keeping her close and hugging her.

"I can no tell ye what it does tae my heart tae hear ye say that. Ye are my happy place as well mo chroi. I dinna think I could ever be happy again after I lost Dair, but ye opened a door for me and I am happier and more at peace than I have ere been. I miss Dair desperately, but I ken he would have adored ye and wanted us tae be happy."

They stood there and waited as the crowd grew and 10:00 am neared. He kept his arms around her and they chatted while they waited. On occasion the redhead would catch his eye and smile. The first time he gave a polite sharp nod, after that he felt no need to acknowledge her. Gwen asked him to play along with her, explained that she played Mairead here, and was very exuberant. She told him that she was more outgoing and silly at faire. He was looking forward to seeing that side of her. Finally the town crier began his introduction. Telling them that King James had come to visit and the year was 1603. There was silliness from peasants mixed among the crowd and he found the whole little display enjoyable. Finally a cannon roared and the gates were thrown open.

Gwen could not believe what was happening. She was about to introduce her highlander husband to her modern friends. It struck her that this morning was the polar opposite from last time. There was not the sense of melancholy, but she did take time to remember Ian. She was overjoyed this morning and it had been wonderful so far. Her husband was a virtual sex god!

Taking it all in, Donnchadh felt like his head was on a constant swivel. The front gate of the festival had been made to look like a castle. While it was not true stone, it still looked quite nice and gave the entrance some style. His attention was drawn when Gwen let go of his hand as she was scooped up and hugged by what looked like a kings guard. He bristled and reached for his sword, which he remembered Gwen had not let him bring so it was still lying on his chest back home. Once the man put her down she was approached by several other people greeting her with hugs and excitement. She finally turned to him and grabbed his hand again to introduce him. It went far toward soothing him. "Soo.. I have to introduce y'all to someone special. This is my husband Donnchadh MacLeod. Sweetheart, these are my friends, Richard, Cassy, Jenna, Michael, Craig, Charlotte, Michelle, Billie and Bobby." The ladies smiled and said hello and the men shook his hand. They all offered Gwen congratulations and some scolded her for not telling them before. She laughed it off. Charlotte kept pushing.

"That is my fault lass. I asked her no tae say anything. I ken that she wanted tae see yer faces when she told ye." He stepped in squeezing her hand which earned him a brilliant smile.

"Oh my God Gwen! His voice! Does he really talk like that or is it just for faire like you?" Cassy was fanning herself. Gwen burst out laughing at that.

"He is the real thing sweetie! Imported straight from the Isle of Skye!"

"I get why you wanted to keep tall, dark, and sexy a secret now." She winked at Donnchadh. He smiled a bit hesitantly. He was not sure what to make of the bold nature of some of these people.

"Yeah, well cats out of the bag now. You will just have to get your own because this one is all mine!" She playfully bumped Cassie with her hip and Cassie returned the favor, knocking Gwen into him. She laughed as he caught her and made no move to leave his arms. I know y'all have gigs to get to so we will see ya later. I am going to show my husband the faire." She gave her friends a small but exaggerated curtsey and they turned to wander down the lane. "I am sorry about that sweetheart. I know that there was some overwhelm there. We all get a bit carried away during faire. We all get bawdier among other things."

"Aye it will take some getting used tae. I did have a bit of concern when that first fellow grabbed ye, but tis alright now. Yer friends seem tae care about ye."

"Yeah Richard is something else. Has a real way with the ladies. I used to be good friends with his girlfriend. I will have to see if they are still together."

"So he has a lady. Well that makes me feel better."

"Oh my God you were jealous!"

"Aye I was. A strange man had his hands on my wife. But I understand now and I promise that I will no act out of jealousy."

"Thank you for understanding sweetheart! Now come on! There are shows I want you to see, people I want you to meet, and shopping to do." She excitedly tugged at his hand. He enjoyed wandering around with her. On occasion people would stop and gawk at them. At one point a family even asked for a picture of them with their son and daughter. Gwen all but beamed at them. "Aye we would love tae. Will ye be using one of those miniature portrait boxes we have heard so much about this day?" the little girl who looked to be around six or seven years old giggled. The father laughed and nodded. The boy who was probably a teenager rolled his eyes. Gwen put her arm around his waist and leaned against him while the children stood slightly to the sides. Donnchadh smiled and enjoyed watching the byplay. Once the picture was taken the little girl turned to Gwen said she wanted to ask her a question.

Gwen squatted on the ground so that she could be closer to the girl's level. "Ye can ask me anything ye like lassie. I am more than happy tae answer."

"Well you are a pirate right?" She asked shyly.

"Aye that I am. Even have the feathers in my hat tae prove it. I will tell ye a secret, pirate captains get feather envy! So I try to keep mine pretty."

The little girl covered her mouth in a shy giggle. Her parents were watching the by play as was Donnchadh. Even a few other people stopped to see what was going on. "Well my big brother says that only boys can be pirates."

Gwen cocked her head at the girl. "What is yer name lassie?"

"Emma"

"Och that is a pretty name. Nice tae meet ye Emma. I am Mairead. Any one can be a pirate dearie."

"But he says that is just in movies and places like here."

"See there is where people misunderstand. There have been girls who were pirates. When ye get home this eve have yer mam or da help ye look up Ann Bonnie or Grania O'Mally. Both were real pirates and both were women. They were pretty awesome. So if ye decide tae be a pirate, ye be one with pride representing a long history of female pirates, or if ye want tae be a princess be that proudly. Just do no be a ninja! Everyone kens pirates are better and can kick ninja butt!" Everyone laughed, including her brother. Emma threw her arms around Gwen's neck. Gwen hugged the girl back for a moment. Her parents were quick to snap a picture. The little girl thanked her and skipped off to her parents immediately telling them that she wanted to be a great pirate like Ann Bonnie, Grania O'Mally, and Mairead.

For a moment, Donnchadh stared at her in wonder. "That was amazing. Ye were so good wi' the lass. It was like ye already kenned what she would ask and what tae say."

"Thank ye. I have done this for a long time. At one point I was even part of a program where I went to schools in the days leading up to them bringing students to the faire so that they would at least ken a bit about the era. And some of them made me work for it. So I did my homework. As a pirate, there are different expectations even at faire. And on occasion ye do get someone who says women can't be pirates. So it helps tae have facts tae back ye up. I love it though. What happened wi' wee Emma does no happen often. That was special. I have gotten asked for pictures on occasion though."

"Ye will be a wonderful mother. I can no wait tae see ye wi' our children."

"That will be wonderful indeed." They went to more booths where she brought bits and pieces, a necklace for Molly here, a pair of earrings for Lottie there. She even tried to buy him a mug but he refused saying that he would rather share hers. She had laughed and promptly took him to the pub and ordered an ale she thought he would like and had them pour it in her mug. They took turns sipping from it as they walked. When lunch rolled around she got some steak on a stake and he opted for one of the turkey legs. She gave him some cash while she waited for her food so that he could go order. Once she had her steak she made her way to one of the large spools that served as tables and watched while Donnchadh waited for his turkey leg. While he stood there, arms crossed over his chest, the red headed woman dressed as a barbarian, meaning in this case that she was scantily clad in bits of leather and fur, approached him. She reminded Gwen of Red Sonja, if Red Sonja had been a goth. She got Donnchadh's attention and stood closer to him than Gwen thought was proper. The woman reached up and put her hand on Donnchadh's arm, and Gwen was not happy. Donnchadh very gently removed her hand, next time she placed her hand on her chest and gestured over her shoulder to her barbarian horde friends. He looked where she was pointing and she could see him shake his head and again remove her hand. He then looked up, saw Gwen watching, and then looked at the woman again. He said something and then gestured in her direction. The woman turned to look and flushed a deep red. Gwen could only assume Donnchadh had pointed out that he was married and that she was his wife. The woman did not seem to like that answer. She stepped closer to him pressing her breasts against him. He stepped back away from her and gladly grabbed the turkey leg the vendor offered.

He quickly made his way across the lane to Gwen. Once he stood next to her, he heaved a sigh and was quite relieved. Then he jumped and spun about as if shocked. Before Gwen could ask what the matter was, she saw the red head.

"What do ye want woman? I told ye repeatedly that I am married and have no intrest in ye!" Donnchadh was thoroughly exasperated.

"I figured if you were over there alone you couldn't be that happily married. Here is my number just in case." She pulled a small piece of paper out of her leather bra. Gwen stepped infront of the woman and intercepted the paper.

"I believe my husband informed ye he was married and no interested in ye. I suggest ye leave and go about yer day now." Gwen gestured down the lane.

"Oh is that what you suggest?" The redhead stepped up so that she was toe to toe with Gwen.

"Aye, t'is. My husband said nay and yet ye put yer hands on him repeatedly and then just now ye harassed him." Gwen purposely raised her voice. She saw one of the security team that she was friends with coming down the lane. Her raised voice caught his attention. He knew Gwen well and realized that there had to be an issue if she raised her voice. She never yelled.

"Can I help you Mairead?" he asked as he approached.

"Indeed ye can good sir. This woman just harassed my husband."

"I did not! I just touched his arm and his chest!" she cried in an attempt at defense.

"Aye and ye kilt checked him in a most inappropriate and unwanted manner if his reaction was anything tae go by! That is sexual harassment." She hissed at the woman.

Donnchadh had been silent to that point. The security guard looked at him and addressed him. "Did she kilt check you man?"

"If by kilt check ye mean put her hand under my kilt, aye. And it was most unwelcome." The man nodded at him and then made a call over his radio for back up as he detained the woman. Her friends approached to argue her case. She began to cry.

"I have this under control. You two go on. I have all the info I need and if I need a statement later I will find you. Glad to see you again Mairead. You take care of our girl!" He pointed at Donnchadh.

"I am so sorry sweetheart!" Gwen apologized as they took their food to the inn where she knew they could be more comfortable and not harassed by the likes of the redhead again.

"Do no ye apologize for that. That was no yer fault and I am glad ye handled it like ye did, I ken nothing of rules here so thank ye."

"I just hate that that happened. You get to come to my faire and get assaulted. Today is supposed to be fun not filled with harassment."

"That was merely a small moment of our day. Tis over now. I do wonder what they will do wi' her though."

"Kicked out of the faire and banned most likely."

"Now there is my favorite wench and her handsome husband!" Chastity made a fuss as she sat down at the bench across the table from them. Gwen shook her head and laughed chagrined.

"Aye tis. What are ye about?"

"The usual. Having fun, causing trouble, and on occasion dodging chores. Oh and flirting!" She said in a wildly obnoxious cockney accent.

Donnchadh was bemused by the whole exchange. He was glad to experience this with Gwen but he would be glad to get home too. Gwen leaned across the table and motioned for chastity to do the same. "Want to know a secret?" she whispered dropping her accent.

"Oh yeah! You know I love secrets! Spill!"

"Do you want to know the translation of Donnchadh's name?"

"Oh this has to be good if you want to keep it a secret. Of course I want to know!" Chastity's eyes shifted to Donnchadh for a moment and then back to Gwen.

"Donnchadh translates to Duncan." Gwen waited a moment for Chastity to process what she had told her.

"Wait wait wait! You mean his name is Duncan MacLeod?" she crowed with laughter. Several people turned to look. "You lucky bitch. That is crazy! Well it has to be fate then. Seriously though," She lowered her voice and dropped her accent, leveling Donnchadh with a hard stare. "You take care of my girl! Things have not always been easy for her and she deserves only the best. And if you hurt her I will hunt you down and fong you!" Donnchadh was confused when Gwen broke down giggling to the point that she was crying. At one point she even snorted which led to more peals of laughter.

"I will fong you until your entrails become your extrails!" the two of them cried out together. They had binge watched A Knights Tale more times than either of them would admit to. It was their pizza and a movie night comfort watch and the loved Wart. Fonging was their go to threat because of their shared love of the movie.

"I can only assume that would be most unpleasant." he said after they had calmed down a bit. That elicited another round of laughter. He was certain now that his wife was indeed crazy as he first thought but he liked this brand of crazy. "That aside. I give ye my word that I will protect Gwen wi' my life and spend my life making her happy."

"Good! I am glad. It is awesome to see her this happy. It wasn't often that she was like this before she left to join the military. I am glad she found you."

The rest of the day passed in a haze of happiness. They saw shows and Gwen even participated in a few since she knew the people on stage. She even managed to get him dragged on stage a time or two. At one point a small man was climbing him in place of a ladder. All the while Gwen was taking pictures of him and pictures of the two of them together. Most of those shows ended in laughter. He began to see why she liked this place so much. She had laughed and smiled more here in one day than she had with him in several months. For a moment he felt a pang of jealousy and then reminded himself that she had years of history with some of these people and he had a lifetime to accumulate even more of her smiles and laughter than anyone else. As the shadows grew long, they walked back to the car and grabbed her basket. They took their time as she guided them to the back of the faire. She told him that she would miss it but she was ready to go home. His heart swelled at that.

They were almost to the back of the faire when they heard a familiar sound. A lute playing She Moved Through the Faire. She looked up at him "I think that is our cue."

"Aye. And just in time. I am ready tae go home." They walked back toward the joust field.

Gwen was confused to see the back fence of the faire still there. It should be gone. She stopped suddenly. Donnchadh looked at her in concern. "Why do ye stop lass?"

"Because of the fence. There is nowhere to go."

"What do ye mean love? There is no fence. I can see Dunvegan from here." He looked into the distance and then back at her. When he looked back, her face was filled with horror and it scared him. He did not understand what was going on. She looked down at their joined hands and he realized he could not feel her hand any more. He looked down and saw that her hand was fading. He looked up and met her gaze. Tears poured down her cheeks as she begged him not to go. He reached out to her but she continued to fade. He called her name and she did not answer. Then the joust field was gone, the vendors were gone, his Gwen was gone. He fell to his knees and roared his pain to the sky. This was worse even than losing Dair. He felt broken. He picked himself up and began the walk home. As he walked, he noticed that something was not right. He could hear sounds of battle. He ran. MacDonalds were attacking his home and his people. He cursed his lack of sword but spied a fallen man not far off, picked up his sword and charged into the fray. He wielded his sword like a mad man, like a berserker of old. It was said that MacLeods had some Viking blood, and

Donnchadh prayed that it aided him now. He cut down men left and right. Hoping that if he shed enough blood that he would hurt less. His clansmen cheered as he helped drive the MacDonalds back. Cameron made it to his side. The two of them fought like men possessed. The sun was low on the horizon when the MacDonalds began to flee. Cameron turned to him with a large grin on his face at the defeat of the MacDonalds, but his grin fell when he saw that Donnchadh had no such response. His eyes were bleak. "Are ye alright man?" he asked putting his hand on his shoulder. Donnchadh patted Cameron's hand and then stepped away saying nothing as he began to walk back to the castle. "Donnchadh, where is Mairead?" He became more concerned. Donnchadh stopped his head and shoulders drooped and then he shuddered and stood tall. He turned his head to speak so that Cameron might hear him but did not meet his gaze.

"Do no speak her name. It is mine and I will hear it from no one else again." With that, he looked toward the castle and began to walk again. His clansmen cleared the way for him, some out of respect, and some out of fear for the black look he wore on his face. Cameron was baffled. He had no idea what was going on. He had adored Mairead. She was a wonderful woman and a perfect match for Donnchadh. But Donnchadh's response had been frightening. His mood had not even been that foul when they had fought before. This was new. Worse even than his response to Alasdair's death. He cried and drank though that one. Now he was cold. He hoped that it was temporary and he would share his pain and details of what had happened. He followed him as they approached the castle. Once inside Donnchadh was bellowing for his aunt. When she did not answer, a maid came forward and told him that she had been injured in the raid. Donnchadh lost all color in his face and ran up the stairs and down the hall to her chamber. Cameron was hot on his heels.

"Auntie! Oh God, Molly please do no leave me! I can no lose ye tae!" He fell to his knees next to her bed and clasped her hand as she lay unconscious. She had been bandaged. She was hit by an arrow when the MacDonalds attacked. She had not woken yet in spite of being treated and bandaged. "My love is gone. I can no lose ye as well! Ye have tae help me bring her home so that we can be a family. So that we can have bairns and ye can spoil them as they deserve." He crumpled then, sobs wracking his body. He had failed them all. Alasdair, Cait, his clan, Molly, and his beloved. He knew of no way to fix this. While the MacDonalds had been routed, they would be back. Had he not gone with Gwen he would have been here to protect his clan and Molly would never have gotten hurt. Had he stayed perhaps his Gwen would never have gone either and they would be celebrating the defeat of his enemy now. But she would not be as happy as he had seen her at the faire. Or mayhaps, she still would have gone but then he would be forever awaiting her return when she could not make it back. There was no outcome that did not hurt. As his eyes dried he sat lost in thought. The joy he had seen in Gwen earlier had been so beautiful. He would not trade that for anything. She held nothing back and gave herself whole-heartedly to the experience. She gave herself whole-heartedly to him. Perhaps the memories of her love and the time they had together would sustain him. He prayed for Molly to wake so that she might help bring Gwen home. Finally he looked up and noticed

Cameron. "Tis Beltane" he sighed "Go and set about it with the rest of the clan. Fires need tae be lit soon. I will stay wi' my auntie. Please act in my stead"

"Aye m'laird. I will see to it. Will ye join us at all?" Cameron questioned, full of worry for his friend and laird.

"Nay, I have no stomach for what the fires will bring tae those around them. Go and find a bonny lass tae celebrate wi'" at that Cameron quit the chamber. Donnchadh pulled a chair near the bed and leaned back propping his feet up on the mattress waiting for Molly to wake. He must have dozed off because he was startled by a hand on his arm where it rested on the bed. He looked over to see Molly looking at him with watery eyes. "Och Auntie! I am so glad ye live!" He got up and sat on the bed to check on her.

"Aye lad. I am a tough old bat. I'll be damned if I let a MacDonald arrow do me in." She was quiet then and took a deep breath. "I am sorry lad. I failed ye." She looked up at him tears spiling over her cheeks onto the coverlet. "I was struck down afore I could see ye both safely back. I ken she is still there and I ken that ye are both heart broken because of it."

"Hush woman. Tis no yer fault. Twas MacDonald treachery. Now when we left I recall that ye said something about a contingency plan should aught go awry." He held her hands and spoke softly to her.

"Aye. I told ye that ye were tae wait at the hotel and help would come. I hope yer Gwen remembers and I hope that it works. I have not the strength for another round of those spell tae send ye back let alone bring ye both home."

"I pray she remembers as well Auntie, and that it works" He sat in the darkness looking at the window waiting to see the Beltane fires lit in the fields.

Chapter Sixteen

Gwen stood staring at the back fence of the faire. She slowly realized that people were trickling to the front gate since the faire would be closing soon. She felt raw as if she had been bled dry. She had no desire to deal with anyone one at all and was relieved to find that some of the exits from the faire that existed for cast only were still there. She made her way around the back of the faire avoiding everyone she could. She remembered what Molly had said and hoped that she had been right about help coming to the hotel.

She made it to her car without too much incident and drove back to the hotel. She was not aware of scenery she passed. She parked and sat in the car loath to go up to the room where she had last slept with him, last loved him. She finally gave in when she realized how late it was and her stomach growled. She trudged to her room and slid the card in to the reader. The door swung open and she swallowed hard as she entered. The housekeepers had made the bed but she swore she could still smell his clean woodsy scent. She sat down on the bed and dug through her pouch and basket for her phone. She could not find it. She remembered then that Donnchadh had taken it from her after she had shown him how to take pictures shortly after lunch. She had taken some selfies of them and then he hijacked the phone and put it in his sporran. She had caught glimpses of him fiddling with it or quickly stuffing it back in to his sporran for the rest of the afternoon. He was adorable when he thought she didn't know that he was up to something.

The lack of her phone hindered her options. She looked over at the table in the corner of the room and noticed a binder. It was the usual hotel info as well as local take out numbers and menus. She didn't really care to dig through the menus so she opted for pizza from a local delivery place. She turned on the TV to find something to watch. When she surfed the channels she wanted to pull her hair out and scream. First she came across Braveheart, then First Knight, then the first Highlander movie. The one that broke her was when she flipped to a new channel and saw that the series was on. It was the episode where Mac proposed to and then lost his love. Gwen was a sobbing mess by the time the pizza guy got there.

She stayed awake most of the night partially because she couldn't sleep, but also because she desperately hoped that Molly's promised back up would come. She dozed off shortly before sunrise, but slept fitfully. Every noise woke her with the hope that it was her rescue. She did not leave her room at all that day. Noone came and nothing happened. She ate a piece of the leftover pizza that evening because she knew she had to eat something. Monday was the same. Tuesday pushed her into depression and she had no desire to even get out of bed. When she woke up on Wednesday she decided to take a new outlook on things. She told herself that she would have faith, and then thought that perhaps the magic only worked at faire. So that meant she had until Saturday to make sure that she had everything in order. She made a list and headed to an electronics store. If Donnchadh still had her cell phone, the battery would only last so long. She knew just the remedy. She bought a small solar panel. Next she went to a superstore and bought some tampons, toothpaste and toothbrushes as well as some oreos and chocolate treats. She purchased a large leather backpack so that she could fit everything. She even stopped by a Victoria's Secret to buy something to surprise Donnchadh with. Her final stop was a bookstore. She bought numerous novels and fiction pieces. She stayed away from any books resembling nonfiction Scottish history. She was terrified that she would read that he remarried or something terrible. Granted he was technically dead at this point in time, she could not even bring herself to consider it.

It was almost dark by the time she made her way back to her room. She was a bit lightheaded and realized that she had not eaten all day and had only had one piece of pizza the previous day. She shrugged and pulled out the remainder of the pizza and at two pieces this time. She went to bed feeling slightly better than she had. Thursday morning came and nothing happened. She had an idea to keep her spirits up. She would go run one more errand and then sit on the lakefront under an oak tree for a while. She loved sitting on the Northshore lakefront of Lake Pontchartrain. There was so much wild beauty there. She stopped by a CVS and picked up a handful of pregnancy tests. It would be nice to know for sure when she and Donnchadh got pregnant instead of guessing. She drove through a neighborhood to the lakefront. It was a lovely afternoon, and people were taking advantage of the lovely weather. There were a lot of people walking and some bike riders. There were also families with small children playing on a nearby playground. She found her favorite oak and clambered up on a branch that dipped just close enough to the ground to act as a bench. She sat there for hours pondering her existence.

Just before sunset she returned to the hotel. It was another long and lonely night. Friday dawned overcast and rainy. She was glad of it. She loved rainy days and it fit her mood. She went down to the lobby and used a computer to purchase a ticket to the faire online. She returned to her room to wait out the day and hoped that tomorrow she would be going home. The rain eased that evening. Just before it was full dark a knock came at her door. Her heart pounded. She prayed that this was what Molly had promised. She opened the door to see the lutenist she had met when she was sent to Donnchadh. "Oh my God! It is you! What is going on?"

He smiled as he stepped into the room. I received an odd message that instructed me to assist you in getting home like I did before. But I don't remember sending you anywhere before. I do remember seeing you last weekend with a big Scottish guy but that is it."

Gwen's face crumpled. "So you can't help me then?"

"NO no no! I didn't say that! I am assuming that if I was sent here, that you have an open mind. My lute was a gift that was handed down through generations. A Scottish woman gave it to an ancestor of mine. He went to some village on the Isle of Skye to learn to play the bagpipes and apparently, he sucked. It was said that he drove the laird at the time nuts to the point that he called my ancestor before him and asked him why the hell he had chosen the pipes. Because there was no way he would ever play well if the best in the world could not teach him. So he told the laird that he loved music and wanted to do his family proud. He even offered to display his talent. He asked if they had any instruments on hand. There was one. A lute. It was brought to him and he played so beautifully that he made everyone in the room weep even the laird. He supposedly told my ancestor that his music reminded him of his beloved that he missed with all his heart. He invited my ancestor to stay at the castle for a time. He stayed for a while and entertained those around the castle until one day an old woman approached him and presented him with this gorgeous piece of art. She said it was very special and would be of great use. She said that it was blessed and would always help find the way home. It played sweeter than anything he had ever heard and still does." He gave it a strum.

Gwen smiled through tears. That sounded like her Duncan and Molly. "That is a wonderful tale! What did she mean by saying that it would help find the way home?"

He smiled then. "That is the good part! My ancestors found out that it was indeed blessed. Even those who are terribly lost with no idea of where to look to get home, find their way home when they hear this beauty play. It is not all the time mind you, because old magic is tricky like that. But there is an equally old journal that was passed down as well that led me here to you. You go by Mairead MacLeod I assume?"

"YES!!!! That is me! What do you need to do to send me home? What needs to happen?"

"Meet me at the faire tomorrow evening toward the back of the site. I am not sure of much more, but I am betting we will figure it out."

"Oh my God I cannot thank you enough! I can't wait!" She hugged him. He returned her hug and then waved as he left. She did not sleep at all that night. She checked on everything she bought and made sure there was nothing else she needed. She sent her family an email telling them that she loved them and giving them a brief watered-down explanation. They had not been terribly close since she joined the military.

Saturday evening could not come soon enough. She loaded everything she wanted to take with her into her car and headed to the festival late in the afternoon. When she arrived, she left a note on the windshield telling her friends that she loved them and would miss them. She told them to use the car however, they saw fit. She entered and did her best to be inconspicuous. A few people called out greeting which she returned but she really wanted to avoid questions about her backpack and basket. Well perhaps not questions about her backpack because she had that hidden under a cloak, so more like questions about her sudden hunchback. She chuckled to herself about that one. As she came around a curve in the lane she saw the lutenist. She caught his attention and practically ran to him. "Perfect timing! I was starting to worry. Any ideas?" he asked her.

"Last time you were playing, and I walked to the back of the site near the joust field and the fence was gone and I was there all of a sudden."

He nodded. "Very well. I think I know the song to play. You go ahead and I will set the mood."

She thanked him and turned to walk back to the joust field. He played a soft mournful tune and she looked back over her shoulder for a moment. He saw and nodded encouragingly. As she walked the tune became more peaceful and almost happy. She rounded the corner to the area that housed the joust field and was overjoyed to see that there was no fence that she could see. She continued to walk and could already make out Dunvegan in the distance. She was glad of her cloak. There was a chill in the air and the sun was setting fast. It would be dark by the time she made it to the castle. She did not stop to look around.

She removed her hood and guards at the gate stared at her as she walked past. She didn't understand their reaction. She went to the chamber she shared with Donnchadh but he was not there. She sat her things down on the chest at the end of the bed. Dinner was long over, and the fire was still stoked. He could not be far. She left the chamber and went to the great hall. More people stared as she passed and it was starting to worry her. When she entered the hall she looked around. Maids were cleaning up. She noticed something different over the fireplace. It was a painting. But not like any portraits painted by artists from this era. It was her and Donnchadh. He had his arms about her and she leaned into him with her head against his chest. She recognized the pose. It was like a picture that Richard had taken of them! It was gorgeous. But how did it get here? She studied it. It was a large piece and pieces of that size and detail took time. More than just the week since Donnchadh had returned. It didn't make sense. She jumped when she heard a yell.

"Can anyone tell me why the bloody hell there is a woman's cloak and belongings in my chamber?! No one is tae enter my chamber without permission! Just because I left the door open does no mean a welcome!" Donnchadh was roaring at top volume as he came down the stairs stomping heavily on each one. Gwen was a little nervous. She had never heard him like that, and it scared her a bit.

Molly came flying around the corner with her back to Gwen. Neither one of them was aware of her presence. "Haud yer wheesht ye great arse! I am sure it was just a mistake or an accident of some sort."

"I do no ask much of my clan but my privacy! And now that is not even respected! I have sacrificed all for ye lot!"

"Oh ye and no one else lad? Ye were the only one tae sacrifice? Do ye want tae rethink that?" She yelled back and gestured to her shoulder.

Gwen had never heard either of them like this. She got a good look at Donnchadh and it scared her. He had dark circles under his eyes and while he was more muscular, if that was possible, he looked sharper. The sweet loving smile in his eyes was replaced by cold hard steel. How could this have happened in a week?

"I want it all gone! Burn it! I do no care! But I do no want any of it in my chamber! Ye and no one else is tae take care of it and ke ken damned well why." He growled. Molly shoved past him angrily. He sank to the stairs and sat there in the middle of the stairs with his elbows resting on his knees and his head in his hands. Gwen was not sure why she didn't say anything. It was as if she had been rendered mute and rooted to the spot.

"Donnchadh! Donnchadh! Ye great arse!!! How could ye be so thick headed and blind? We need a search party!" Molly yelled as she ran back to the stairs.

"What now woman?" He sounded so tired. He did not look up until he heard her gasp. He raised his head to see what had caused his aunt to respond like that. His heart stopped. He just stared for a moment and then opened his mouth to say something but nothing came out. He stood and slowly approached Gwen leaving Molly on the stairs to gawk. "Are ye a ghost come tae torment me since the veil is thin this night?" his voice was low and sounded broken.

What she had just seen of Donnchadh scared her. "I would never torment you and I am not a ghost." She said softly as she took a step back.

*   *   *

"OCH ye great lummox!" Molly cried at him. "Can no ye pull yer head out of yer arse long enough tae see that it really is her. She came back tae ye! I told ye she deserved none of yer blustering! She has done naught tae earn this treatment. Ye even said that her friend told ye her life had no been easy, and she herself even stipulated once that she would not have ye yelling around her. I can no imagine how she feels about ye speaking tae her as ye did let alone just yelling at her. The lass needed yer love and yer tenderness. She needed the sweet lad I helped tae raise, no this hard and bitter man."

Donnchadh shook her hand off of his arm. "Leave off woman! Is it really ye lass?" his voice was a whisper.

She shook her head confused. " It was only a week since you left me and in that week I was broken. The only thing that kept me going was the thought of you and the hope that I would be able to come home. To return to this though, I don't understand."

"Christ lass! I am sorry mo chroi! I have been drinking and the site of a woman's cloak in my chamber put me over the edge. It is my sanctuary. It is where I put all the things ye left and remember every little moment wi' ye that I was blessed wi'. No one is allowed in my chamber because of what I have hidden there. Ye ken well enough that some of it would raise more than a question or two. I could no bring myself tae get rid of any of it, while it would probably be safer, it would mean giving up a part of ye. And I could not lose more wi' out breaking. I thought that something might have happened and I could no handle even the thought of losing more of ye. So aye, I flew off the handle and I will always beg forgiveness for that."

He noticed that she was looking up at him now. "Please come back up tae our chamber and just sit wi' me a bit and let me tell ye what happened while I prayed ye would come home." He offered her his arm and was relieved when she took it, and he led her back upstairs to their chamber. He gestured to the two chairs before the fire place. She hesitated but then sat down and curled up into as small as space as she could manage in one of the chairs. Donnchadh sat in the other and leaned forward. Molly had been behind him in the hallway and her heart broke for both of them. They both deserved to be happy. She softly shut the door so that they could have privacy.

"When I came home it was in the middle of the MacDonalds attacking. It was horrific. I joined the fray and we fought them off. When I made it back tae the castle I found Molly gravely injured. She had taken a MacDonald arrow. That was why ye did no come back wi' me. She was only halfway through when she went down. She told me that there would be help sent tae ye at the hotel and for a long while I kept up hope. I hoarded everything that reminded me of ye, everything ye left behind. I even had a traveling artist sworn tae secrecy wi' a great deal of money and threats against his life." He gestured to the fireplace. There hung another large piece. It was just of her. She was turned to the side looking over her shoulder at him with a half-smile on her face in front of a booth full of garlands. She remembered that moment. He had not expected her to turn at that moment and she caught him fiddling with the phone. She said nothing and looked back at him. "As time went by, I gave up hope. I figured that there was no way ye would have stayed at the hotel that long. Cameron thought I was going mad. I would come in here at the end of the day and talk tae ye."

Perhaps she was being too hasty. While she was still deeply unhappy with how he had treated her, he was not a horrible person. "I have a question for you. Did you have a young man come to train with the McCrimmons who was awful despite all training efforts?"

Her question confused him. "Aye we did. Sounded like the lad was murdering a bag of geese when he tried tae play. Why do ye ask?"

"And did you speak with him and discover that he played the lute like an angel?"

"Aye just so. He made all those listening in the hall tear up. Even I got a bit choked up at his talent. Again, why do ye ask this and how do ye ken?"

"That is not exactly what I heard. I heard you cried outright and said the music reminded you of me." Donnchadh was staring at her in disbelief. She gave him the half smile that he loved. "I met his ancestor. Molly gave him a lute while he was here and it was handed down through generations. He plays as beautifully as his ancestor did, I am sure. He and his music are what brought me home."

Donnchadh blushed a bit. "I can no tell ye how glad I am he found ye. I also cannot tell ye how sorry I am. I ken it seems as if I am always begging yer forgiveness." He scooted off his chair and knelt before her chair offering her his hand but not daring to touch her first. She placed her hand in his and he kissed it. "My love, I thought ye lost tae me entirely and I jealously guarded anything and everything I had left of ye. Ye are my very soul and wi' out ye I am lost."

"I will be honest, you startled me this evening." He flinched at her statement. "But that does not mean I love you any less and it would kill me to lose you. I don't know how the magic worked or why it took months on your end but only a week on mine, but at the end of the day, I am glad it worked Duncan. While this was not the homecoming envisioned, I am glad to be home."

"I can no tell ye what it does tae my heart tae hear ye say that. Tis no the home coming I envisioned either." He stopped suddenly and then jumped up and pulled Gwen with him. "Ye stand here lass. He stood her by the chest where her things lay and handed her her cloak and then dashed out of the room closing the door behind him. Gwen was thoroughly perplexed. A minute later he opened the door a serious expression on his face that changed to one of wonder as approached her. "Och Christ I have missed ye mo chroi!" He took her cloak, tossed it across the room, and swept her up in to his arms. "Welcome home my love!" He kissed her deeply then.

It took Gwen a moment to realize what he was about and when she did, she could not get enough of him. "I have missed

you so very much my Duncan" she said against his lips. He sat
her back on her feet and set about unlacing her bodice.

Chapter Seventeen

The sunlight woke them the next morning. Gwen looked around and surveyed the destruction. Clothes had been flung everywhere; the contents of her pouch were strewn across the floor and Donnchadh's sporran hung haphazardly from the back of the chair where it landed with a piece of fabric hanging out. She shook her head and cuddled back against her husband. Donnchadh tightened his arm around her and kissed the top of her head. "Good morning wife."

She looked up and kissed him. "Good morning, Husband."

"Mo chroi I have a serious favor tae ask of ye. I ken it is no easy for ye and I do no want to upset ye. But, I do no want tae time travel ever again and I do no want ye tae either. I would be tae afraid of losing ye."

"That does not upset me at all sweetheart. I am in full agreement. And I think it would put too much of a strain on Molly. I am happy right here with you. I tied up my lose ends in the week without you. Sometime today, I want to show you everything I brought back. Some very useful stuff." She winked at him. They did not leave their chamber that day at all except to use the privy. Cameron brought up their lunch and was overjoyed that Gwen was back. He hooted and squeezed her in a bear hug.

"Let go of my wife ye oaf!" Donnchadh chided him teasingly.

"Och I am so verra glad ye are back m'lady. We have needed someone tae keep him line!" Cameron dodged Donnchadh's halfhearted swat. "I will leave ye love birds tae it then. I will see that all is as it should be and have meals sent up here for ye. Consider yerselves free of any obligation for a few days. I will take care of things."

Gwen gave give him a quick kiss on the cheek and he was out the door leaving them alone together then. "Hmm so you are all mine then sir," she disappeared behind a divider on the far side of the room. When she stepped out she was wearing a black lace confection that covered everything and nothing.

"I...I...Good God Gwen!" Donnchadh could barely get a word out. He had never seen the likes of what she wore now. He was glad he was sitting on the bed. "Ye are beyond stunning! Come here and show that tae me upclose. I fear my eyesight is going and I need a much closer look." He leered at her. "I will probably need tae touch it as well."

She slowly walked to the bed and then crawled to him. He was as hard as a rock as he watched his wife advance on him. She crawled over him so that she ended kneeling over his lap. She was covered in delicate black lace. Well not covered so much as accentuated by the black lace. He ran his hands up her sides and cupped her breasts. She leaned forward then so they were quite close to his face. He gave in, pulled the lace out of the way, and licked her nipple. She shuddered and pushed closer. He pulled away and then tongued her other nipple. They were both moaning by then. His hands pulled her to him, tracing her spine, squeezing her hips. "I want ye so bad I can taste it love!"

"The feeling is mutual!" She pulled the covers out of the way and wrapped her hand around his hard length. His breath came out a strangled cry and he kissed her more fiercely. It was as if they could not get close enough to each other. She stroked the length of him bringing him to the brink of release and then stopping.

He growled and nipped her neck causing her to shiver "If ye do no stop teasing me woman, ye will no be able tae wear this ever again!"

"No need to worry about that." She winked and slowly lowered herself onto him. He gave a guttural cry as she sank down. She sighed with pleasure as he filled her.

"God ye are so hot and tight! Ye drive me wild!" He grabbed her hips and began to thrust into her. She met his thrusts and leaned against his chest. She rode him much as he expected she would a stallion with ecstasy and a sense of control that was on the verge of shattering. He dug his fingers into her hips thrusting harder. Her breath was coming in gasps, moans punctuating some of his thrusts. He could feel her body tightening around him.

Gwen threw her head back and moaned as she rode him. There was a delicious pleasure laced with the tiniest bit of pain that sent her over the edge as she connected with him. She gasped and shuddered, her body seemed as if it was no longer under her control for a moment. And Donnchadh kept pounding into her.

He reveled in her pleasure, loved how she responded. He stopped for a moment and reversed their positions. Now he had her where he wanted her. He tucked the lace beneath her breast and sucked first one and then the other as he thrust into her again. She gasped at his intrusion and then wrapped her legs around his waist. She dug her nails into his back. He was sure he would bear the marks of this love making for some time, and he would be proud to honestly. As he neared his peak he kissed her fiercely and then pulled away for a moment. He could feel that she was close as well. Her movements were becoming more frenzied. "Look at me mo chroi. Look at me as we cum together, ken that I love ye above all else!"

"Oh yes Duncan! As I love you!" She cried out as she shattered again and Duncan roared his pleasure, their gazes locked. Finally he collapsed atop her, both of them breathing hard. "I have missed you so my love!" she whispered as she stroked his sweat damp hair. "Oh, what does mo chroi mean?"

Laughter rumbled through Donnchadh's chest as he shifted his weight so that he could look at her. He pushed a stray lock of hair off of her brow. "It means My heart. Which is what ye are and always will be.

The next few weeks saw the clan relaxing around their laird again and welcoming Mairead back. There was a sense of relief that seemed to wash over everyone. It was as it had been before. Gwen and Donnchadh were nigh inseparable, and the clan could not have been happier. Donnchadh doted on his wife. The harvest was plentiful and they were preparing for the winter.

Gwen had been home for about a month when she realized that not only had she missed her period, but she had been sick in the morning a few times. One morning she snuck away while Donnchadh was training to dig through her bag that was hidden deep in one of their trunks. She pulled out a pregnancy test and went to the privy. It was quite possibly one of the longest five minutes of her life while she waited for the results. They were positive, she was pregnant! She was in tears of happiness. When she exited the privy she sought out Molly to enlist her help with herbs to make sure she stayed healthy, but also in surprising Donnchadh.

As Christmas approached Donnchadh was excited at the prospect of this being their first holiday together. He wanted to make it special for her since he knew how much she loved it. He made sure that the decorations in the hall were over the top, holly and ivy and ornaments everywhere! She and Molly had been busy as well. She was so excited that she was practically glowing, and he loved seeing her like that. She had been ill with a stomach ailment but that seemed to have passed for the most part and he was immensely relieved. Christmas morning, they sat in the library sipping hot chocolate that she had brought back with her. She knelt and pulled a box out from behind some books that she had used as a hiding place. "Merry Christmas my love!" she handed him the beautiful leather box as she sat herself on his lap.

He squeezed her hip and kissed her and then opened the box. Within there was a beautiful silver mug engraved with trefoils and "World's Best Da". He read it and then peered at her quizzically. "What is this mo chroí?"

She laughed delightedly, "It is a mug for your ale sweetheart!"

"Aye, I ken that dearest!" he snorted. "I just dinna ken what ye mean by "World's Best Da"!"

She laughed again and kissed him on the nose. She took his hand and placed it on her stomach. "You are going to be a da my Duncan. I am pregnant." His eyes went wide as he looked at her and then at her stomach and then at Molly who could not contain her grin.

"I am going tae be a da?!" He whispered in wonder. He pulled Gwen to him and kissed her deeply. "I can no believe it love! Are ye ok? Do ye need anything? Christ am I holding ye too tight?!"

Gwen and Molly giggled about his concern. "Everything is fine sweetheart. We are all fine, and you will be a wonderful da!" She kissed him then and they sat holding each other enjoying the roar of the fire in the fireplace, the snow outside and the family gathered around.

About the Author

Ashleigh Shelton has been going to and been obsessed with renaissance faires since her dad took her to the Georgia Renaissance Festival for the first time as a child. She has since been part of a cast and still frequents numerous renaissance faires a year. She started writing with pen and paper in middle school and dreamed of becoming a published author since then. She has finally achieved that dream and now she types her spicy historical and renaissance faire inspired works on her sticker laden laptop. She is excited to share all the romances she has waiting in the wings to be written. When she is not writing her next book at her local Starbucks, she spends her time fixing her family's computers, going to renaissance faires with her besties, hanging out with her ultra fluffy maine coon, and harassing as well as being harassed by her teenage son.

Acknowledgements

This book started out as a dare to myself, could I write a romance novel in a month? I love reading them so why not try and write one? (Spoiler alert; I did). I only hope that my readers enjoy it as much as I enjoyed writing it. And it would not have happened without the village of people I am lucky to call friends and family. Whitey and Kat, my beautiful Fandom Fatales, I cannot thank you enough for going to ren faires with me and putting up with my info dumping about this book and helping me fix bits and pieces. Whitey you were a life saver. And Kat I am so glad you were there with me that day at ren faire when the universe smacked me across the face telling me to get off my ass and make a go of what I love, and you took me to the Line by Lion tent and introduced me.

Dad, you lit the match that became a burning lifelong obsession with renaissance faires for me. I treasure our memories at the Georgia renaissance festival when I was little and they still fill me with wonder today and inspires so much of what I write.

Mom, I may not say it enough, but thank you for supporting me in this. Your input and ideas and tweaks helped so much. Having an English teacher for a mom pays off when you are a writer.

I am immensely grateful to my romance novel writers group at a Novel Romance. You ladies have given me so much amazing advice and helped me grow my confidence in my writing.
Amanda, my amazing publisher, there are not enough words to thank you and Thomas enough for taking a leap of faith with me and making my dream come true!

Zhalet, Lauren, Julie, Nastasha, and Mary I can not thank y'all enough. Y'all supported me and had faith in me even when I did not and that means the world to me and I won't ever forget that!

Thanks to my amazing cover artist Adam Prack! You made me cry so many times when I first saw the mock up. I am enamored of it!

A huge thank you to my editor Susan Travis, your help was invaluable and your suggestions really helped me round some things out!

And finally thank you to my Conn man, my son. Thanks for putting up with your crazy romance novel reading and writing mom. Love you sweets. Just don't tell me if you ever read this!

My thanks and love to you all,
Ashleigh